FATAL PROGNOSIS

by

Dr. Edmund G. Andracki

AmErica House
Baltimore

First printing.

ISBN: 1-58851-017-4
PUBLISHED BY AMERICA HOUSE BOOK PUBLISHERS
www.publishamerica.com
Baltimore
Printed in the United States of America

Dedication

To all the dedicated doctors, nurses, and other health care providers who work so diligently so that others might live.

Acknowledgments

Many thanks to my brother Zenon who was so helpful in editing and helping to prepare the manuscript for submission to our publisher.

And thanks to Lois Holmstrom for her review and editing of the final manuscript.

Chapter 1

INTENSIVE CARE, GOOD SAMARITAN HOSPITAL...The young patient lays in a semi-coma, his hands and face twitching every so often as if he were prodded by a pin. His eyes are open but unseeing, nervously flicking from time to time when light shocks the optic nerve into action. His expanding and contracting chest wages a war against the accumulating fluid that floods his lungs. Lack of oxygen in the blood stream gives his skin an ashen gray-blue color. His heart muscle, afflicted by the strange disease that has overtaken it, works laboriously in a futile effort to pump blood through the arteries to the brain and other vital organs that cry out for the life giving oxygen that is not there. Intravenous fluids carry drugs into his veins battling to keep him alive. Death stands nearby, waiting to pick up the pieces as the young man is slowly being torn apart by his disease.

Lisa Clarke monitors the EKG oscilloscopes that constantly record each beat of the hearts of the patients under her care. The scope that is monitoring the heartbeat of the young man is recording a slow, erratic, wave pattern, just as it had been doing for the past six hours, only now the pattern is even more erratic and the heart rate is sinking even lower.

Suddenly the oscilloscope becomes a picture of turmoil. The young man's heart has gone into ventricular fibrillation, a wild electrical pattern that means that the heart muscle is not capable of pumping blood through the young man's arteries. Then, asystole, no electrical activity whatsoever. The young man's heart stops beating. He is clinically dead.

"Code," yells out Nurse Clarke, "Module six." Lisa Clarke rushes to the young man's bedside. Within seconds the young man's bed is surrounded by activity, resuscitation activity, in an effort to bring him back to life.

"Code Blue.... Intensive Care," shouts the hospital page system. And again, "Code Blue... Intensive Care."

Dr. Steve McKay is making rounds on his patients on the third floor when he hears the "Code Blue" call. Acting instinctively, he hands the patient's chart that he has in his hands to a nurse and makes a dash to ICU. Dr. McKay bolts through the double doors and into the Intensive Care Unit. The Respiratory Therapy team has already placed a tube into the young patient's trachea and is ventilating his lungs with oxygen. They are literally breathing for him. A nurse is rhythmically compressing the chest to circulate the blood with an artificial pumping action.

"I think that you are familiar with this patient, Dr. McKay," said Lisa.

Dr. McKay makes a rapid assessment of the patient's condition. "I know, Lisa. I saw him with Dr. Lowe. Has Lowe been notified?"

"I have a call in for him now," answered Lisa.

Dr. McKay rechecks the EKG monitor. "A flat line...bad news. Give adrenaline, I-V."

"How much?" asks Lisa.

"Ten c.c.s." Dr. McKay observes the young man's pupils. They are widely dilated and unresponsive… another terribly bad sign.

Lisa plunges the needle into the rubber dam of the I-V tubing, then looks up. "This is a pretty big dose."

"Give it."

Lisa slams down the plunger of the syringe, sending the drug rapidly into the young man's vein.

Dr. McKay anxiously watches the monitor. "No response." In rapid succession he orders other drugs to be given as the resuscitation team continues to ventilate the patient's lungs with oxygen and to circulate the blood with the chest compressions.

Dr. McKay continually assesses the EKG monitor and the patient. "Nothing...not a thing," he mumbles in frustration.

He orders more drugs. He orders the team to continue resuscitation as he watches the EKG monitor with an ebbing hope that it might, just might, show some faint evidence of activity.

Finally in a fit of frustration Dr. McKay yells out, "Here, let me do that," as he shoves away the nurse who was performing CPR chest compressions in a very satisfactory manner.

Dr. McKay compresses the chest hard, too hard.... much harder than he knows is necessary. It is an exercise in futility, and Dr. Steve McKay knows it. But he continues banging on the chest in a wild attempt to make the dead heart alive. "Beat, come on baby, start beating!"

Lisa Clarke leans over and says softly, "Steve...he is dead...he was dead before we started all of this."

Dr. Steve McKay gives three more hard stabs at the chest, the last one fractures three ribs with a crunch. Then he stops compressing. He leans on the chest for a second, then straightens out. "Yeah, I know." He orders the resuscitation attempt to cease.

Dr. McKay takes the chart from the nurse and makes a note. "Patient pronounced dead at 1400 hours after unsuccessful resuscitation attempt to reverse cardiopulmonary arrest...cardiac asystole." He scribbles his signature at the bottom of the notation, then throws the chart on the desk.

Dr. Steve McKay argued with death every day, and he was a poor loser. And this was the second time he had lost that day...two patients dead from similar causes, and the twentieth to die at Good Samaritan Hospital under similar circumstances in the past twenty-five days. Dr. McKay had been involved in all of the cases.

Chapter 2

It was mid-afternoon of the following day and Dr. Jacque Marten, chief pathologist at Good Samaritan Hospital, sat in his office peering into his microscope. Every now and then he tapped his foot against the switch, which activated the dictating machine, so that he could record his observations.

Dr. Lowe stomped down the hall and into the Pathology office and did not even stop at the secretary's desk but went right into Dr. Marten's private office. He spotted Dr. Marten hunched over his microscope. Jacque Marten knew who was rattling his door. The heavy footsteps had announced his visitor long before he came into the office.

"Jacque, what kind of a report is this?" asked Dr. Lowe, wildly waving the paper in the air. "The second autopsy in a week, and the second time that you tell me nothing about why my patient died."

Dr. Marten continued to examine the slides under his microscope. He made one more dictation note before turning toward Dr. Lowe. Dr. Jacque Marten looked questioningly into Dr. Lowe's eyes. "Would you rather that I fabricate a death report to your liking?"

"Come on, Jacque. Get off of that kind of stuff. You know what I mean.

"Cardiomyopathy, cardiomyopathy…cardiomyopathy, that does not tell me anything, and you know it."

"Well, that is why your patient died. He had cardiomyopathy. I cannot tell you exactly why he had the myopathy, but he had it."

Dr. Lowe withdrew a large handkerchief from his hip pocket, and mopped the beads of sweat which were bursting with profusion from his forehead. Still holding the handkerchief in his hand, he drew a deep breath and collected his composure. "I'm sorry, Jacque. But this was no ordinary case. This patient was only twenty-eight years old.... too young to die from cardiomyopathy. And besides that, he is the son-in-law of the publisher of our paper…he has two small sons at home. The family is a personal friend of mine. I am more than just a little upset over this."

"I know you are, and I can appreciate your concern." Dr. Marten scooted his chair away from the microscope table. "But, I am sorry Gordon, I just cannot give you any more information now. Maybe after the reports are back..."

Dr. Lowe loudly interrupted. "Maybe later, maybe later. That's what you told me after you did the post-mortem examination on McFarrell. It was cardiomyopathy on that one, too. Your needle is stuck on a broken record, Doctor. Holcombe is going to call me in about fifteen minutes and he is going to want to know exactly why his son-in-law died. And what am I going to tell him? Cardiomyopathy, and he is going to say, 'and what in the hell is cardiomyopathy?' And then what do I say, Jacque? Your son-in-law died of a flabby heart that quit beating? No way, Jacque. No way at all. Bill Holcombe is no ordinary person. He is well educated, well read, and inquisitive… and smart. He is going to want to know why his son-in-law died, and we had better have a better answer than cardiomyopathy. That is a result of something, not a cause."

Dr. Marten showed no emotion whatsoever throughout Dr. Lowe's outburst. "Don't worry about it, Gordon."

"What do you mean, don't worry about it? I have to talk to this man in about fifteen minutes," Dr. Lowe glanced at his watch, "ten minutes."

"I have already talked to Holcombe."

Dr. Lowe was caught by surprise. His hands fell to his side; his mouth opened as if he were about to say something, then it closed again. Before he could muster any kind of reply, Dr. Marten continued. "Bill called me early this morning, and I took the liberty to talk to him about his son-in-law. I felt free to do so since you had asked me to see the patient prior to his death. I had talked to the family about the case at that time, as you are well aware. Bill knew that I had done the post-mortem, and he thought that he would rather talk to me about it. He realized that you were very upset about the whole matter."

Dr. Lowe did not know whether to be relieved because now he would not have to face Bill Holcombe or to be angry because Dr. Marten had performed a task that was rightly his responsibility. The relief of not having to explain his son-in-law's untimely death to Bill Holcombe overcame any animosity he might harbor against Dr. Marten. Dr. Lowe calmed down. "I'm sorry, Jacque. I did not know that. I guess I should thank you. You really did not have to do that, you know. It is really the place of the attending physician to make the report to the family, no matter how uncomfortable it might be." He mopped his sweating brow again. "What did you tell him?"

Dr. Marten retained a relaxed composure. "I told him just what I told you. I told him that his son-in-law died from a cardiac condition, cardiomyopathy, but that we are not sure about the exact cause of the problem. Then, without going into any great detail, I had a short discussion about cardiomypathy with him. And you can be sure, Gordon, that I emphasized that you did everything possible that could be done under the circumstances, and that you could not have done anything more. I especially stressed the fact that we are not sure about the etiology of his son-in-law's myopathy. Bill Holcombe seemed to accept what I told him. I think that he understands the problems that we face in medicine. He realizes that we do not always have all of the answers."

"Very well, Jacque. But I would rather have a better explanation than we have as to the way the patient developed the myopathy in the first place, for my own knowledge if for no other reason. I would hate to think that I had missed something which would respond to therapy." Dr. Lowe paused, and then questioned him, "You are not holding back on me, are you?"

"No, Gordon, I do not know anything more than what I have already told you, but I wish that I did know more. We know that there is a close similarity between the McFarrell case that you attended and this one. That similarity is bothersome, especially since I have had other autopsy cases similar to these two in the past few weeks."

Dr. Jacque Marten rose from his chair. "I'll let you know if anything turns up."

Dr. Lowe stuffed the handkerchief back into his pocket, muttered a farewell, and left. His last words faded into the hall as he passed through the door, "I will be at my office if you need me."

Dr. Lowe brushed past the ruggedly handsome Dr. McKay, whose ruffled hair, loosened tie, and wrinkled, white lab coat contributed to his youthful appearance. The usual abrupt "Hello" of Dr. Lowe seemed even more abrupt today, thought Dr. McKay as he watched Dr. Lowe, disappear around the corner. Steve McKay shrugged his shoulders and continued to his destination, the Pathology Lab.

Dr. Steve McKay stood in the doorway of Dr. Marten's office. "What did you do to Gordon Lowe? He was colder than usual, even for him."

Dr. Marten did not answer Dr. McKay immediately. When he finally jarred himself from his thoughts he said dolefully, "Dr. Lowe lost a patient and wanted to know why. I could not tell him."

"Bill Holcombe's son-in-law?"

"Yes."

Steve McKay found a chair in the corner of the room and slouched in it in the easy manner that was characteristic of him. He lifted the test tube in his hand up to the light, then held it at arm's length in the direction of Dr. Marten. "I have an interesting and perplexing case myself. Think that you can help me?"

"Depends on what kind of case you have. What do you have in the tube, spinal fluid?"

"No, pericardial fluid." Dr. McKay handed the specimen tube to Dr. Marten.

Dr. Marten took the tube from Steve. "Want to tell me something about the clinical history and clinical findings."

"A twenty-eight-year-old guy with flu like symptoms about a week or so ago. Went to his family doc., got treated, but didn't get any better. His doctor sent him to the hospital where he is now getting worse with cardiac failure and probably cardiomyopathy. No special clinical findings except those that confirm what I just told you."

The pathologist fingered the test tube nervously as he listened to what Dr. McKay was saying.

Steve buried himself a little deeper into the chair. "And now this patient is acutely ill with congestive heart failure and his heart rate is slowing down. I think that he is going to die, and soon."

Dr. Marten pushed a button and called loudly into the remote microphone that transmitted his voice into the main laboratory. "I need a lab. tech. to run some tests.... Right now."

Dr. Marten then turned toward Steve. "Your case sounds familiar."

Dr. McKay eyed the pretty, white clad, tight skirted, technician as she entered the room. Dr. Marten handed the tube to her and said, "Run a complete profile on this, immediately. It is pericardial fluid." He paused just a moment, then added, "And refrigerate two c.c.s. I may want to run some viral studies later."

Steve McKay's eyes had followed the technician as she entered the room and he was still watching as she disappeared through the doorway when Dr. Marten joggled his thoughts, "You still have that eye for a pretty girl, don't you, Steve?"

"He who covets his neighbor's wife commits adultery in the heart. I can't believe that, can you? I never really believed that thinking about it was as good as the real thing." Steve was now looking at Jacque Marten. "And besides, I doubt that the pericardial fluid will reveal anything helpful in our diagnosis."

Dr. Jacque Marten managed a faint smile. "If you say so, Steve." He swung his chair around. "I did post-mortems on both Holcombe's son-in-law and the McFarrell case. Both had similar clinical histories as yours."

"Did Gordon have anyone else see McFarrell?"

Dr. Marten wrinkled his forehead as he answered. "Yes. He asked Dr, Welsch to see the patient."

Steve rubbed his hand over his face and drew in a deep breath. "Lowe is a good guy, a good doctor, conscientious, dedicated; but he sometimes picks poor consultants."

"He wanted you, Steve. But you were out watching the sports cars races. Where were you this time?"

Steve McKay's eyes brightened whenever an opportunity arose to talk about his avocation and hobby, sports car racing. "Glen Haven. You should have seen the Alfa that was racing. They really had it tuned perfectly. It beat the Porches out of the turns every time. I don't know what they did to the suspension, but it held onto the track like nothing I have seen in a long time. I would have given a lot to get my hands on that wheel."

"Did he win?"

"Nah! Hit the guardrail on the fourteenth lap. Misjudged the turn. Do you think that Lowe would care if I looked at the McFarrell record? Actually I did see McFarrell briefly before I left. Then I told Lowe that he could either handle the case himself or get someone else. The symptoms of McFarrell and Holcombe's son-in-law and others I've seen have been very similar."

Dr. Marten spoke with deliberation. "That similarity bothers me too. The most frightening common aspect in all of the cases is that they all have died. And they all have had Cardiomyopathy, but why?"

"Jacque, but do you think that Dr. Lowe will allow me to examine the McFarrell chart?"

"I have no doubt about Gordon allowing you to see the chart, but Dr. Welch was in on the case as a consultant, and you should get his permission as well Welch will probably question the request, but I am sure that he will not object. As soon as I get their permission you can pick up a copy of the chart here in my office." Dr. Marten paused, then rose from his chair. "As Chief of Staff, you could look at the chart without Welch's permission you know."

"I would rather not go that route," said Dr. McKay as he began to head for the door. Then he abruptly stopped and looked at the Pathologist. "Jacque, if this patient dies with cardiomyopathy, it may be a marker that this community is in trouble, deadly trouble. This many people coming down with a disease that is invariably fatal…that is a nightmare."

Dr. Marten watched as Dr. McKay disappeared from the room. He sat back in his chair and rubbed his hand through his thick hair. There was no need to await the death of Steve's patient. They were already on a collision with death, and both he and Dr. Steve McKay knew it.

Chapter 3

Good Samaritan Hospital was not the kind of institution that you would expect to become headline news. It was situated in a midwestern city with a population of forty-five thousand with diversified industry and surrounded by rich, rolling farmland. It was a prosperous community and a pleasant place to live and raise a family. Good Samaritan was the only hospital in the area.

Good Samaritan Hospital had a medical staff that was good, if not outstanding. Dr. Jacque Marten, chief pathologist, was the most notable member of the medical staff. He was six foot tall, stocky, walked with stooped shoulders, and had thick, gray hair. His face was wrinkled and hardened from the weather. He was slow and methodical in all that he did, and he looked older than fifty-two. Jacque Marten was brilliant. He could have been the head of the pathology department in many of the best medical schools in the country. But Dr. Marten was not academically oriented, even though he still continued to do research and wrote numerous articles for publication in medical journals. He was born and raised in a small midwestern town, he liked the outdoors, he despised the pressures of big hospital administration, and besides, he commanded an excellent salary at Good Samaritan. He also had a very good, upcoming associate. All of this added up to a comfortable practice with adequate time to enjoy a good income in a semi-rural area, with time to do the things that he liked to do most…hunt and fish and spend as much time as possible on his farm.

Dr. Steve McKay was Chief of Staff at Good Samaritan. He was just over six feet tall, slim and by all means athletic in stature. Dr. Steve McKay had dark brown, piercing eyes that were highly communicative. They could tear into you with anger and rip you apart, or, they could tranquilize you with a melting glance of sympathetic understanding, or, they could burn your soul with love. He was in his mid-forties, but looked younger. Dr. McKay maintained his excellent physical status by jogging five miles five times a week. He also played a rugged game of racquetball, and was a competitive tennis player. His dark brown hair always had a wind blown look that made his already handsome features even more attractive. His heavily sun bronzed skin gave him a sportive look that emphasized his indefatigable lifestyle based on a very busy medical practice. He also managed to take a very active part in hospital affairs and in teaching medical students and medical residents. He was always at the hospital making his rounds at least by six each morning, and he was a frequent night visitor at the hospital, checking on his patients or consulting on patients for other physicians.

Like Dr. Marten, Steve McKay was one of the outstanding members of the Good Samaritan medical staff. But unlike Dr. Marten, Dr. McKay was oriented toward clinical medicine, and he had an extraordinary clinical acumen that made him the envy of other members of the medical staff. He commanded the respect of the other staff physicians because of his hard work, and because of his ability to unravel the secrets of puzzling medical cases and come up with the correct answers most of the time. Dr. McKay was not as medically knowledgeable as Dr. Marten or some of the other members of the staff, but he was able to get the most out of every bit of medical knowledge that he had ever known. He admitted to having no interest in research. He had done post-graduate study in infectious diseases, and he was considered the consultant of choice in this field of medicine in his community.

Dr. Jacque Marten personally knew many well-known medical personalities and specialists in all parts of the country, and even the world. But he still collaborated with Dr. McKay on difficult cases that were referred to him, both from local and from out-of-town physicians. It was a somewhat strange, but effectual medical partnership that these two physicians enjoyed; Dr. Marten, the brilliant, nationally known pathologist, and Dr. Steve McKay, the medically wise clinician, famous only at Good Samaritan.

Steve McKay had at one time raced sports cars, but he gave up racing after an accident four years prior that disabled him for three months. He was still an avid follower of sports car racing and was frequently out of town watching the races, much to the chagrin of other doctors on the staff who somehow felt that he was never available when they needed him most.

Dr. Winston Welsh, another notable member of the Good Samaritan hospital medical staff, was overtly famous in state and national medical politics. He had spent years in post-graduate medical training at various medical centers in this country and abroad. He was independently wealthy, thanks to an advantageous marriage to the daughter of a famous local industrialist, the president and owner or Bio-Medical Technologies. BMT, Inc. was the largest designer and producer of custom and standard technical equipment for medical research and industry. Dr. Winston Welsch did not have a very solid background for research, but he did have access to the vast, well-equipped laboratories at BMI, and because of this he had managed to acquire research grants that allowed him to do experimental work from time to time. Most of his research had been unproductive, but he still liked to dabble on research projects.

Dr. Winston Welsch was not an outstanding clinician, but he was a very influential person, both in medical and in political circles. He was the type of person who could make the right phone call and get you an appointment with the president of the State Medical Society, the President of the AMA, your Senator or Representative in Washington, and sometimes even the President of the United States. He remained at Good Samaritan because his wife liked living in her hometown.

It was late in the afternoon when Dr. McKay came back to the hospital to see his patient. He rapidly examined the young man and saw the obvious; his patient's condition was rapidly deteriorating. He was in congestive heart failure and had to labor with every breath. He was hypoxic, in spite of the fact that he was receiving 100% oxygen by mask. His body organs and tissues were not getting enough oxygen and were slowly deteriorating. The fluid collecting in his lungs prevented inspired oxygen from crossing into the blood stream so that it could be transported to the cells of the body where it was vitally needed. The drugs that he had been given had not been effective, and it seemed useless to give more. When he was responding, which was becoming less and less frequent, he was confused. The remainder of the time the patient dipped into varying degrees of coma.

Dr. McKay carefully examined his patient. He had examined the patient frequently in the prior two days, but he had been unable to detect any clues as to the underlying disease process that was the cause of the presenting symptoms and clinical findings. The patient had an infection, that was clear. Even a second year medical student would have come to that conclusion. But the most vital question remained, what kind of an infection, and why could it not be pinpointed more accurately? Examination of the chest again bore evidence of congestive heart failure. Dr. McKay listened to the heart again. The bradycardia was worsening. The heart rate was slowing down, just like in all the other patients shortly before they died.

Dr. McKay turned to the nurse who had accompanied him on his visit to the patient. "I want another EKG right away. But first, let's transfer him to Intensive Care."

"I thought you would do that," commented the nurse as the two walked out of the room. "He is pretty sick, isn't he? The family wants to talk to you again."

"I just talked to them this morning," replied Steve in a somewhat irritated tone of voice.

"Well, you know how it is with a sick patient. The family wants a minute-to-minute report."

Steve was somewhat annoyed at himself for becoming short tempered. "I guess that they are entitled to it. But next time tell them to contact their family doctor."

"They already did," answered the nurse as a small grin crossed her face. "He told them to talk to you."

The two met with the family in the hall. Dr. McKay carefully explained the situation in as precise and clear a manner as he could. He felt pangs of guilt, or something, in that he could offer them so little in the way of consolation as to the prognosis.

The patient was dying, and he knew it. But he did not know why his patient was dying, and this bothered him. Dr. Steve McKay was doing all that he and medical science could offer, and still the patient was on a slippery slope that would carry him over the edge to his death. Dr. McKay finished talking to the family, then struck out for pathology.

Dr. Marten put down the phone when he saw Dr. McKay enter his office. "I was about to ring you up and let you know the results of the pericardial fluid tests."

"Negative, right?"

"Correct," replied Dr. Marten. "The same pattern that we have seen in the past. I would say that your patient is in near extremis now and that he will probably die today."

"Thanks for the encouragement. I just saw him and I sent him to Intensive Care. I don't know why, except that is where you are expected to send critically ill patients these days." He sarcastically added, "It seems that it is against the law to let a patient die in a regular hospital room anymore." Steve shuffled in his chair, then continued. "I am sure that we are getting the same cardiac changes we have seen in all the cases that you autopsied. You know, Jacque, if we just could have gotten these patients past the bradycardia stage, I believe that a lot of them would have survived."

Jacque Marten swung his chair around. "I think that you are right. All the cases that I have seen developed a fatal bradycardia that led to cardiac standstill and death. And every time we have found cardiomyopathy at autopsy. But, it is the arrhythmia that is killing the patients. In the patients who have come to autopsy the cardomyopathy was already in the healing stage. In about week or so and I think that the patients would have completely recovered from the myopathy. It was the arrhythmia that killed them, not the myopathy. I've never seen this before in a myopathy. The conduction system is especially hard hit in these cases."

Steve replied, "And that is about all that we know about this thing, whatever it is. But what is causing the myopathy?"

Dr. Marten said, "I can tell you with near absolute certainty that this is not an ordinary bacterial disease process. Our cultures would have picked up something by now, Steve. We are already doing some viral studies, but getting results is pretty slow."

"I think that we should pursue that aspect more aggressively."

Dr. Marten added, "I have sent samples to the Contagious Disease Center in Atlanta. We have not gotten any result back yet, and it may be a few more weeks before we do." Then Jacque said, "Get another blood sample from this patient in about a week, then we can compare the initial sample with the second."

Dr. McKay put his hands in his pockets, wrinkled his mouth to one side; "This guy ain't going to be here in a week, Jacque."

"O.K. then get another specimen every day until he dies. Get one today. In the future I think that we should get immediate blood specimens, and daily, on anyone we suspect of having this disease, whatever it is."

Steve said, "I ordered another EKG." Steve thought for a second, and then added as an afterthought, "There is no use kidding ourselves, Jacque, we know that the EKG will only confirm what we already suspect, that the patient has cadiomyopathy and that his heart is slowing down." Steve stared blankly out the window as if he might suddenly sight something in the summer sky, which would give him the answer to his problems. "How about enzyme studies? Think that you have anything new to offer in that field of investigation?"

Dr. Marten swung back and forth in the swivel chair. "Enzymes will tell us that your patient has a heart muscle problem, myocardial damage, but not the etiology. Anyway, we've already done enzyme studies."

"I know, Jacque. I guess that I was hoping that you might have something new." Steve was stalling for time. He dreaded having to go back to his patient. He had nothing to offer the dying man, and he was reluctant to admit defeat. He was looking for moral support. "Come on up to ICU with me, Jacque. Maybe you can add something."

Dr. Marten wrinkled his forehead and again rocked back in his chair. "I am not a clinician, Steve. But I'll go with you anyway, if it will make you feel better."

"You underestimate your abilities, Jacque. You have helped me with clinical problems more than a few times. Come on."

Dr. Marten accompanied Dr. McKay to Intensive Care. Lisa Clarke went over the chart with the two doctors, then went with them to the bedside of the patient who was now in critical condition. He was in even greater distress than when Steve had seen him less than an hour before. Oxygen was being delivered through the special mask that covered the patient's face, but the patient still labored with every breath. He was semicomatose, cool, clammy and ashen in color. Strapped to one arm was the blood pressure cuff linked to the electronic apparatus that automatically inflated and measured the blood pressure every five minutes. As the three approached the bed, there was a loud hiss from the instrument as the blood pressure cuff inflated then deflated. The blood pressure measurement numbers presented themselves on the screen.

"Eighty over forty. He is near shock now," said Dr. McKay. Steve looked at the EKG monitor on the shelf above the bed. "The heart is slowing down even more. That's trouble, real trouble."

Lisa looked up at Steve. "Anything you want done now that we are not already doing?"

Steve turned toward Dr. Marten who stood at the foot of the bed staring at the EKG pattern. Jacque Marten murmured quietly and sarcastically, "Shift gears, stay close to the wall, and hope that you don't hit it."

As Dr. Marten walked over to the desk to go over the patient's clinical chart, Steve re-evaluated his patient. He rapidly performed his examination focusing mainly on the chest and heart. Having completed his examination. He walked over to Dr. Marten and they studied the EKG record.

"He has cardiomopathy like the rest," said Dr. McKay.

Jacque Marten did not look up, but he nodded his head in agreement.

Lisa Clarke had been following the doctor's conversation very closely and was aware of the patient's precarious condition. "Anything that you want done, Dr. McKay.?"

Steve tossed the EKG onto the desk. "We have a real problem. If we try to increase cardiac output with inotropic agents and vasodilators, we will probably control the shock, but we will also be compromising an already compromised myocardium, and we could worsen the arrhythmia."

"I hate to just have him just lie there and do nothing, Steve."

Steve McKay blew an audible rush of air from his mouth. "I guess you're right. We have to try something."

"He is going to die in spite of what you do," said Dr. Marten.

Dr. McKay took the chart and wrote some new orders, changing some of the drugs that were being delivered and changing the dose of others. Then he walked over to the dictating booth and dictated a lengthy report of his visit, findings ending with, “Prognosis…”very poor.”

“Anything else?” asked Lisa.

“Pray!” retorted Steve.

At 4:41 that same afternoon, Dr. Steve McKay’s patient expired. The body would be sent down to the morgue where Dr. Jacque Marten would perform an autopsy and diagnose the cause of death…”Intractable Cardiac Arrhythmia ending in asystole; secondary to Cardiomyopathy, etiology undetermined.” This was the same diagnosis that he had written after performing eight post mortal examinations in the past two weeks, and Dr. Steve McKay had been involved in all of the cases.

Chapter 4

Steve McKay and Lisa Clarke lay quietly in bed, married, not to each other, but very much in love. Lisa turned over lightly, then carefully propped herself up on one arm, her hand lazily sifting through Steve's ruffled hair, her eyes gazing affectionately upon him; his face bronzed with the sun and the wind, his eyes closed, his hands cradling his head. He looked so much at ease, so relaxed that Lisa hesitated to disturb him.

Steve and Lisa met five years before when Lisa first came to work at Good Samaritan. "Mrs. Clarke, this is Dr. McKay, one of our better doctors. Mrs. Clarke is from Kent Community Hospital. Shê will be working with us beginning next week." The Nursing Supervisor was introducing the new Intensive Care Nurse to the staff at Good Samaritan, and Dr. McKay happened to be making patient rounds at the time.

"Are all of the nurses at Kent Community as pretty as you?"

Lisa blushed, but did not answer.

The Nursing Supervisor answered, in a protective, motherly like voice, "Dr. McKay is a good doctor, but sometimes outspoken about the wrong things."

Lisa Clarke and Steve McKay held more than a casual interest in each other from the time of that initial meeting. At first, the only contact that they had with each other was strictly professional when Steve had a very sick patient confined to Intensive Care. It was not too long, however, before Dr. McKay began to find excuses to spend more time than usual in Intensive Care, especially when Lisa Clarke was on duty. Many times he visited ICU even without an excuse. During this period of time the relationship between the two of them had grown from a casual friendship to their being very, very close friends. Both Steve and Lisa began to realize that a deeper feeling for the other was developing, feelings deeper than either cared to admit. Meetings "by chance" became more frequent. There was even an occasional telephone call, and then came the consequential moment that was to become the foundation for their future intimate relationship.

Steve had admitted a seriously ill patient to Intensive Care and had come to the hospital late in the night to care for him. It was Lisa's regular duty night and ICU was busy, so Lisa was working overtime. Steve attended to his patient for over an hour and had successfully resuscitated him after his heart had stopped beating. Lisa assisted Steve throughout the resuscitation, and during critical periods when the patient's life balanced on a thread of uncertainty, Lisa felt more than a professional admiration for Dr. McKay. Lisa would literally melt when Steve's eyes met hers and exchanged a feeling of growing mutual attraction.

Steve took Lisa home that night; a drizzling rain, a slow, rambling ride, congenial conversation. Nothing really happened. But the two of them felt so comfortable, so much at ease, so content; just riding, just talking, enjoying each other's company. The rain stopped, the drive ended and Steve, in a gentlemanly fashion, escorted her to the door. Nothing more. Each had halfway hoped that the other would give some small sign of affection, or caring, but none was to be given that night, and Steve bid Lisa a Platonic good night. But Platonism was about to be transformed in their affaire d' amour.

The following day Steve phoned Lisa. "How would you like to go to lunch today? I can meet you, say about 11:30."

"I don't know, Steve."

"I won't take no for an answer. I'll be finished seeing my patients at the hospital by then and I am not due in the office until two."

"I thought that you started office hours at one."

"By some strange coincidence, my first hour's patients all cancelled. I can meet you and then we can drive to Old Towne and have lunch at Jeans. The food is excellent and the atmosphere, well romantic. I promise to have you home by 1:30."

They met, they drove to Old Towne, they lunched at Jeans, and they had an enviously good time. They terminated their first date by arranging for another, and then to a third and in a short time Steve and Lisa found themselves seeing each other on a regular basis. A drive home on a rainy night had insidiously opened the gates for the initiation of a most intimate relationship, a love affair.

Lisa's hands were affectionately caressing Steve's face now.

Steve shifted a little. Then with his eyes still closed, he mumbled, "Nothing, really."

"Your wife?"

Steve lay still for a moment, and then he turned toward Lisa until their eyes met. "What made you say that?"

Lisa, her silver streaked, short, black hair disordered ever so slightly, continued stroking Steve's face. "I don't know. But I would be jealous if I thought that you were thinking about Carole."

"I hardly think about her when I am with her. How could I possibly think about her when I am here with you?"

Lips touched, and Lisa felt a warmth sweep through her as Steve pressed a little harder and a little longer. He whispered, "I was thinking about you, about me, about us."

"I do that all the time." She put her arms snugly around Steve, smiled and bit her lower lip in a manner that was characteristic of Lisa. "What about us?"

Steve pulled her even closer, kissed her tenderly, once, twice, three times, whispering softly as he did. "I love you...you are in love with me, and yet"...one more soft caress and a soul searching kiss... "Here we are in bed, illegitimately."

"I don't agree with that. We are in love, and we deserve to be here, together, loving." Lisa pulled back from Steve momentarily, and then she surrounded Steve with her arms again. Her lips busied themselves with his, "I love you, Steve, and I am so afraid that I will lose you. I am so afraid that something will come between us. I could not live without you." Lisa pulled away from Steve again. "I miss you so much that I could cry, and sometimes I do." She looked sadly into Steve's eyes. "I wish that we could do something about it. But I know that we cannot, at least not right now."

As Lisa lifted away from Steve, the crisp sheet slipped downward exposing her soft well-formed breasts, the nipples erect and firm. Steve's hand caressed them softly, and the firmness increased. Steve could feel his own firmness beginning to rise. Steve pulled Lisa closer to him. Bodies shifted so that thighs pressed firmly against each other. Their lips met. Passions quickened an excitement that erupted with an incredible, sensual pleasure. Caressing hands brought them even closer together and Steve could feel Lisa's breasts against his chest, and new emotions fired an already overheated soul. Lips and tongues touched again and again, exchanging passion...love. Steve's hand flowed slowly over Lisa's shapely body, outlining for him every curve and hidden crevice. Lisa gently guided the hand to the right places at the right time, to evoke the utmost sensual excitement in each of them. Finally, Steve embraced Lisa firmly, then gently, with mouths buried in each other, their bodies floated downward...for the second time that night.

At 3:30 in the morning, hospitals are quiet. The routine care of the hospital patient takes place between seven A.M. and five P.M. when laboratory work is ordered and evaluated, x-ray examinations are done, elective surgery is performed and the general care of the patient is determined and carried out. In the case of the seriously ill patient, nothing in the hospital ceases to operate no matter what time of day or night. The laboratory, x-ray and surgery departments all remain in constant readiness to take care of the patient who is in need of any of these services, twenty four hours every day, seven days of every week, twelve months of every year. The Intensive Care Departments usually stayed active, taking care of patients who are seriously, and often times critically, ill.

Dr. Steve McKay strode toward ICU, the noise of his footsteps vibrating in his ears as he moved through the night-silent hospital hallway. He slipped quietly into ICU and was greeted by the pleasant voice of Diane Vaughan, head nurse for the night. "Hello to the long missing Dr. McKay. I think that everyone except the FBI and the CIA has been looking for you, and maybe even they have been out tracing your whereabouts." She walked over to the chart table. "Dr. Lowe wants you to check his patient."

Steve answered in a slightly irritated tone of voice. "I know. That's why I am here instead of in bed where all nice people are at three o'clock in the morning."

"Depends on what you are doing in bed," answered Diane.

"I'll stick to my first statement. I think that anything you do in bed can be nice, even sleep."

Diane shook her head and smiled. "Dr. Lowe is a little worried about this young woman. Here, you can read the chart. Dr. Lowe has a pretty complete history and extensive progress notes."

"He always does." Steve took the chart from the nurse. "Is that the patient in the last bed by the window?"

Diane leaned against the chart table, her arms crossed against her chest. "Good guess, module six."

"She looks pretty comfortable to me, and pretty alert."

Diane looked toward the patient, then at Dr. McKay. "She looks fine, but..." Diane paused, looked at the patient once again, then she grabbed Steve's arm. "Come on to the consult room. I can chat with you better in there."

In the consult room Diane leaned against the desk as Steve went over the chart very carefully. Every now and then he asked a question of, and got an answer from, Diane. The story sounded familiar. A young individual, in good health up until two weeks prior to hospitalization. The patient developed an illness that was very much like an attack of the flu, but unlike a patient with the flu, she did not get better. There was a slow deterioration in her condition for no apparent reason. There were no clinical clues as to the cause of the initial illness or as to why there was no improvement in her condition in spite of adequate treatment. The X-Ray and laboratory data up to that time were all non-contributory. No definite diagnosis had been established. And when the patient developed shortness of breath and mild congestive heart failure Dr. Lowe became very concerned; especially since he had other patients who had similar findings and who later died. The patient was admitted and transferred to ICU. Steve looked over the electrocardiogram then read Dr. Welsch's report out loud. "Myocardial damage, minimal, early, cause undeterminable from this tracing alone. Possibly early cardiomyopathy. The clinical history and clinical findings must be correlated with these findings for a more precise evaluation."

Dr. McKay put the chart on the table. "Come on, Diane, let's check the patient."

Diane watched as Steve carefully examined the patient. The patient had a low-grade fever and showed an anxiety out of proportion to her apparent illness. Her chest had some fine rales in the bases that testified to the congestion that was building up in her lungs. The heart had an occasional extrasystole, an extra beat in the heart rhythm, but nothing more. The heart rate was still within acceptable limits…68 per minute. Steve could find no acute problem of a severe nature, but the patient was too young to have the problems that she was developing. Deep down, Dr. McKay was worried.

After he had completed the examination, Steve and Diane walked back to the consultation room. "This girl is sick alright, but why did Dr. Lowe insist that I come over at this time of the night to see her? He has things well in control right now with the drugs that he is giving her. She certainly is not in any immediate danger."

Diane was crisp in her answer. "I'm sorry, Doctor, but you know Dr. Lowe. He worries a lot about his patients, and since his other patients with these findings had died, he became quite concerned. It seems lately that Dr. Lowe attracts this kind of patient. He thinks that someone has something against him."

"Beelzebub?" asked Steve.

"Anyway, Dr. Lowe has a thin skin and it seems that Dr. Welsch got him a little excited."

Steve looked around the room. "Coffee?"

Diane beckoned to one of the aids and in a short time each was holding a cup of strong, steaming hot, black coffee.

"How did Dr. Welsch get Lowe upset, Diane, and how does Dr. Welsch fit into this anyway?"

"Well, I'll tell you. But don't quote me, or you may get me into trouble."

"Your secret is our secret. Shoot."

"Dr. Welsch came to the hospital late last night to read his EKG's. He was out of town all day, and that is why he did not get here till late to do his routine work." Diane sipped hot coffee, then continued. "When he saw the tracing from Dr. Lowe's patient, he checked the chart and thought that the patient may be developing CM Disease."

"CM Disease. What is CM Disease?" asked Steve.

"That is what Dr. Marten has labeled the malady that is killing patients these days. CM Disease...Cardiomyopathy Disease."

"That sounds like Jacque."

"Dr. Welsch speculated that this patient was developing CM Disease."

Steve interrupted, "I'm sure that she is, but go on."

Diane flinched and hesitated after Dr. McKay confirmed her ominous expectation, but she continued. "Dr. Welsch did call Dr. Lowe, and I think that Dr. Welsch thought that Dr. Lowe would ask him to see the patient in consultation. But Dr. Lowe merely thanked Dr. Welsch for calling, and hung up."

Steve set down his coffee cup. "And Dr. Welsch stormed away, very angry."

Diane's face took on a sudden look of surprise. "How did you know?"

"I know Dr. Welsch."

Diane made a few quick notations on the chart, then moved a little closer to Steve. "Dr. Lowe called in later and asked us to call you. We tried to get you, but you were nowhere to be found."

"I was busy."

Diane picked up her cup, and as she was walking through the doorway she stopped and turned toward Dr. McKay, and with an all- knowing look on her face she said, "And please, let you wife know where you are so we can find you." Diane left, but a second later poked her head around the corner. "And for your information, Dr. Marten is doing a post mortem examination downstairs. He said to tell you to come down, if you happened to show. Another one of 'those' cases."

The echo of Steve's footsteps followed him down the empty hall and three flights of stairs to the basement. The partially opened door to the post mortem room left a crack of light which informed Steve that Dr. Marten was still working. Slowing his pace, but not stopping, Steve pushed open the door.

Without even turning, Dr. Jacque Marten said, "Hello, Steve."

Steve, hands in pockets, stood near the door staring at the sheet covered body that lay on the stainless steel autopsy table under the bright, overhead light in the center of the room. "How did you know it was me?"

"At three-thirty in the morning, who else? And besides, I was expecting you. I told the girls in ICU to send you down. I knew that you would be here...sooner or later." Dr. Marten finished drying his hands. He walked over to the autopsy table and slipped the sheet from the head of the body. "Recognize him?"

Steve angled toward the table, looked at the ashen face of the corpse, then at Dr. Marten. "Dr. Welsch's patient. I saw him in consultation yesterday."

Dr. Marten replaced the sheet over the cooling body. "Not Dr. Welsch's patient, Steve, your patient. The whole hospital has been looking for you, all night... after this patient became critical."

Steve was puzzled and looked the part. He answered defensively, but not apologetically. "He was not my patient, Jacque. I saw him in consultation with Welsch, that's all." Steve reached for the chart and flipped page after page in rapid succession until he came to the pink physician's order sheet. "There." Steve shoved the chart in front of Dr. Marten, at the same time reading. "Consult dictated. I feel that the patient has an influenza-like infection that is affecting the heart in a way that we have seen in other similar cases recently. Prognosis poor in the light of what happened in prior cases. The family is advised of these findings." Steve had finished reading and was staring at Dr. Marten who merely stared back. Steve, seeing no response forthcoming blurted out, "Well?"

Dr. Marten answered, "Look at the order that Dr. Welsch wrote."

Steve took the chart and read, "Dr. McKay will now be in charge of the patient. Please call him for any further orders or if complications develop." That is about par for the course thought Steve. Welsch has me see a patient in consult, then turns him over to my care, to die, with me in charge. Steve closed the chart and handed it back to Dr. Marten. "Nobody notified me about that. And anyway, Welsch never did ask me if I would, or wanted, to take over the care of the patient."

"Come on up to my office, Steve, I'm finished here."

In his office, Dr. Marten shoved aside the papers and journals from a corner of his desk to make a place for the two cups of coffee that Steve was bringing from the other room. "Put them down over here, Steve."

Steve took a sip from the cup, but finding the coffee too hot for his liking, quickly put it back down. "Now, what is this all about Jacque?"

"Simply that Dr. Welsch assumed that he had turned the patient over to you. The hospital called him after they could not reach you tonight, and he just said that it was your patient, not his. The nurses tried to find you, but could not. In the meantime, the patient died…without a physician being present."

Steve gulped the coffee, in spite of it being too hot. "Just because Welsch says that the patient is mine does not necessarily mean that it is. He should have asked me first."

"Maybe. But you are the unofficial specialist in this disease."

Steve gulped hard at the coffee again. "What does that mean?"

The only one who has seen more of these cases is me," said Dr. Marten, "And all of the cases that I have seen were dead. You have more experience in infectious diseases than any one else around here. You have post-graduate training in infectious diseases. The staff looks to you whenever they have a problem in that field. Dr. Welsch had a CM Disease problem case last night, so, logically, he gave it to you."

"Welsch still should have asked me to take the patient, or at least I should have been notified that he wanted me to take over the case. He has never turned a patient over to me before. I'll bet that he was at one of his cocktail parties and did not want to leave."

"I don't know, and that is beside the point. I just thought that I would let you know the whole story. You will probably be hearing more about it in the morning. Let's go home and get some sleep."

In the medical staff parking lot behind the hospital, Dr. Marten was already at his car and Steve was heading toward his when he stopped, turned, and called out, "Jacque!"

Dr. Marten looked toward the voice.

Steve blurted out, "Just saw another one of 'those' cases for Lowe in ICU. You will probably be doing the post in a day or so."

With those words still hanging in the air, Dr. Steve McKay continued walking toward his car leaving Dr. Marten fumbling nervously with his lock.

Chapter 5

In the next week there were more deaths at Good Samaritan attributed to what was now commonly referred to as CM Disease, Cardiomyopathy Disease. All were relatively young people, and all had a similar history and clinical course, and Dr. McKay had seen all of them in consultation. All developed heart failure, a slowing of the heart rate, and finally cardiac asystole, a complete stoppage of the pumping action of the heart when the electrical system that stimulated the heart to beat failed. Dr. Marten or his Associate had performed a post-mortem exam on most of these patients after they died. The heart of each of the victims was affected so that the fibers of the cardiac muscle had become weakened thereby making it incompatible for the heart to function properly. But it was becoming more and more obvious to Dr. Marten that the damage to the heart muscle showed evidence of significant healing in all cases. The immediate cause of death was a slowing and finally a complete stoppage of any pumping action of the heart. The cause of death was not the weakened heart muscle, but an electrical failure.

Dr. McKay had a survival batting average of zero for patients who had CM Disease. Not even one of the CM Disease patients whom he had seen in consultation had lived. Questions began to crop up among some of the staff physicians, and even among other personnel, as to whether Dr. McKay was the one to consult in these cases. Dr. Welsch had been heard to comment that perhaps it would be better to get other consultations. He was not sure that he himself could do any better since the treatment of infectious disease was not really his specialty. But he did point out that, since he was a cardiologist, perhaps he might be of some assistance as a consultant since the eventual cause of death was from cardiac complications. This was notwithstanding the fact that he had asked Dr. McKay to see all of his own patients with CM Disease. It was now beginning to be an embarrassing situation for everyone involved.

The medical and nursing personnel were all extremely frustrated, and now even the hospital administration was beginning to question the significance of the deaths. There had been an increasing number of inquiries from numerous sources about the strange disease that was invading the community and causing all of these untimely deaths. The Emergency Department was becoming increasingly busy seeing patients who were unable to get appointments with their own physicians who were swamped with patients. Patients appeared who thought that any little sniffle, cough, ache, pain or fever was sure to develop into the fatal CM Disease. The newspaper was beginning to demand some kind of an explanation from the hospital and the medical community.

Even though Dr. McKay was Chief of Staff at Good Samaritan, it was Dr. Welsch who, more often than not, was able to strum the strings and lead the medical staff to play a tune that he thought was appropriate at any given time. He usually did not even have the support of the majority of the staff, and he was not well liked, but he could politic very skillfully and was frequently able to influence enough doctors to vote with him when the occasion arose. And recently, Dr. Welsch had shown increasing signs of getting involved in the CM Disease problem in the hospital and in the community.

Winston Welsch was about to leave the hospital when he saw the hospital administrator, Jim Street. "Jim, I would like to have a few words with you, if you don't mind."

Jim Street cursed to himself, wishing that he had stayed in the men's room a few more minutes so that he would have avoided meeting Winston Welsch. "Sure. Do you want to talk here or in my office?"

"We can go down the hall to the doctor's lounge."

The two men sat down facing each other across the round coffee table near the center of the room. There was no one else in the lounge.

"Anything special that you want to discuss, Winston?" Jim Street knew from past experience that whatever it was that Dr. Welsch wanted to discuss, it would not be cordial. Winston Welsch seldom sought out the Administrator unless he had some criticism to make about hospital affairs.

"No need to tell you that there have been a number of unusual deaths in our hospital, including the son-in-law of the publisher of our newspaper."

"Yes, I am well aware of that, Winston."

"Somewhat disturbing, isn't it?"

"You're damn right it's disturbing, and I am just as disturbed by all of these deaths as anyone on the medical staff."

"In your opinion, as a hospital administrator, do you think that we are doing enough to solve this problem?"

Jim Street took a long, deep breath. "Winston, I have conferred with our Chief of Staff, Dr. McKay, more than once on this very issue. I have spoken innumerable times with Dr. Marten about these deaths. Everyone is doing all that can possibly be done under the circumstances."

Dr. Welsch spoke in a biting tone of voice. "I think that perhaps more could be done, if not in the treatment of the patients, at least in trying to make a better diagnosis and evaluation. I know that the cause of the deaths has been cardiomyopathy, and although I am not an expert in infectious diseases, I am a cardiologist, and perhaps I could be of some assistance in the future."

Jim Street was smart, knowledgeable, and not easily intimidated. "No one knows for sure that this is an infection. You yourself have had an opportunity to treat a few of the cases and I am sure that Steve McKay will let you do whatever you want in treating your CM Disease patients in the future. Do you think that you have an answer to the problem?"

"Maybe my connections with various universities and medical centers, and with some top-flight researchers, would be of some value. I do have acquaintances in many special fields you know."

Jim Street was quick to answer. "Look, Winston, I think that this is mainly a medical staff problem but if you want, I will talk to Dr. McKay and discuss the problem with him again." Jim Street was trying to appease Dr. Welsch so that he would leave. "Or, maybe you can talk to Dr. McKay yourself."

"As a matter-of-fact, I was planning to talk to Steve about this, soon. I can be prepared to discuss my views on the matter at the next staff meeting."

Jim Street would rather Dr. Welsch not present his views at any staff meeting, but he could do little about that. "If that is what you want to do, Winston, go right ahead."

Dr. Welsch glanced at his watch. "I have to get back to the office. Thank you for your time, and I will be in touch with you and with Dr. McKay."

Jim Street spent most of the afternoon cloistered to the confines of his office. The conversation that he had with Dr. Welsch earlier that day bothered him. He wondered just how many other staff physicians were that deeply concerned about the recent deaths in the hospital from CM Disease. He also wondered about the seriousness of any epidemiological problem that might be developing. A discussion of the problems at a staff meeting could be catastrophic if emotions and short tempers overtook reason. He mulled over the various aspects of the events that had taken place in the past days and weeks. He rang for his secretary. "Get Dr. Marten and tell him that I want to see him this afternoon, the sooner the better." He then sat back in his chair and waited.

Jim Street stood when Dr. Marten entered. "Come on in, Jacque. I want to talk to you about a few things."

"I understand that you talked to Dr. Welsch earlier today. He said that you are concerned, like all of us, about the recent deaths from CM Disease."

Jim Street was not surprised that Winston Welsch had talked to Dr. Marten about their conversation, and he wondered just what Dr. Welsch was planning. "That is correct, Jacque, I did talk to Winston this morning. But he asked me, I did not ask him. Sit down, Jacque."

Dr. Marten hated the politics of anything, including hospital politics and the politics of hospital medical staffs, and he would do his best to detach himself from these matters. He was adamant in his own mind about not being put into the middle of the present situation that was beginning to sound like a confrontation. He would remain as neutral as possible. "What is it that you want to talk to me about?"

"As a pathologist, you come in contact with a lot of cases, either because you evaluate their laboratory work, or, if a patient dies, you often do a post-mortem. Now tell me, Jacque, and I want you to be honest, do you think that everything possible was done for these patients with CM Disease, or whatever you call it? Was everything done that was medically possible and acceptable?"

"If you are asking me as to whether there is any basis for malpractice in any of these cases, the answer is positively no."

Jim Street frowned. "No, Jacque, I don't mean that. I am interested in patient care not legalities. Dr. Welsch indicated that maybe we ought to get some outside help, from one of the universities."

"Dr. Welsch always knows somebody who would do better. I know just as many important specialists as he does. As a matter of fact I have had phone consultations with pathologists at the Armed Forces Institute of Pathology and with pathologists in other parts of the country, and no one has been able to give me an answer to our problem. An infectious process is probably responsible for these deaths, and it will take some time to sort it out, that's all."

"Well, that's not all, Jacque. What about the people who die in the time that it takes to 'sort things out,' as you put it?"

"Sorry, Jim, I can't help you. We are doing all that we can, and I don't intend to let Winston Welsch push me into doing something drastic just to be doing something. We don't want to lose it now."

"I think that I am going to talk to Steve McKay and have this put on the agenda for the next medical staff meeting. I do not want to give Winston Welsch the opportunity to bring it up and make it look as if he was the only one concerned with the problem. And I don't want him to insinuate that the administration, Steve McKay, or you, did not do everything possible to solve the problem."

Jacque Marten agreed with the administrator. He looked at his watch, and stated that if he stayed any longer he would be late getting all of his laboratory reports out on time. Before Dr. Marten had a chance to leave, Jim Street spoke once more. "Jacque, I hope that we can count on you to help us when the chips are down. I know from the past experience that Winston Welsch can make things pretty ugly."

"Jim, what is it you really want me to do? We have talked over these problems a dozen plus times. I call you every morning and report to you. I have made myself available to you at any time, day or night. I just don't know what more I can do."

Jim Street really wanted a commitment from Dr. Marten that he would support the hospital's position and that of Steve McKay if a confrontation did develop. But he knew that was not to be. "Thanks for coming, Jacque. I have nothing more for now."

Dr. Marten went back to his office and buried himself in his work. He managed to hide his frustration and concern to Jim Street. He was overworked, over-tired, and just plan worried. He was hoping that somehow the problem of CM Disease would disappear from Good Samaritan Hospital.

More cases of "it." More fatal cases of "it," CM Disease. Not a good description, but at least a label to identify a disease that was killing a lot of people. It was a disease for which there was no known cure, and worse yet, a disease for which the cause was not yet known. Drs. McKay and Marten strongly suspected a viral etiology, but they had not been able to prove it. He and Dr. McKay recently had taken additional steps to try to identify a virus, or any other organism that might be the causative agent. Multiple cultures had been taken, but no growth patterns appeared that were either consistent or significant. Dr McKay and Dr. Marten had spent hours reviewing the medical literature trying to find some information that would help them identify the exact nature of CM Disease, its cause, diagnosis, treatment, and most of all, its prevention. They found nothing, absolutely nothing, of any practical value that would help them solve the problem. If CM Disease was not a new disease, it certainly had not been recognized before. But there was one more possibility. They could simply be dealing with a more virulent strain of a known virus.

Doctors McKay and Marten were reaching point of frustration. Patients with CM Disease continued to filter into the hospital, not a large number numerically, but too many considering that none of the victims of the disease survived. Ominously, the number of patients admitted with CM Disease was slowly, but steadily rising. Dr. McKay would not admit it to Dr. Marten and Jacque would not admit it to Dr. McKay, but each was alarmed at the instability of the situation over which they had no control.

Epidemically they had run into a brick wall. They had been unable to find any pattern of distribution of cases that would hint as to the method of spread. There were no cases where more than one person in a family had acquired the disease, and there was not any obvious contact between the victims of the disease thus far. It would take a lot more hard investigation to make a significantly more accurate study, but Dr. Marten had neither the means nor the time to do so. The Department of Health would have to make a more intense study of the mode of transmission of CM Disease. Dr. Marten had briefly investigated the possibility of a chemical toxin, or perhaps some industrial poison as the cause of the disease. But, after lengthy discussions with Dr. McKay and with other health officials, that possibility seemed very remote. So far, CM Disease harbored mysteries that had not yet even begun to be resolved.

In spite of the frustration and the feeling of helplessness that they had, Dr. McKay and Dr. Marten were still in the battle. Multiple blood samples were being drawn from all patients suspected of having CM Disease. The specimens were being sent to the State Laboratories as well as to the United States Center for Infectious Diseases (CDC) at Atlanta. But viral studies are somewhat difficult to perform, and sometimes can take weeks to process and obtain results. The problem was accentuated by the fact that no one knew exactly what he or she was looking for. Although Steve and Jacque were becoming more and more convinced that they were dealing with an infection caused by a virus, they could not be absolutely sure until they could prove it. The main obstacle at that particular point in time was the fact that they had been unable to get the people at CDC to be seriously interested and involved in the problem. Good Samaritan Hospital was getting cooperation, but it could have been better.

As Dr. Marten was finishing signing his reports, a secretary brought in a special delivery letter. Jacque Marten opened the envelope and peered through fatigue-aching eyes. He read the letter for a second time.

Dear Dr. Marten,

The Department of Statistics is requesting confirmation as to the cause of death of a number of patients who died in your hospital within the past two months. The final diagnoses and cause of death in these cases was "Cardiomyopathy, Etiology Undetermined." We also note that most of the patients were under forty years of age, and that a significant number had post mortem examinations confirming the cause of death.

This would seem to be an unusual diagnosis for so many patients in this short time span, especially for this age group.

Please confirm the diagnosis and add any additional information that you think to be significant in the attached enclosure.

It might be of some interest to you to know that recently, this same general diagnosis has been made in other parts of the state.

We therefore believe that your cases, and those from other parts of the state, should be investigated more closely.

Hoping to hear from you in the near future, I remain,

George F. McCloed, M.D., Director
Department of Vital Statistics
State Health Department

Dr. Marten reached for his phone and began dialing.

Chapter 6

Steve McKay entered the outer office of the hospital administrator. He stopped in front of Jim Street's secretary, forty three-year-old, attractive, neatly dressed, and widowed, Bernie Pryce. "Bernie, tell your boss that his Chief of Staff wants to talk to him."

Bernie was working at her computer. She looked at Steve and said, "He is expecting you." She glanced at the phone and saw the signal light was still lit. "But he is still talking to Dr. Marten on the phone."

"I'll wait." Steve began to sit down, then walked to the desk where Bernie was working. "How long has he been talking to Dr. Marten?"

About ten minutes," answered Bernie as she continued working.

Steve spoke in a lowered tone of voice. "If you were not having an affair with your boss, I'd ask you out myself."

Bernie blushed. She was attractive, but rather "prissy." Only Steve kidded her, and although she would not admit it, she did enjoy it. Steve looked up as the door of Jim Street's office when it opened and the good looking, African American hospital administrator emerged. He immediately saw Dr. McKay standing at the desk. "Come on in, Steve."

They entered Jim Street's private office and Steve made himself comfortable in one of the leather-covered chairs in front of the desk. He and Jim Street had worked closely as a team in recent years and they knew each other pretty well, both as personal friends and as professional associates. They sometimes disagreed, but they respected each other's opinion and they had always been able to work out their problems and come to a satisfactory conclusion, and still remain friends. But now events were rapidly closing in on them, and both were edgy.

"Jacque received a letter from the State Department of Health. They are asking for confirmation of the diagnosis on a number of deaths in the hospital. You know, all of those who have died with that cardiac problem."

"I am not surprised. We had to expect that sooner or later." Steve was trying to downplay the problem and its repercussions. He knew that Jim Street was under a great deal of pressure from many sources; the medical staff, his Board of Directors, hospital personnel, and more recently, the news media.

The job as hospital administrator was not a medical position in the true sense of the word, but the administrator is closely associated with the medical staff. As the administrator of Good Samaritan Hospital, Jim Street was an administrator of people and of things. He had two hundred plus beds in his hospital. He was responsible for nearly eight hundred employees. It was his job to see that there was heat, light, water, personnel, drugs, and a variety of services, both medical and otherwise, for his patients. He found himself forever bickering with numerous governmental agencies, insurance companies and HMO's, over charges and fees. In addition, he had to monitor his medical staff to make sure that they were delivering medical services with high ethical and professional standards. Keeping everybody happy was not easy. His medical background was limited and he had to rely on staff members such as Dr. McKay and Dr. Marten to keep him informed and advised on medical matters. He frequently heard a variety of views on medical problems from different members of the medical staff. He had to weigh all of the information, confer with medical staff committees, and then join with them in deciding which alternative to take that would be best for the staff physicians, the hospital, and most of all, for the patient. And now, topping the mountain of everyday, complicated, hospital administration was a new snowstorm. Patients were dying in his hospital and no one on the staff could tell him why. His dilemma now was whether as hospital administrator he could, or should, be doing more to solve the problem.

Jim Street leaned forward on the desk. "Steve, just how big of a problem is this cardiac disease that we have in our community? Winston Welsch thinks we could be doing more to meet the problem and now the State wants a closer look."

Steve wrinkled his forehead. "When something like this happens, there is always someone looking over your shoulder and observing as to whether you are doing everything according to the book. The looker has a lot easier job then the doer because he has no decisions to make. Maybe some of these patients are dying unnecessarily, but I doubt it. Jim, we know that we have a problem. Our whole medical staff knows that we have a problem. Our staff is handling it as well as anyone could. Just don't push the panic button…yet."

Jim leaned back. "Hell, I am not sure what to do, if anything." Jim Street swung his swivel chair around until he was facing the window, his back to Dr. McKay. "And how about your not taking care of that patient Dr. Welsch turned over to you?"

It took an extraordinary amount of restraint to keep Steve from exploding. He spoke in a rather low and almost an angry tone of voice. "Jim, we have already gone over that, three times in fact. You don't think that I was negligent, do you?" He now turned inquisitive and surprised, "Or do you?"

Jim Street swung around so that he was facing Steve once again. " Guess not. But that damn Welsch keeps bringing it up, insidiously, subtly." He paused, then continued. "You know, the hospital and you could be sued for abandonment."

Steve McKay began to show impatience. "Look, Jim, I am not going to worry about a law suit that might happen. I have too many other things to worry about, important things. And anyway, Welsch is not going to trouble us legally about that case. If anybody abandoned that patient, he did. It really made no difference who, if anyone, saw that patient that night. The patient would have died even if Dr. Welsch, or I, or both of us were there. Patient relations wise, it was bad that no doctor was there to see the patient leave this world. But medically, that patient was doomed."

Jim Street seemed to be satisfied with that, at least for the moment. "Okay. Now about this public health thing. Anything that I should do?"

Dr. McKay was still in a cooling off process from the last discussion. "Let Jacque handle that. He knows his way around. I am sure that you are going to get some public health people down here. You have to expect that to happen in a case like this, and we really need their input and expertise." Steve was interrupted by a phone call aimed at the administrator.

After a short conversation, Jim Street set the phone in the cradle and with a worried look on his face said, "Dammit."

"He just did, but what did he damn?"

"That was the paper. They want to talk to us about all of these people dying at Good Samaritan Hospital, unnecessarily, as they put it. The bastards."

"That's a medical problem. Tell them to talk to the Medical Society if they want information."

Jim Street was disgruntled. "They have already spoken to the Medical Society president, the great and all knowing, Dr. Winston Welsch. He talked for an hour with the reporters, and when they apparently got him backed into a corner, he begged off by telling them to see me here at the hospital, that we have all the answers. The bastard."

Later that day, Steve McKay found himself in Jim Street's office once again. Jim had asked him to be with him during the interview so that he could help to clear any medical questions that might arise.

Jim Street, as hospital administrator, was the official spokesman for the hospital, so the reporters pointed their initial questioning at him. "You have had an inordinate number of deaths from some strange disease recently. Any comment?"

"What you say is basically true, but I don't know if a 'strange disease' is the best way to describe it."

"It has been uniformly fatal though."

Jim Street referred the question to Dr. McKay.

"Yes, it has. As far as we know, there have been no recoveries. But people may have had the disease, recovered, and we might not necessarily know that."

"Our publisher's son-in-law died from this disease, is that correct?"

"You know that we are not able to divulge any information about a particular patient by name without explicit permission."

The interview went on for thirty minutes. Both Jim Street and Dr. McKay had the feeling that the reporters seemed to already know what they were going to write. They had a hefty amount of information about CM Disease, due undoubtedly to information that had been given to them by Dr. Welsch. They seemed to be seeking confirmation of what they already knew.

Near the end of the interview, a few soft spots were touched, and Jim Street almost blew his cool. But years of experience as an administrator told him that you never aggravate the press.

They again turned their questioning to Steve. "We understand that you have been in on almost every case of CM Disease, Dr. McKay."

Jim Street, holding back his aggravation, answered before Steve could collect his thoughts. "Gentlemen, we must leave individuals out of this completely. Medical ethics dictate that it would be better not to use the name of any physician or any patient in any interview that you plan to publish in the paper."

The reporters would not retreat. They knifed forward. "No mention of this in the paper. We merely would like to ask Dr. McKay a few questions since he apparently has had the most experience with the disease."

"I have no objection," answered Steve. "But bear this in mind. I have been a consulting physician for the attending physicians, so I feel that it is very important that you not refer to any particular patient unless you have the permission of the attending physician who was in charge of the case, and of course the family of the patient."

The evasive answers indicated to the reporters that they were definitely on to something. "Tell us what you think of all this, Doctor. I mean these patients dying from this heart disease, this CM Disease, or whatever you call it?"

Dr. McKay continued to word fence with them. "I cannot add anything more than what you know. Dr. Welsch, as president of the Medical Society, should be the official medical spokesperson in these matters. I am sure that he has already told you everything that we know about this problem."

The reporters were not getting any new information. The lengthy, and what they considered to have been a productive interview with Dr. Welsch had already given them a great story. But they were unsure that Dr. Welsch had told them everything that was going on with CM Disease in the community. Rather than pursue a questionable situation any further they chose to close the interview. But they left with a note that was disturbing to Dr. McKay. As the reporters were leaving, one turned and said, "Dr. McKay, we will be in contact with you again since you are the expert around here on CM Disease."

These words brought back to mind similar words spoken by Jacque Marten a few days before. Steve McKay felt uncomfortable in the position of being an expert in a disease whose etiology was unknown and for which there was no known cure.

The following evening Jim Street drove into his driveway, earlier than usual. He had left the hospital at four so that he could eat a leisurely supper and relax a short time before appearing at a Woman's Club meeting where he was scheduled to give a talk. He was not looking forward to spending an evening away from home for the seventh day in a row, but a very close friend of his wife had asked him to speak, so he could hardly refuse. Ellen Street met her husband at the door, holding a folded newspaper in her hand. "Now, Jim, don't get angry when you read this. Remember, you have to give that talk tonight."

Jim Street read the lead line from the article about the interview that he and Dr. McKay had given the day before. "The Chief of Staff of the hospital and the hospital administrator admit CM Disease is on the brink of becoming an epidemic." Jim Street did not even finish the article. He flung the paper half way across the room and stormed upstairs to take a cold shower.

The next few days were near chaos at Good Samaritan. Jim Street's office was deluged by phone calls from doctors, nurses, patients and people who were panic stricken. Doctor's offices were packed with people who were afraid that they might have CM Disease. Day after day the Emergency Department set records for the number of patients they saw. The newspaper had printed a follow up story in an attempt to calm the stormy waters generated by the first article, but they had underestimated the public's reaction to what was intended to be an interest generating story. The reporters had colored Jim Street's and Dr. McKay's remarks for two reasons. They thought that the hospital was hiding the whole truth about what they actually knew about CM Disease, and secondly Dr. Welsch had insinuated that something more could have been done and should be done about CM Disease.

Jim Street was not sleeping well so he got up and went to the hospital earlier than usual. He picked up the packet containing a daily report from a computer service that was used to audit patient care in the hospital on a day to day basis and went to his private office. He threw the packet on his desk and hung his coat in the closet. He sat down at his desk and took a big gulp of the coffee that he had brought with him from the cafeteria. He set the cup down and opened the envelope with the computer-generated information and skimmed through it. The report was routine until the final page. The bomb was dropped in bold, large, type: OUR SURVEY INDICATES THAT CM DISEASE IN YOUR HOSPITAL AND COMMUNITY HAS REACHED EPIDEMIC PROPORTIONS. ACTION APPROPRIATE TO THE SITUATION IS INDICATED.

Chapter 7

A young family physician in upstate New York is in the medical library of his hospital. He is reading the medical journals as he waits for one of his obstetric patients to deliver. He reads a short article about recent deaths at a Mid-western hospital. The etiological cause of the deaths could not be determined but the affliction is referred to as CM Disease. He notes the similarity of the clinical course of those cases and the clinical course of two patients who had died in his hospital in the previous week. He makes a copy of the report and plans to present it together with a summary of the hospital cases at Family Practice Department meeting that would be held the following week.

Wonder Gap, Washington. A pathologist sits in his office reviewing a number of recent deaths at his hospital resulting from an acute flu-like illness terminating in cardiomyopathy and cardiac arrest. His interest in the cases is heightened when he remembers reading of similar cases at Good Samaritan Hospital. The pathologist makes extensive notes as he carefully reviews his charts once again. He then makes copies of the charts, dictates an extensive summary letter and faxes everything to Dr. Jacque Marten, at Good Samaritan Hospital.

Two physicians in Bridgeton, Iowa, are having coffee in the cafeteria at the hospital where they practice. A third physician joins them. The conversation soon turns to a discussion of the similarity of the clinical findings and general downhill course of three patients recently admitted to the hospital. All three patients died. In all three patients the immediate cause of death was an arrhythmia leading to cardiac arrest. All of the cases went to autopsy, and a severe cardiomyopathy was noted. The hospital's pathologist had not been unable to dctermine a definite etiology for the myopathy.

"It has to be more than sheer coincidence that we should have three cases of cardiomyopathy in so short of time," said one of the physicians. "And all three of the patients were pretty young."

Another physician added, "I wonder why our pathology department could not determine an etiology. They are generally quite competent." Unbeknown to the doctors, there were three more patients with CM Disease in their hospital at the time of their conversation. All three patients would die that week.

A scheduled weekly staff meeting was being held at the Center for Disease Control at Atlanta. At these meetings, problems are discussed and sometimes decisions are made. If the problem had far reaching consequences, or was of a complicated nature, it was referred to a superior committee for further discussion and decision making.

The staff members attending the conference had already finished reading the report and were in the process of carefully evaluating its content. A new disease had apparently manifested itself, a disease that was killing people in scattered parts of the country. Patients with the disease first experienced an influenza-like syndrome, but instead of a slow recovery, the condition of the patients slowly deteriorated and they died of cardiac complications. Cardiac arrest secondary to Cardiomyopathy was diagnosed as the immediate cause of death in all of the cases.

Dr. Cathy Chen, Chairperson, opened the discussion, and immediately focused on the reports from Good Samaritan Hospital. "They seem to have had more cases at Good Samaritan than anywhere else in the country. CM Disease...that is what they call it. Dr. Marten, their pathologist, and Dr. McKay, their Chief of Staff, have written us an exhaustive report of their experience with the affliction, whatever it may be. I studied under Dr. Marten," continued Dr. Chen, "And he is very competent."

Vice-Chairman Dr. Zenon Ambrose added, "They would like to present their findings in the *Journal of the American Medical Association or the New England Journal of Medicine*."

Dr. Chen stopped to take a drink of water, then continued. "I think that this is important enough that we should contact Dr. Marten and Dr. McKay personally about this. Actually, I would like to see Marten and McKay come here so that we can discuss this with them personally. Might even suggest that some of their Administration and nurses come with them."

Julie Smyth, an Administrative Assistant added, "CM Disease. That is a good name for it, whatever it is. I believe that we should officially refer to this particular disease entity as CM Disease, at least for the present."

All present agreed that they would refer to whatever this fatal disease was as "CM Disease" in all future reports and communications.

Dr. Zenon Ambrose spoke again. "I would like to suggest that we contact the NIH. I'd like to know what information they have on CM Disease, and if they intend to become involved."

Dr. Chen stacked her papers to one side. "I'll try to arrange for the Good Samaritan group to meet with us, then go on to the NIH. I'll call the NIH and get their input.

Julie Smyth asked, "Just how big a problem is this anyway?"

Dr. Cathy Chen answered. "It appears that it is a very serious problem. An epidemic may be erupting in some parts of the country, especially in the community served by Good Samaritan Hospital. No national epidemic in sight, yet. But this CM Disease is on the rise, and it appears to be uniformly fatal. I think that this should go right to the top immediately."

"The Executive Committee had their regular meeting last week, and they are not scheduled to meet again for two weeks," said Julie Smyth.

"I will take care of that," said Dr. Chen. "I will deliver our recommendation in person to Dr. O'Brien, and I will suggest that they meet and discuss this tomorrow."

"Hi, stranger. Where are you going so fast?" Lisa greeted Steve as they met on the staircase between the first and second floors of the hospital. "It is nice to see you, Steve. You have not even called in three days."

"I thought that I would see you in ICU, but I guess that you have been off for a few days. You needed that time off, and you still look tired."

Lisa spoke as they climbed the stairs to the fourth floor. "I am on my way to surgery. I need a special intravenous catheter for Dr. Welsch's patient." They walked into the lounge of the surgery suite. 'Sit down, Steve. I am in no rush and you look as if you have not slept for days."

Steve needed no second invitation. He was tired, really tired. He had never been this tired since his Residency when it was common for him to routinely put in eighteen hour days. "It does feel good to sit down. If I close my eyes, I think I'll fall asleep."

"You sound as if your ship has just capsized. Anything wrong besides being tired?"

"I have just been pushed, that's all." Steve kicked off his loafers and threw his feet on the table in front of the leather sofa where they were sitting. "I don't know how many more mothers I can face and tell them that their son or daughter is dying, and that there is not a thing that I, or anyone else, can do to prevent it. After awhile it just gets to you."

"I know," said Lisa. Then she looked at Steve with a sad look on her face, "Frustrating, isn't it?"

"Lisa, there has to be an answer, there just has to be. "I've read, and read, and read. I've been on the Internet, I've made phone calls, and I still have not come up with anything that compares to this. Jacque has called half way around the world, and no one can even come close to giving us even the slightest clue as to what in the hell we are facing."

Lisa looked at Steve; his head thrown back, his eyes closed.

"You could let someone else do it. Take a few days off, Steve. You need some time to catch up on your rest, and you will never get it here at the hospital. People depend too much on you."

Steve spoke lazily now, but with more confidence. "Our break will come." He was quiet for a few moments, then continued. "And how are we set for Friday night? Is it still on?"

"I think so, unless something unforeseen happens to change our plans. David will leave Thursday night and will be gone for the whole weekend. I'll call you tomorrow and let you know for sure."

It rained off and on all day Friday, and it was still drizzling as Steve sat in his car in the doctor's parking lot. He checked his watch again. It was nearly midnight. He looked out the window at the dark sky with no visible moon and a thick overcast covering the city. His mind was still dull with fatigue and shifted frequently from thought to thought. Lisa was late. ICU was full and there was a shortage of nurses. There were a lot of extremely sick patients in ICU and Lisa was helping the night shift get organized. "She is efficient as hell," thought Steve, "and she would never leave until she was satisfied that everything was in proper order for the night." A ribbon of headlights cut through the night and interrupted Steve's chain of thought.

Steve's brain landed on the problem of CM Disease and on the fact that the State Department of Health had officially declared the community in which he lived an epidemic area. A shudder went through Steve as a haunting thought entered his mind; no one as far as they knew who had CM Disease had survived. Not a single patient had lived after contracting the damnable thing. Could it possibly be that they were in the early phases of a pandemic that would match the "Black Plague" of the Middle Ages? One quarter of the population of Europe died in that one. Could such an epidemic occur in the twentieth first century, even with all of the modern advances in medical technology that had taken place? It was impossible. Or was it?

Steve looked toward the door of the hospital. No sign of Lisa. He glanced at his watch again. He was tired and he was becoming impatient. Then the door opened and Lisa emerged and walked quickly toward his car. Steve stepped out in the drizzling rain to meet her, then he drove to her place.

*

Steve and Lisa sat on the softly carpeted floor, half dressed, crossed legged, and sipping Asti Spumanti. Quiet music from the stereo filled the background and the sound of the rain that splattered the window was interrupted every now and then by the faint roll of thunder that echoed from a distance. It was a delightful night for two people in love to spend together making love. Steve and Lisa were enjoying every second of this precious, quiet moment.

Steve leaned over and poured wine for Lisa and then for himself. He raised his glass in Lisa's direction, "To us."

Steve drank lightly from the glass then set it down. "I thought that you were off all of this weekend."

"I was, up until tonight. We had one nurse call in sick, so I will cover."

"Can't you get someone else?"

"Not this weekend. It seems that it is harder and harder to get anyone to work extra hours any more."

"Afraid that they will get stung by CM Disease?"

"Maybe."

"No one has yet," said Steve.

"Not yet," answered Lisa. "But one of these days."

"One of these days, what?" asked Steve.

"Someone is going to get stung," replied Lisa.

Steve took a long breath. "Yes, and I wonder who it will be?"

"Let's not talk about it, Steve. Not now anyway?"

Steve moved closer to Lisa. The music turned more romantic, the rain touched the windows a little harder, the thunder rolled closer. "How many years has it been now, Lisa?"

"Five, more or less."

"A long time," answered Steve.

"Not long enough," replied Lisa as she emptied her glass.

Steve reached for the wine and poured again for Lisa. "You have taken a greater interest in the Asti Spumanti than you usually do, Lisa. Drinking is not your thing."

"I know, but I am in that mood. I would like to get cloudy and forget. I'd like to forget the hospital; forget the hospital and all of the death that is there."

"You are really morbid tonight." Steve leaned over and kissed Lisa gently on the cheek. "You need some time off. Let's leave for St. Louis, tonight."

Lisa smiled a caricature smile. "Funny, very funny. And how do you think that you will manage to get away?"

"Carole is gone for a week, you know."

"You are too valuable to her. You are quite safe. I am the one who she would shoot, if it were to come to that."

They rolled into each other's arms and swam in each other's caresses and kisses. Passions flared and heated exchanges of love passed between them. The circumstance surroundings and the wine releasing them from the tensions of the pervious week fired the furnaces of excitement that overwhelmed the two lovers. Their remaining clothes were haphazardly thrown aside, their bodies entwined into a rapturous tangle of limbs. Tongues explored each other and sent spine tingles that begot greater passions and eager explorations. Soft caresses and touches of vital areas signaled new spices of covetousness to explode and sprinkle the two of them with lustful pleasure. Again and again they buried themselves into each other as deeply as they could. Their love play sent them flying into luxurious, sensual ecstasy. And then, the final penetrating act of love, and they both were devoured in a ravishment that sent thunders of pulsations emanating to all parts of their spent bodies. They lay still, and quiet…fulfilled.

Diane Vaughan was charge nurse in ICU. She had relieved Lisa Clarke earlier that night. The Intensive Care Unit was busy and all the beds were filled. Two of the patients were in the terminal stages of CM Disease and there was one more patient who was suspected of having the fatal disease.

Diane looked up when Dr. Welsch, wet with the rain, walked into the unit. He walked over to the desk and to Diane. "Is that patient still alive?"

"Yes, but I am glad that you came over to see him. He is slipping fast. I have done everything that you told me to do, and he still is filling up with fluid. His last blood gasses were horrible. I don't see how he can survive much longer."

"Did you ever get in touch with Dr. McKay? He has been seeing this patient also, and I think that he should be here."

"Dr. McKay has signed out for a few hours. He will call in when he returns."

"Did you try his home?"

"We usually do not do that. We always call his answering service, and they have him call back. We do not like to disturb his wife, especially at night. His answering service is usually quite good about having him call."

"Do you know where he is?"

Diane thought that she knew, but she would not call there under any circumstances. "Not really. We always work through the answering service.

You know Dr. Welsch, Dr. McKay has been putting in a lot of hours these past few weeks. He has practically been living here at the hospital. I think that he just wanted a few hours of rest." Then she rapidly reversed the conversation back to the patient. "Here is your patient's chart. I'll help you if you want."

Dr. Welsch reviewed the chart, and then he and Diane went over to the bed where the young man was dying of CM Disease. Dr. Welsch checked the EKG monitor. "He has a bradycardia with frequent PVC's. Is his heart slowing down to any significant degree?"

"Yes, it is definitely slower than when I came on duty. But Lisa Clarke said in her report that Dr. McKay saw the patient earlier last night and was worried about the developing ventricular slowdown. He was sure that the patient would go into cardiac a bradyarrhythmia, then standstill, just like all of the others have done."

Dr. Welsch examined the patient who was obviously dying. The patient was cyanotic and his chest was congested. Intravenous fluids were running into his veins and oxygen was being administered by mask. He was restless and in extremis. You would think that Diane and Dr. Welsch would be extremely anxious about the patient, but they were not. No one at Good Samaritan became anxious over CM Disease patients anymore; frustrated yes, but they were past the panic stage of seeing so many dying young patients. The staff had come to the point where they expected these patients to die. The only question that remained anymore was, when? The staff tried to remain aloof of the patient, as if by doing so the problem would go away. But aloofness only served to dim the reality of death that would invariably come to visit, and to conquer.

Dr. Welsch walked back to the desk. "I do not think that there is anything more that I can do. He will probably die in the next few hours." Then he asked again, "Are you sure that you cannot reach Dr. McKay? He should talk to the parents."

"The parents are in the waiting room. You can talk to them yourself, if you wish. In fact, they were hoping that they would have a chance to talk to you tonight. Dr. McKay had a long conversation with them this afternoon, and he did not give them any hope for survival. So, they are prepared."

"I don't think that it would do any good for me to see them. When he dies, be sure that we get a post-mortem. It is important that we collect as much information as we can in these cases."

Diane tried once more. "Are you sure that you don't want to talk to the family? I think that they would appreciate it."

"I don't think so. I have another patient to see before I go back home, and

I have to get up early to get back here to the hospital to see my patients. Try and get in touch with Dr. McKay. Ask him if he can come out and check the patient once more, and then he can talk to the family again."

Diane was not happy about Dr. Welsch leaving without talking to the family, but she could not do anything about it. She held a great deal of empathy for the family of the dying young man, and she thought that they were entitled to at least some consolation from the attending physician, even though the doctor could not offer any hope for recovery. She picked up the phone and began dialing Lisa Clarke's home. She stopped half way through and replaced the phone in its cradle. Then she took up the death vigil that finally ended at 0600 when the young man's heart went into cardiac asystole… his heart stopped beating. The family consented to have a post-mortem examination performed.

Chapter 8

It was still raining early Saturday morning when Jim Street arrived at the hospital. He collected the numerous reports that had accumulated in his box overnight then went downstairs to the cafeteria for breakfast. Dr. McKay was already there and on his second cup of coffee as he waited for the hospital administrator to appear.

"Any new cases of CM Disease during the night, Jim?"

"One suspect, on the second floor."

"Negative. I have already seen that one."

"You don't think that it is a case of CM Disease then?"

"I am not one hundred percent certain, but it does not act like it. Not yet anyway. We will keep a close watch on him today just to be sure. I have transferred him to ICU."

"You have been filling ICU with those suspect cases, Steve. We are overloaded up there."

"I know, and that is one of the reasons why I want to talk to you this morning. I think that we should take four or five rooms on the second floor and use them as a CM suspect ward. If a patient takes a significant turn for the worse, then we will transfer them to ICU, or some other designated intensive care area."

"That's a good thought, but we may have trouble staffing such a unit. We are starting to get repercussions from the Nursing Office. It seems that some of the nurses are not too eager to attend CM cases in fear that they themselves might get the disease."

"I suspected as much from the way that some of the nursing staff has been talking. I think that it is probably their families that object to their working with these cases rather than the nurses themselves."

Jim Street called for a second cup of coffee. "I don't give a damn why we can't get people to staff, I just want nurses to do their job."

"Well, work at it then," replied Steve in a somewhat annoyed manner.

"Goddamn it, Steve. Sometimes you are no help at all."

Steve sipped coffee. "I have medical staff problems to think about let alone nursing staff problems to worry about."

"Like what? What medical staff problems are you talking about now?" asked Jim Street.

"Like Dr. Welsch has asked to present his 'abandonment case' at a staff meeting," said Steve.

"That dumb bastard. Here we are, a deadly disease stalking our community, patients dying all over the place, and we don't know why, and he gets his ass in an uproar over an abandonment case that is not even an abandonment case. What the hell is the matter with that guy?"

"He also thinks that we should be doing more about this epidemic"

"We all think that, goddamnit. If we only knew what to do that we are not already doing. I suppose he will get the whole damn staff in a turmoil over this." Jim Street swallowed hard at his coffee. "Anything you want me to do?"

"I don't know what you can do. I have heard rumors that Winston has some new information on that abandonment case. But, I have no idea what new information it might be, and I have not been able to find out anything more. If any of his pigeons know anything, they are not spreading the information."

"Keep a tight lid on the meeting if you can. If I learn or hear anything I'll get in touch with you." Jim Street stood at the table before he left and said, "And don't worry about it. I will back you one hundred percent on this. We have to get it out of the way as soon as we can so we can get back on track with the really important problems that are drowning us."

"Like CM Disease?"

"Yeah, like CM Disease." Jim Street turned and left the cafeteria and headed for his office.

At eleven a.m. that morning, Dr. Welsch was entering the pathology office. He appeared to be hurried and anxious as he spoke to the secretary behind the desk covered with laboratory reports. "I would like to talk to Dr. Marten. Now, if at all possible."

The secretary responded promptly to the air of authority that made the request. "Dr. Marten has just completed an autopsy, but I will check to see if he can see you now."

"Tell him it is very important," said Dr. Welsch.

Dr. Welsch nervously took a chair and fumbled with a medical journal that lay on the table alongside. He did not have to wait very long. Dr. Marten entered the room, unhappy about having been interrupted in his work. Still wiping his hands, Dr. Marten motioned to Dr. Welsch. "I suppose that you would like to talk in private. Come into my office."

Dr. Welsch closed the door, but he did not take the seat offered to him. "Jacque, I have a meeting this afternoon with three other staff members. We want to discuss the upcoming staff meeting. We want to know where you stand on all of this."

Jacque Marten leaned back in his chair. "Just what you are driving at, Winston?"

Dr. Welsch leaned on the desk. "I think that you know what I am talking about. We have a terrible problem with this epidemic, and our Chief of Staff, who is also our so-called expert in this field, is doing nothing."

Jacque Marten did not hide his anger. "What do you want Dr. McKay to do? We don't even know what kind of a disease we are dealing with. We don't even know what it is, let alone how to treat it."

"I am well aware of all of that, Dr. Marten. I am no dummy. But we have taken no precautions for our staff, our nurses, and our personnel. We have taken no public health action. The community expects us to do that, and I think that we should."

Dr. Marten was still angry. "What do you want me to do? You are the president of the County Medical Society. Why don't do something?"

"I just want to know if you will stand with some of us when we bring this up at the meeting. We have to have some kind of action."

"I won't promise anything. I don't know what you are planning and I am not taking sides. I do not see anything that could have been done up to now that has not been done."

"Okay, Jacque, but just remember you may end up being responsible for some of this, if disaster strikes."

"I'll take that chance. I will stand on whatever we have done so far, and defend it."

Dr. Welsch's tone of voice changed. He became more subdued and quiet. "You know that we are presenting that case of Dr. McKay's. You know the one I mean. The patient that died the night that they could not find him. It looks as if the patient may not have had CM Disease after all. And if he did not, Doctor, then the patient might have lived if he had more intense and proper treatment." Without saying anything more, and without waiting for a reply, Dr. Welsch left the Pathology Department.

Dr. Marten returned to his work. Pathology was his business, not hospital politics.

It was becoming obvious to Doctor McKay and Doctor Marten, as well as to Jim Street, that Dr. Welsch was setting up some kind of confrontation with the administration and Dr. McKay. Two issues were involved. The one concerned the developing epidemic of CM Disease, and the other was an apparent attempt to discredit Dr. McKay by blowing out of proportion the alleged abandonment of the patient on the night that Dr. McKay could not be found. Up to that time none of the medical staff had considered this to be a case of abandonment under the circumstances, but Dr Welsch had continued to keep the issue alive. And now it seemed that he was about to bring the matter to the entire medical staff for action.

Steve found himself in Jim Street's office that same Saturday afternoon, keeping the appointment he had made at breakfast that morning. "Bernie, how is your boss doing on time? You notice of course that I am right on time for my appointment."

"He is a little behind today. I will let him know that you are here as soon as he is off the phone."

The light on Jim Street's telephone line went off, indicating that he had finished his phone conversation. His authoritative voice blared over the intercom, "Has Dr. McKay come in yet?"

Steve motioned to Bernie to be quiet, then he depressed the button and answered in a high pitched voice in imitation the secretary. "Dr. McKay phoned and said that he would be late, and that he would meet you at your girlfriend's house."

"Goddammit, Steve, get in here so I can get the hell home some time tonight."

"He must have had a bad day," said Steve as he reached for the door leading to Jim Street's office.

"Sit down, Steve."

Steve slumped into a chair at the side of the desk. "You sure are gruffy today. Any special reason?"

"Special? Hell no. Just the same goddamn stuff. CM Disease is killing people all over my hospital. Winston Welsch is stirring the trouble pot, and I don't know the hell why. The bitch of a newspaper bugging my ass all day." Jim Street leaned over the desk. "And what bad news do you have for me to contemplate about now?"

"Nothing," answered Steve. "But you seem edgy today."

"Nothing. Nothing, hell," replied Jim Street. "When you say nothing, that means something." Jim Street leaned back in his chair. "Okay, Steve. So I am edgy. I have good reason to be edgy, and you know it."

Steve slouched in the chair and drew a deep breath.

Jim Street asked, "Coffee, Coke, tea?"

"Tea, iced if you can."

Jim Street shoved down the intercom button. "Bernie, have someone in the cafeteria bring up a pitcher of iced tea and two glasses." Then he turned toward Steve. "It will be here in a minute. Now, what is on your mind? You would not tell me over the phone why you wanted to talk to me and that is unusual for you. This must be something really special."

"Not really. I just did not want you to get all upset early in the day. I want to talk to you about calling a special meeting for the staff. I knew that if I told you this morning, you would have wanted to settle the matter right there, and I had other things to do."

"What in the hell kind of special meeting are you talking about? You have a General Staff meeting coming up in a couple of weeks."

"I know that, Jim. But Welsch is stirring up the medical staff, so I thought that it be best to get this whole thing settled, now, before the medical staff starts taking sides. What we don't need now is a disorganized staff."

Jim Street hardly gave Steve a chance to finish. "I am against any damn special meeting. A special meeting is just going to make Welsch feel even more confident. He will think that you are being defensive."

"I don't think that this has to be a confrontation at all. We just meet, both sides, present their views and that will be about all that will be necessary. Once everybody, including Welsch, has a chance to sound off, I'm sure everyone will be happy."

"Hell, yes, they will be happy. They'll have your head on Welsch's plate. Steve, I've been...." Bernie bringing in the iced tea interrupted him. "Let's see now, where was I?"

"You have my head on Welsch's plate."

"Oh, yes. Steve, I have been here long enough to know that you can't come out ahead, even if you win. There will be a lot of nasty things said, and some of them are bound to stick in the minds of some of the doctors, whether you like it or not."

"It would be the same at a staff meeting," said Steve.

"Not really," answered Jim Street. "There you would have other things to discuss and there would not be that much time to discuss your abandonment case. But in a special meeting, there would be no other business. Now, Steve, you are the Chief of Staff, and you can call the special meeting and I can't stop you, but I can advise you against it, and I do."

"I don't understand your objections," said Steve.

"You are going to discuss the problem of CM Disease in the hospital and community. And Welsch is going to say that more can be done, and that he can do it. He is going to say that he knows a bunch of university professors who will come out here and give us their opinion, and maybe, just maybe, solve the problem. That's a bunch of bullshit, but there is enough truth in what he will say so that it will sound good, and a bunch of the guys will buy it. And then when that is all tumbled through the wash, he is going to bring up that abandonment business."

"Jim. There is nothing, absolutely nothing, to that. After you mentioned it to me two or three times I talked to the family. They were upset on the night that the patient died, but they naturally would be. But they are not upset now. They understand the situation and they understand that everything was done that could have been done to save the patient."

"Steve, your problem is that you are too trustful. You have been around Welsch long enough to know that he will not sit still and let this die. He is power hungry and his ego will not allow this to go on without his bringing it up. He does not want to kill you, hell no. But he does want to wound you. He knows damn well that you are becoming a very influential person on the medical staff and he does not like that. He has been king pig around here for too long and he does not want to lose that."

Steve shifted a little, then reached into his inner coat pocket and withdrew a folded paper that he handed to Jim Street. "Thanks for the support, but here is the notice that I want to put out tomorrow."

Jim Street unfolded the paper and quickly read it. He looked up at Dr. McKay. "You want this meeting this coming Tuesday?" He asked in a surprised tone of voice.

"The sooner the better. I want to get this off the ground so that we can all get to work on this problem of CM Disease. I think that it is going to get worse, Jim."

"I agree with you. About the CM Disease problem getting worse, I mean. Any closer to an answer, yet?"

Steve was sort of slow to respond. "Not unless we have had some new breaks in the past hour. Dr. Marten and I have some ideas, but nothing definite. Up to now we have not had the full cooperation of CDC. They are so busy that it is difficult to get their attention sometimes."

"Maybe Dr Welsch can move CDC," said Jim Street in a sarcastic tone of voice.

Dr. McKay smiled. "Ironically, he has absolutely no, and I mean no, influence whatsoever at CDC. I don't know exactly why, but I suspect that they had some kind of a run-in with him in the past."

"I know that he did, and I will not say why, for personal reasons," answered Jim Street.

"I think that Jacque has CDC so stirred up now that we will be getting prompt action, and soon."

Jim Street looked at his watch. "Time to go home, Steve. Have Bernie get this out to the staff, tonight. And I hope you are doing the right thing in calling this meeting. I think that you are wrong, but it is your prerogative to call meetings whenever you feel that one is necessary. Good luck."

On the way home, Dr. McKay thought about his talk with Jim Street. He was not confident about the success of a special meeting before he talked to Jim Street, and now his confidence in his ability to keep control of the situation was shattered even more.

Chapter 9

It was the day that Dr. McKay had scheduled for the special medical staff meeting.

There was absolutely no doubt about it now; Good Samaritan Hospital was the focal point in the country for the rapidly expanding epidemic of CM Disease. The situation seemed to be worsening by the hour. The number of new cases was increasing at an alarming rate. And now it was getting difficult to get nursing personnel to work, especially in the Intensive Care Unit, the Emergency Department, or any area that was involved in the care of patients who actually had CM Disease, or who were suspect of having CM Disease. The mode of transmission of CM Disease was not known and a subconscious cloud of fear cast itself over the hospital and hovered in every corridor and patient room. Up to now, no one working with CM Disease patients in the hospital had contracted the disease. Jim Street had urged the nursing department office to use this argument to encourage nurses to continue to report to work at the hospital. Before the end of the day, this argument would have been shattered and inconsequential.

"What a miserable way to begin the morning," thought Dr. Marten as he covered the corpse with the white sheet. He had just completed an autopsy examination on another case of CM Disease. A similar history as all the others. A young patient, a thirty-three old female, a mother, a wife. She had no indication of illness until ten days prior to her death. At that time she developed flu-like symptoms, just like everyone else who had contracted the disease; a sore throat, headache, a low-grade fever, and a feeling of weakness and fatigue, especially on exertion. Her attending physician had suspected that CM Disease was developing, but he did not tell her or her family. What if he did? He could offer her no hope of cure. The only thing the doctor could do was to watch her die as he filled her failing physiological systems with fluids, antibiotics and other drugs that would prove to be worthless in combating CM Disease. The patient's condition predictably deteriorated. She developed congestive heart failure; the lungs filled with fluid and her tissues became progressively more hypoxic. She slipped into a coma and developed the cardiac arrhythmia that was the ominous sign of impending severe Cardiomyopathy that terminated in cardiac asystole and death. She died at one a.m. Dr. McKay had been asked to see the patient in consultation. He did, but he requested that he not be expected to follow the case. He had seen too many patients die lately. He was frustrated by the fact that he could do nothing but stand by and watch life ebb away. And now Dr. Marten felt the same helpless frustration as he and his associates continued to do the post-mortems on the patients dying with CM Disease. The situation was becoming almost commonplace, so much so, that someone had left a morbid note on the morgue door: ANOTHER DAY, ANOTHER POST ....SIGNED, CM DISEASE.

Steve McKay stopped outside the morgue and was reading the handwritten sign taped to the door when Dr. Marten stepped out. He read the note, quickly tore it off and threw it into the wastebasket in one quick motion. "I don't think that is so funny," he said.

"Jacque, you look a little pale, and tired."

"Two post-mortems last night. My associate did the first one, but I came in at five to do this one. We have so much other work to do that I did not want to let it go till later. Anything in particular that you want to see me about?"

The two were walking past the cafeteria. "Come on, Jacque, I'll buy you breakfast. Jim Street should be here soon."

Dr. Marten looked at his watch. "I really should not. I have a frozen section to do at eight."

They stopped at the cafeteria door. "Your associate can take care of it. You look like you need the break, and I'd like to roughly cover the agenda of the special meeting that we are having at noon."

Jacque Marten was tired and almost overwhelmed with fatigue. He offered no resistance to Steve's suggestion. He called the laboratory and made arrangements for the frozen section to be done, then he collected his tray of juice, toast, bacon and hot tea and joined Dr. McKay and Jim Street.

"Right here," motioned Jim Street as he pulled the chair out for Dr. Marten.

No one spoke for a short period of time. Jim Street finally broke the silence. "Steve, did you change the agenda or is it the same as before?"

"Only one item changed. We will have you lead the opening prayer."

"You may be joking, Steve, but you sure as hell might need all the help you can get before the meeting is over. Even prayers by an unbelieving Christian."

Dr. Marten looked up. "I hope that you two are not planning on getting me involved in this meeting. I know you very well, Steve, and I respect you. But you know that I will not take sides in any controversy. I will just present any facts as I know them and that is all."

Jim Street was more short-tempered than usual. "Goddamn it, Jacque, you can't go through your whole life with your head up your ass. You have to lean sometimes, and this is one of those times. I know damn well that you are the smartest physician that we have on the whole staff. You're one of the best pathologists in the whole Midwest, maybe the whole goddamn country. The staff respects you and they will listen to you. We are in no position to have a divisive staff. We have problems, big problems, and they are getting bigger. All we ask is that you do your best to keep things in perspective that's all. Welsch is going to bring up that abandonment bit, and that is going to undermine Steve, and maybe you, too. That whole damn case is irrelevant. It will cloud the real issue that we have to wrestle with; what to do with this goddamn CM Disease that is stalking us."

Steve felt a little embarrassed over the outburst. "Take it easy, Jim. You are getting all steamed up and that is not going to help matters."

There was a short silence as Jim Street rapidly gulped his coffee while Dr. Marten wrung his napkin, his way of sublimating his urge to offer an outburst in retaliation.

Silence for a short time, then Dr. McKay looked at Dr. Marten. "Jacque," he leaned over the table, "I must know one thing. Dr. Welsch has spread the rumor that the patient in question may not have had Cardiomyopathy as originally presumed, and that prompt and vigorous treatment that night might have saved him. Is that true?"

Dr. Marten did not immediately answer. When he did speak, he spoke in a subdued voice. "Yes, that is true. There is a path. A report questioning the diagnosis of Cardiomyopathy."

Jim Street flung his napkin onto his tray. "What in the hell are you talking about, Jacque? If there is something screwy about this case, why in the hell didn't you tell me or Steve before? Here it is, the day of our meeting, and you tell us that Steve may have been wrong all the time and that Welsch is right. Jesus Christ, sometimes I just don't understand you, Jacque."

Steve also was surprised. He leaned back in his chair. "Just what do you mean Jacque. I was under the impression from the report of the postmortem examination that the patient died from CM Disease."

Dr. Marten spoke quietly, but powerfully. "Both of you read into the post report what you wanted to read. If you read the report closely you will note that it says that the patient apparently has Cardiomyopathy, and that specimens were to be sent to the Department of Pathology at the University for review and for their opinion."

Jim Street had calmed down to a gale from the hurricane he was moments before. "So now you are going to tell us the University says the guy did not have Cardiomyopathy."

"Is that correct, Jacque?" asked Steve.

"The report came in late yesterday. In fact, I had to call them to get it over here. I had to know for sure before the meeting."

"But if you just got that goddamn report yesterday, how in the hell did Winston Welsch know all about it before?" asked Jim Street.

Dr. McKay answered, "As usual, he knew somebody over there who leaked the report to him."

"That is exactly what happened," confirmed Dr. Marten.

Jim Street leaned back in his chair. "So where does that leave us, especially you, Steve? This could make you look pretty bad."

"I know." Steve then turned again toward Jacque, "Are you going to present this report to the staff, Jacque?"

"Only if someone asks for it. In that case I will have no choice but to present the University report." Jacque looked at his watch. "I'm sorry, gentlemen, but I have a lot of work to do in the lab." He got up and left.

Jim Street and Dr. Steve McKay sat opposite each other, staring over each other's shoulder into space. Steve spoke. "I've got rounds to make. See you at the noon meeting." He got up and left Jim Street still staring into space.

Jim Street was still stunned by Dr. Marten's revelations at breakfast. Besides that he was tired. He had not slept well the night before. It seemed as if the whole world was closing in on him from all directions at once. It was near the beginning of the fiscal year and he had to prepare and submit a budget to his Board of Directors. This alone was a big job under ordinary circumstances. But with the weight of the CM Disease epidemic added to his shoulders, his life as the hospital administrator was more stressful than ever. And now there was a strong possibility that his medical staff would be broken into factions of doctors with conflicting opinions. And just at a time when he needed all of the help that he could get from a united medical staff.

When Jim Street arrived at his office, he found a special delivery letter waiting for him, this time from the CDC. He threw the stack of papers that he held under his arm onto the desk and picked up the letter. "Now what in the hell do those bastards want?" he muttered to himself as he sliced open the envelope.

*

"I am glad that you see things in the same light as I do." Dr. Winston Welsch was talking to a young staff physician in the doctor's lounge. "I really do not think that we are going to have a problem, and we do not really want to create one. But we must make it clear to the administration that the staff is concerned about the care of patients in this hospital, and that when the quality of care is at stake, then we must investigate, and sometimes reprimand. All of us have been guilty of mistakes in judgement and I think that this is what has happened in this case. Dr. McKay is a very capable doctor. We all know that. And we must make it clear that our only interest is to bring this type of problem out in the open so that we might all learn from it. The matter may not come up at all, but if it does, I hope that you will not hesitate to speak up." Winston Welsch looked at his watch. "You will have to excuse me now, I have to read some EKG's before nine so that the record department can get them on the charts this morning."

Dr. Welsch was on his way to the Medical Record Department when he spotted Dr. Marten's associate in the hall. "Dr. Lane, may I speak to you for a minute?"

Dr. Lane did not want to talk to Winston Welsch at any time, but especially today. He stopped and waited for Dr. Welsch to catch up. "I suppose you want to know about your patient with the severe myocardial infraction?"

"Not really; I have already seen your reports. What I do want to know is whether or not your department has received a report from the University on that suspect case of CM Disease. You know the one I mean. The one that Dr. McKay is involved."

"I was not involved in that case. You had better ask Dr. Marten." Dr. Lane had read the report, but he knew better than to get involved in any matter with Dr, Welsch.

"I'll try to see Dr. Marten before the meeting," replied Dr. Welsch. "You will be there I presume."

"I really am not sure that I will be at the meeting. I have to be at another meeting at the same time. Now if you will excuse me, I have a lot of work to do this morning. We have been extremely busy the past few weeks." Then Dr. Lane quickly turned and walked away.

Dr. Welsch was interpreting EKG's in the record room. One of the family physicians on the staff, Dr. Charles Hillary, interrupted him. "Sorry to bother you, Winston, but have you read the EKG on the twenty-nine year old lady I have up on third?"

Dr. Welsch turned around. "Hello, Charles." He shuffled through the EKG tracings that lay on the table in front of him.

"Yes, I just finished reading it. Quite interesting. Here it is." Dr. Welsch went over the tracing with Dr. Hillary, pointing out the changes then came up with his diagnosis. "I have not seen the clinical findings, but from these tracings alone, I would have to say that your patient is a victim of CM Disease."

Dr. Hillary answered pensively. "I was afraid of that."

"Would you like for me to see her in consultation?" asked Dr. Welsch.

"I was thinking of asking Dr. McKay, but if you want to. I guess you might just as well. It does not seem to make much difference who sees these patients or what treatment they receive, they all just die regardless of what anybody does."

"I have to agree with you. And by the way, you are going to the noon staff meeting?"

"I was not planning to. I have just returned from a post-graduate course in Chicago. We are way behind in the office."

"Charles, you are an up and coming physician on this staff. This is going to be a very important meeting and I think that you should try and be there."

"It's about our epidemic of CM Disease isn't it?"

Dr. Welsch paused and thought a little before answering. "That, of course, is one of the topics, but more importantly, there will be a discussion as to how we are going to handle these cases in the future. It seems that what we have been doing has not been very effective and we have to do more. We should be getting more people involved, more doctors like you."

Dr. Hillary was young, inexperienced, and did not quite understand hospital politics. The old guard was conservative and quite jealous of its monopoly in the development of hospital policy and usually apprehensive about change or new ideas. He did not understand what Dr. Welsch was aiming at. "If Dr. McKay or Dr. Marten want any assistance, I will be glad to do anything that I can to help. I have given them full reports on my three cases of CM Disease, this one included."

"I am sure that you did, Charles, and I am sure that you are willing to help. But you really should come to the meeting. There have been some inconsistencies in the care of these patients and I think that it is important that we formulate some definite guidelines in the way we handle future cases. Every case of chills and fever is not CM Disease. We cannot be completely overwhelmed by this problem to the extent that we neglect other patients; patients who have a disease that can be treated successfully. We don't want to throw spears at anyone, but at the same time we have to maintain a high quality of care in this hospital."

"I didn't know that we had a problem of that nature. But since you say that we do, I guess that I will be there. And thanks for the EKG report."

"I will see your patient as soon as I am finished reading these EKG's," said Dr. Welsch as Dr. Hillary was leaving.

It was just past noon when Lisa stepped off the elevator and walked quickly to the nurses' station. "Hello, Lisa," said the nurse sitting at the charting desk.

"Where did they put Diane?" asked Lisa

The nurse put down her pen, then got up and walked over to the counter where Lisa was standing. "In 246. I wondered why you were here. We don't see you ICU girls very often. Diane was just taken to her room. Come on, I'll walk down there with you."

"Diane did not want to come in," said the nurse. "Her husband called me and was really so upset. Diane did not want to come to the hospital so he asked me to talk to her. So I went out to see her. She only lives a block away. She looked awfully sick, and scared."

The two stopped in front of Diane's room. Before they entered the floor nurse said, almost in a whisper, "I'm scared, too, for her. No one has said it yet, but we are all thinking the same thing. CM Disease."

"God, I hope not. Dr. Lowe is her family physician, isn't he?" asked Lisa.

"Yes. And I'm sure that he will ask Dr. McKay to see her in consultation."

"Steve knows her so well and has worked with her for so long. He is really going to be upset."

"Lisa, why don't you go in alone. You are probably her best friend and she needs somebody to hold her hand. Her husband is downstairs in the admitting office filling out papers."

Lisa slowly opened the door and quietly entered. Diane was the only patient in the room. "Lisa, I'm so glad to see you. I'm so frightened. I feel terrible and I can't help thinking about all those people with CM Disease. The symptoms are the same, Lisa. They are. I just know it."

Lisa knelt beside the bed and took Diane's hand in hers. I'll stay as long as you want me to."

"I want you to stay, at least for awhile. Craig is in the admitting office. He should be back here soon. I feel so sorry for him. He is more frightened than I am."

"What did Dr. Lowe say, Diane?"

Diane smiled for the first time. "I feel sorry for him, too. I know that Dr.

Lowe thinks that CM Disease has something against him. He has had more cases than anyone has. He feels so helpless and he worries so much about his patients. He ordered a lot of tests and I think that he is going to do a spinal tap after their meeting. He asked if I would mind if he asked Dr. McKay to see me with him. I knew then for sure that Dr. Lowe thought that I had CM Disease. Up to that time it was just a fear lurking in the back of my mind. But it all fits, Lisa. All the symptoms. All the signs, they all fit." She threw her arms around Lisa and sobbed violently. "I don't want to die, Lisa, not yet."

Tears welled up in Lisa's eyes as she held Diane close to her. "Come on, perk up. Let's try to be optimistic, if for no other reason, let's do it for Craig. He will be back in a little while."

Diane quit sobbing, but she still had tears in her eyes when her husband came into the room. The three waited in subdued silence for Dr. Lowe to return.

The special medical staff meeting had been in progress for at least thirty minutes. After Dr. McKay had called the meeting to order, Jim Street asked for the floor so that he could make an important announcement. "This morning I received a letter from the Center for Disease Control. They have requested that we send representatives from our medical staff, the administration and the nursing staff to the Center for Disease Control in Atlanta to discuss our experience with CM Disease with them. It seems that our community is in the throes of an epidemic of the damnable thing, and it seems that we have had more cases of CM Disease than anywhere else in the country. I hope then, that you will proceed with your meeting bearing in mind that what you say here today will be reflected in what information we take with us when we go to the Center for Disease Control next week." Jim Street thanked the doctors for their attention and sat down.

Dr. McKay and Dr. Marten then made their presentation of a typical case of CM Disease and how the cases have been handled thus far at Good Samaritan. It was emphasized that they had reviewed the literature and that they could find no precedent of a disease like it. They were at a loss as to what more could be done for the patients who develop CM Disease until they were able to better determine the etiology.

Winston Welsch inquired about the possibility of having myocardial biopsies done on these patients.

Doctor McKay answered, "There is no doubt that we have the capability of performing a myocardial biopsy while the patients are still alive, but that procedure would not be very helpful to us. We can usually ascertain clinically that a patient has developed CM Disease. And even if we did make a more positive diagnosis by biopsy, it would not alter the course of the patient's disease process since we have no treatment for CM Disease. But there certainly is no reason why they could not be done in some cases, just for the record."

Dr. Welsch said nothing more and since there were no further questions or comments, the discussion was turned over to Dr. Marten. Dr. Marten gave a report of the problem as he saw it. He again summarized the clinical findings that were present in the patients who had died of the disease. He then gave a report of the autopsy findings that were found in all of these patients, and he emphasized the fact that the findings were much the same in each case so that it was certain that there was a common etiological factor causing the myopathy. He went on to explain that sometimes it is difficult to establish the diagnosis of a disease with a viral etiology. If the cause of the disease was bacterial, then they certainly would have been able to isolate the causative agent in a relatively short time, and would possibly be able to treat it with one of the available antibiotics after appropriate sensitivity tests. There was of course an outside chance that the cause of the disease was neither viral nor bacterial. Another etiological agent such as a Ricketsea, a fungus, or yeast could be the cause, but this seemed unlikely. Dr. Marten concluded his discussion with two statements. First, he stated that, in his opinion, the cause of CM Disease was a virus, not yet isolated, and as yet unidentified by anyone in the past. He had reviewed the world's literature and he could find no report of a disease similar to CM Disease. He had, in addition, been in contact with the top experts in communicable diseases in the country and they had been unable to give him any information that would be of any value in solving the riddle.

Dr. Marten concluded his discussion with his second statement, an ominous one. "There has been a definite decline in the number of days between the onset of symptoms in patients with CM Disease and their deaths. Gentlemen, it appears that the virus, if it is a virus, is becoming more virulent."

Dr. McKay thanked Dr. Marten and he then asked for questions from the floor. A few physicians did have questions that Dr. Marten answered clearly and precisely. When there was no further discussion of CM Disease, Dr. Welsch rose and asked for the floor.

Jim Street shifted uneasily in his chair when Winston Welsch began to speak. Jim Street thought that he knew what was about to come, and he was not happy. Up to this point, the medical staff had been attentive and had seemed to comprehend the complexity of the problem as Dr. Marten had presented it to them.

"That silly son-of-a-bitch," thought Jim Street to himself, thinking in the same kind of language that he often used a language that had remained with him from his youth. Jim Street was born and raised on the south side of Chicago, and he often times had to literally fight his way to and from school. His parents were poor; his father a heavy drinker who died when Jim was seven. His mother struggled to keep the small family together in the best way that she could, but her education was limited, and she could never find a way to remove her family from the ghetto that she hated with a passion. Jim Street did have the advantage of having a superior I-Q and was befriended by the Christian Brothers who operated the school that he attended. They arranged for him to enter an all boy's secondary school for college preparation, and after his mother died when he was sixteen, the Christian Brothers took over his guardianship and sent him to college where he excelled in all subjects and graduated with honors.

Following his graduation from college Jim Street served as an assistant administrator at a number of hospitals in Chicago before taking over the reins at Good Samaritan. His main reason for leaving his former position was to get away from the city that did not offer many happy memories for him. He left the memories in Chicago, but he took with him the street language that was engraved deeply into his subconscious. It was embarrassing to many people who did not understand him. Jim Street, too, was embarrassed by what shot out of his mouth when he spoke, especially when he was upset, or angry. Still, he was an outstanding administrator and his associates at Good Samaritan overlooked his language and accepted him for what he was.

Dr. Welsch commended the medical staff for the fine work that it had done under very difficult conditions. He also congratulated Dr. Marten and his Pathology Department for the outstanding work that they were doing in trying to find a cause for the dreaded CM Disease. He even managed to commend Dr McKay for the work that he had done in attending to patients with CM Disease and for being so kind as to act as a consultant so often.

"Buttering the bread for the final ingredient," thought Jim Street. "And that sure as hell is going to be some kind of poison. The bastard!" Jim Street looked over toward Dr. McKay but he could not get his attention. Dr. Marten was busy going over the papers that lay on the table before him

"But we must avert a stampede," continued Dr. Welsch. "Not every patient who comes into the hospital with a fever has CM Disease. Not every flu-like episode is going to progress to CM Disease with its death dealing Cardiomyopathy. Evaluating each patient is still important so that no mistakes are made. And mistakes have been made. We know of at least one case where the physician in charge of a patient assumed that the patient had

CM Disease. CM Disease is fatal, but if the patient does not have CM Disease, then vigorous therapy may save a life. In this case the physician assumed that the patient had CM Disease and he was not available when the patient needed him most and the patient died. And we now know that the patient did not have CM Disease. The patient may have lived if the attending physician had been available to vigorously treat the patient."

Jim Street shuffled in his chair and had a difficult time in controlling himself and keeping the volcano that was churning inside from erupting. "That goddamn son-of-a-bitch. What in the hell is he trying to prove."

One of the physicians at the meeting asked the question, "Are you saying that one of the physicians on our staff allowed a patient to die without adequate care?"

Dr. Welsch answered, "I do not think that it is in the best interest of the staff to mention names. There is an important lesson that we should learn from this case, and bringing personalities into the discussion is not going to help in solving the problem?"

Jim Street shook his head. He glanced over and caught the eye of Steve who had a helpless look on his face. Jim Street felt like blurting out what he thought. "Welsch, you are a real ass. You know damn well that you don't have to mention any names. You have already told everybody on the staff that it was Dr. McKay whom you are talking about. You've already told your story to everybody you met in the hallway."

There was a rising crescendo of accusations and counter-accusations. The meeting was deteriorating into a discussion of the quality of care by some physicians in the community, and again no names were ever mentioned. But there was developing a rising tide of disenchantment of Dr. McKay in the undercurrent that was flowing with the discussion.

Finally a staff member posed the question. "Dr. Welsch, you say that there was a misdiagnosis in this case that you are referring to. How do you know that? I believe that I know the case you are talking about and what doctor you are talking about. It was my impression that at autopsy the diagnosis of Cardiomyopathy and CM Disease had been established."

Dr. Welsch had planted the bait and it had been taken. He had a slight smile on his face, an all-knowing kind of smile that said he was ready for the kill. "Dr. Marten tentatively, and I say tentatively, made the diagnosis of CM Disease. But, he was not certain and he sent some of the tissue to the University for their opinion." Dr. Welsch then turned toward Dr. Marten. "Jacque, would you care to read the report that you received from the University?"

Dr. Marten rose to speak. His voice was usually saturated with confidence, but Steve McKay could detect a troubled tone in the way Jacque presented his facts, as if he were afraid that someone might at any moment attack what he was saying. Dr. Marten continued to speak. "That this is the summary of the findings of my autopsy." He read the report word for word. "On microscopic study, the heart showed involvement of the myocardium suggestive of, but not diagnostic of, myopathic disease highly suggestive of that found in patients dying with CM Disease." Dr. Marten looked at the audience. "I then sent specimens of the heart muscle tissue to the Department of Pathology at the University. It was their opinion that the heart involvement was not that usually found in CM Disease." Jacque Marten finished speaking, but he did not sit down.

Jim Street looked toward Dr. Welsch who was sitting with an awkward smile on his face. He then glanced toward Steve who looked grim and worried. No one in the room stirred.

Then Dr. Marten continued. "Dr. Bresnovich, the University Pathologist who made the report, served under me when we both were in our Residency training in pathology at the Peter Brent Brigham Hospital in Boston. I was the senior resident, and Dr. Bresnovich was my junior. He is a capable pathologist, and I have the utmost confidence in his judgement."

Dr. McKay was puzzled and somewhat apprehensive as to what Jacque would say. Jim Street was thinking, "Now what in the hell is Jacque up to?"

Dr. Marten then said powerfully and positively in a tone of voice that reeked with confidence. "I do not agree with those findings. I carefully reviewed the slides once again and I scrupulously reviewed the history and clinical course of the patient. There is no doubt in my mind, none whatsoever, that the patient died of CM Disease. And since no other patient has ever survived the disease, I see no reason to believe that this patient would have survived in spite of any medical treatment that any doctor could offer. I have submitted my final diagnosis in this case: Cardiomyopathy secondary to CM Disease." Dr. Marten sat down. The room reverberated with silence. An uneasy feeling spread over the meeting room like a gathering storm cloud that would break loose at any moment.

Dr. McKay broke the silence. "I really do not know what we have accomplished today. We have been here close to an hour and a half, and we are exactly at the same place that we were when the meeting began, confused about a disease that is killing our patients, CM Disease." Then the meeting abruptly adjourned.

Lisa was waiting for Steve in the hall. At the same time that they met, Dr. Marten came by. "Just a minute, Jacque, I want to thank you for what you said in there."

Jacque Marten stopped. "Don't thank me, Steve. I did not say anything just to make things easier for you. I only said what I thought to be the truth. I would have done the same thing for Welsch if the circumstances were reversed."

"Well, thanks anyway."

Lisa looked at Steve. "Steve, I have some very bad news."

"Come on up to the lounge and we can talk about it."

"No need for that." They stopped walking. "Steve, Diane is ill. She is up on the second floor. It looks like she has CM Disease." Lisa broke down and cried softly.

Steve gripped her shoulders firmly. He lifted her chin with a finger and looked into her eyes and saw the deep concern that was there and he felt like crying himself. "I hope to God that you are wrong."

The two struck out for the second floor to see Diane.

Chapter 10

The big shiny jet lumbered onto the runway, its engines whining, its wings shuddering lightly with vibration. The jet engines whinnied louder; there was an easy tug and the MD 80 began to gather speed as it rolled down the black asphalt ribbon. In minutes the jetliner was banking to the left and heading south toward Atlanta.

Jim Street stared out the window as the ground receded below. Dr. Marten gazed blank-eyed at the FASTEN YOUR SAFETY BELT sign on the bulkhead up front. Steve and Lisa sat together, quiet and engrossed in deep thought. The four were heading for a meeting at the Center for Disease Control.

Jim Street had been invited by the CDC to bring some of his staff to present everything that they knew about CM Disease before a gathering of infectious disease experts. Cases of CM Disease had been reported from all parts of the country, and the officials of CDC decided to meet with medical personnel who were most familiar with the disease. And since no other institution in the country had reported as many cases of CM Disease as Good Samaritan, it was logical that they were among the first to be invited.

CDC hoped to collect as much information as possible in an effort to develop a plan of attack to stem the tide of the spreading epidemic of the strange malady, CM Disease. Jim Street asked Dr. McKay and Dr. Marten to go to Atlanta because they had been involved, in one way or another, in nearly every case of the always-fatal CM Disease that had been diagnosed at Good Samaritan. He also decided that the Nursing Service should be represented at the meeting, and Diane Vaughan, the supervisor of ICU, was the logical choice. But now, she was dead...a victim herself of CM Disease. Her funeral service had been held the day before.

Jim Street asked Lisa Clarke to take Diane's place at the CDC meeting. Lisa declined at first. Later she relented and agreed to go, hoping that she might be able to add some meaningful information to the battery of data that was being collected about the dreaded Disease.

The jet droned on. Lisa sat with her seat tilted back. Her eyes looked glassy, as if she were in a trance. It was apparent that Lisa was still visibly shaken over Diane's death, her friend, nursing associate, and confidante. She had spent many hours with Diane in the final days of her illness, and Lisa was nearby when death finally came to visit Diane.

Steve McKay did not perceive what his eyes were seeing. His mind was distressed with thoughts of Diane's death. He had been the consulting physician with Dr. Lowe in Diane's case, and knowing Diane personally had made attending her in a disease process that he knew would lead to her death psychologically difficult for him.

Steve turned toward Lisa. "We should be in Atlanta in about two hours."

Lisa did not answer. She continued to stare blankly at the bulkhead at the front of the plane.

Steve placed his hand on Lisa's. "I know that the past few days have been difficult for you, Lisa, but they have been difficult for all of us. There are so many things that are still undone. There are a lot of things that need our attention.

Lisa nodded, did not answer, and continued staring straight ahead.

"Look, this will never do," said Steve. "We live with death every day. Patients whom we know very well die. Friends die. People very close to us die. We are all on the same ship, Lisa, and all of us will one day fall overboard and join all of those who preceded us into the ocean of death. But in the meantime, our lives must go on."

Lisa continued to gaze straight ahead, saying nothing. Finally she spoke, almost in a whisper. "I know. You seem to accept it so much better than most people, including me. But it scares me, Steve. Diane was a friend, and she died. I can accept that, but it is hard for me to accept the fact that we are still under the shadow of the disease that killed her. You or I, you and I, either one, or both of us, we could be next, Steve. Our friends, our family, they too could become a victim and die. Diane's death just brought a reality a little closer, that's all."

Steve listened intently to what Lisa was saying. He managed a feeble comment. "I'm sorry, Lisa. I understand what you are saying."

"Don't apologize, Steve. You can sublimate your feelings so much better than I can. But I also know that it bothers you as much as anyone else. The only difference is that you will not allow yourself to get upset by it, at least not visibly."

Steve matter of factly answered, "There are situations that we can alter by our actions, and there are situations over which we have no control whatsoever."

Steve and Lisa withdrew back into the privacy of their own thoughts.

After awhile, Lisa turned toward Steve. She smiled for the first time in days. "I wish that we could do something about us."

Steve did not immediately release himself from the grip of his reflective thoughts. When he did, he gently took Lisa's hand into his again and gave it a gentle squeeze in reply. Then they both closed their eyes as their minds tried to blot out the problems that surrounded them.

Jim Street came back to where Steve and Lisa were seated and sat down in the empty seat next to them. "After we get to Atlanta we'll check into the hotel, have a bit of lunch, then head off for CDC. How late we will be tonight...well, I just don't know."

"Any idea as to what they want to cover?" asked Steve.

Jim Street ruffled his thick black hair with his hand and thought for a few seconds before he replied. "I am not sure. They asked me to bring as much data as I thought we would need, and Jacque collected a lot of material for us. I have it all in my brief case." He was silent for a moment before he continued in a low tone of voice. "I would have asked both of you to contribute to the preparation of this, but I did not have the heart to bother either of you with Diane being sick, then dying. I know that both of you have been under a great deal of strain."

Lisa mumbled a faint, "Thank you."

Jim Street spoke again. "I am very worried. Up until the time that Diane died, we did not have any of our employees contract CM Disease, so, we had no serious problems with staffing. Sure, we had a few minor problems, but, in retrospect, they were not really all that bad and did not hamper hospital operations to any great extent. But now, well, I think that we are going to have one hell of a time trying to keep nursing personnel in the hospital."

"Have you any indication that this is happening?" Steve asked.

"Hell yes! I called the Director of Nursing before we left. Twelve people called in sick today, and that was at five in the morning." Jim Street left for his own seat when he saw the attendants coming down the aisle with coffee.

At the hotel Lisa finished straightening her hair, then tuned the room's FM receiver to a quiet kind of music and made herself comfortable in the big, soft chair next to the window. She decided that she would take a short respite from the tensions of the past few weeks and just sit back, close her eyes, and relax for awhile. This was the first time that she really had a time to unwind in a long time without the tensions of her job in Intensive Care and CM Disease bearing on her mind.

As Lisa began to relax, her mind began to wander into thoughts of today and of yesterday. Then she eventually settled on the thoughts that often washed across her brain...the why of her, Lisa Clarke, and him, Steve McKay.

Lisa opened her eyes in an almost startled manner. She was about to regress into memories of her and David, memories that always left her with mixed emotions of regret, antipathy, and more than anything else, frustration. She was frustrated at being trapped in a marriage that was shallow and meaningless to her, and she was frustrated at not being able to have the one person whom she loved and wanted more than anyone else...Steve McKay.

Lisa never did completely discover the answer as to the why of her marriage to David. But deep down she realized that she never really loved David, but that she was attracted to him for reasons that were not entirely clear to her. David held an engineering degree and had a good position with one of the local industrial plants. He was physically attractive, and like Lisa, he liked to go places and see new things. At first Lisa thought that marriage for her and David was nearly ideal. They traveled. They had a lot of fun together. Eventually the things that held them together seemed superficial and Lisa began to wonder if she had married the right person.

Lisa wanted to be independent in what she did, and in what she thought. She wanted to be herself, to be Lisa, and David would not allow her to do that. David looked upon Lisa's nursing career as a rival and he discouraged her from working. In fact, he told Lisa time and again that he would like to see her to give up her nursing career altogether. But that was impossible for Lisa. Lisa loved nursing; she loved the challenge of the changes that were taking place in medicine and in nursing. The intense activity and responsibility of critical care nursing, with its demanding dedication to excellence, fascinated Lisa. She greatly enjoyed working in the Intensive Care Department even though it meant that she often had to study to remain current with the ever expanding and changing concepts of nursing care that exploded in a seemingly endless flow. Being a competent Intensive Care nurse meant that Lisa sometimes had to take time away from David to attend conferences and seminars, sometimes a long way from home. David could not quite understand how Lisa could get so involved and interested in her work. But to Lisa, nursing was more than a job. To her, nursing was taking care of people who were desperately in need of the expertise that she had to offer when it was needed most, when patients were critically ill and often times hovering at the edge of death.

When Lisa became pregnant for the first time, both she and David were very happy and Lisa thought that having a child would help to mold their marriage into the image that she expected and wanted. Both Lisa and David were disappointed when she miscarried in the second month. It was not long before Lisa was pregnant again, and a second miscarriage was even more disappointing to them. It was a year before Lisa was pregnant for a third time. She reluctantly took a leave of absence from her position as an Intensive Care Nurse, hoping that by eliminating the tensions and stress of working she would have a better chance of carrying her child to term. She miscarried one month to the day after she had resigned her position at the hospital.

After the last miscarriage Lisa was very depressed and still wanted a child very much. David was completely frustrated, and did not want to undergo the trauma of Lisa having another miscarriage. He was beginning to think that they were getting too old to begin to raise a family anyway. Lisa and David argued, almost violently, about this. David ended any further arguments about the matter of their having a family when he had a vasectomy. Lisa, at first, was very angry with him, but then she reluctantly acquiesced to the fact that she and David would never have a child. After that, Lisa and David drifted further and further apart. Their marriage soon became a matter of convenience rather than love.

David accepted a position with a new company as plant supervisor. Lisa knew that Good Samaritan Hospital was noted for its outstanding Intensive Care facilities and she was anxious to get back into nursing. She saw this as an opportunity to launch her back into the mainstream of nursing in very progressive medical surroundings. She inquired about a position in the Intensive Care Unit at Good Samaritan, and with her exceptional credentials and experience she was immediately offered a position as a staff nurse in ICU. It was there that she met Dr. Steve McKay.

There was a soft knock on the door that aroused Lisa from her thoughts. It was Steve. “Feel a little better?” Steve asked as he entered the room.

Lisa smiled. “Yes. I always feel better whenever I am with you.”

Steve held her close. He knew that this was a time when Lisa needed someone to hold her, to give her a hug to help her erase the dreadful events of the previous few weeks that had scratched her soul. He held her firmly, then pressed a soft kiss onto her lips. “You look lovely when you smile.”

“And this is Lisa Clarke, one of our ICU nurses who has been involved in the care of many of the patients with CM Disease.” Jim Street was finishing with the introductions.

Dr. Cathy Chen of the CDC Staff stepped to the rostrum and opened the discussion. “I want to begin by thanking all of you for coming. I understand that a very close friend of some of you has died recently from CM Disease, and so it appears that an urgent matter has become even more urgent.”

Jim Street removed a sheaf of papers from his well-worn leather briefcase. He handed the folder of papers to Dr. Chen. “This is the information that you requested that we bring with us to this meeting. I hope that you already have received the preliminary material that I forwarded to you last week. I thought it best that you should have the information ahead of time so that you could review it before we arrived.”

Dr. Marten was asked to summarize his reports. The CDC representatives were impressed with Dr. Marten’s presentation. He spoke without using written notes but he used his laptop computer to present his outline and pictures of his tissue specimens. He presented case after case of CM Disease, including the history, the clinical findings, and then waded through the details of the clinical course of individual cases. He took them into the autopsy room where his slides painted pictures on their mind as he showed them how he focused on the pathological findings of the heart and the myopathy that was invariably found at autopsy. They peered into the microscope with him as he pointed out cellular changes and disruptions from the normal. He painstakingly summarized the laboratory findings in patients and what had been done in an attempt to find a clue as to the cause of CM Disease. He described how they tried to find any organism that might be the etiological agent causing CM Disease. He took them into his laboratory as he studied possible toxicological etiologies of the dreaded disease and showed them that he did not find any indication that it was a toxic substance that was the cause of CM Disease. “And so,” he explained, “it has become more and more evident that it is in all probability a virus that is the underlying cause of CM Disease.”

The room was infinitely quiet as Dr. Marten finished his presentation. It was so complete a presentation that no one could wager a question that had not already been answered in anticipation. Finally, Dr. Chen cleared her throat and intervened on the silence. “Now, Dr. Marten, you indicate that you have made some preliminary studies in an attempt to discover an infectious organism as the cause of the disease. Have you had any positive results?”

“No, not really. Cultures have not been of any help. They have all been negative. And we have not found any indication of a toxin as the etiology.”

“Viruses?”

Dr. Marten answered the question about viruses that had been put to him by Dr. Chen in his usual blunt reply, “None, as far as we have been able to determine. But, we have sent cultures for viral studies to you here at CDC. But as of now, we have not received any reply.”

Dr. Cathy Chen spoke as she wrote on her note pad. “I have some important information about the specimens that you have sent us. But I would rather leave that to the end of the discussion. Right now I want to get as much raw information as I can so we can later put all of our facts together and come up with some plausible course of action that we might take in this matter."

Dr. Marten volunteered. "It appears to me that we may be dealing with a very elusive virus that has a strong affinity for the heart, the myocardium in particular. It also appears that it affects the conduction system of the heart in some yet undetermined manner so that the electrical impulses that control heart rhythm are disrupted and the heart goes into asystole. But we have not been able to prove this, not yet anyway."

Dr. McKay added his observations. "From what Dr. Marten has been able to discover in his post-mortem examinations, the Cardiomyopathy is not all that serious. Our experience indicates that the death-dealing blow is delivered by a disruption of the electrical system of the heart. It is possible that if we could just get the patient through the arrhythmia stage, then we could be saving the lives of a lot of these people."

Dr. Marten added, "Dr. McKay is correct. From the specimens that I have seen, the myopathy will heal in time, and in fact it has shown definite signs of significant healing in the patients whom we have examined. We have been able to control the heart failure with an acceptable degree of success, but the arrhythmia, the asystole, well, that has been a different story."

Dr. McKay emphasized, "Cardiac asystole is almost always impossible to reverse, and that is what we are dealing with as a terminal event."

"I must commend both of you for your work. It is seldom that we see work of this caliber done outside a medical center.

The CDC Staff would not admit it, but it was easy to see that they were very much impressed by the large amount of work that Dr. Marten had put into his attempt to trace both the etiology and the transmission of CM Disease. They were even more impressed by the knowledge that Dr. Marten displayed, not only about the cases of CM Disease that he had presented, but also by his general knowledge of the entire subject of infectious diseases, and especially virus diseases.

Dr. Chen now turned her attention to Steve and Lisa and began the discussion of their clinical experience with CM Disease. "What have been the principle symptoms that you have found in patients with CM Disease, Dr. McKay?"

"We have found that the early symptoms are the same as with any viral infection such as the flu: sore throat, a feeling of chilliness, a lowgrade temperature, and most of all, general achiness and severe fatigue and weakness."

"Then what?

"There follows a period of remission. The patient seems to improve for a few days. After that, there is a rapid downhill course. And what is bothersome to us is that the downhill course ending in death seems to be shorter in the cases that we have seen in the past few weeks than in the cases that we observed when CM Disease first appeared. The patients that we have treated in the past week have had a very rapid deterioration."

Dr. Chen interrupted. "Your story of what your patients have clinically experienced with CM Disease is the same that we have found in reports from other parts of the country. We are convinced that we are dealing with a single disease process that is reaching epidemic proportions in all parts of the country, an epidemic that seems to be spreading more rapidly than we would like to see."

Dr. Chen broke a silence that had overtaken the room. "Mrs. Clarke, is there anything that you might want to add to what Dr. McKay has said?"

"No. I have worked on many of these cases with Dr. McKay. He has done just about everything that he knows in treating these patients, but the CM Disease victims just keep dying in spite of what is done for them. I just don't know what I can say that would add to what has already been said by the doctors."

Dr. Chen returned the discussion to Dr. McKay. "Have you used any drugs, Doctor, besides the usual cardiac drugs and usual supportive measures?"

"I am not sure what you mean, Dr. Chen," replied Steve

"I thought that perhaps you might have used some experimental drugs."

"I am sorry, Doctor, but we do not have experimental drugs in our hospital."

Jim Street frowned as he asked Dr. Chen. "What are you driving at?"

Dr. Chen continued. "I just thought that perhaps Dr. McKay might have used some non-approved or other drugs or treatment in attempting to save a life."

Dr. McKay leaned forward as he spoke. "We are well aware of the rules concerning the use of non-approved drugs."

Dr. Chen said in a tone of voice suggesting an admonition. "In cases like this there is sometimes a tendency to try anything possible. You must be careful about experimenting, even in difficult circumstances. The rules concerning experimental drugs are pretty clear."

All was quiet for the moment. Dr. Chen continued writing on her notepad, Steve McKay sipped on his soft drink, Lisa Clarke wondered what she was doing there, and Doctor Marten was bored and anxious to get back to work.

Jim Street just sat, stewing in the frustrations of weeks of dying patients, a dissident Medical Staff, and now what he often referred to as the goddamn stupidity of Washington bureaucracy.

Dr. Chen could feel the animosity stirring, so she thought that it was time to toss her newfound information into the ring. "We have good news, I think. Today I received a report regarding the viral studies that you had sent to Atlanta sometime earlier. You were absolutely correct. It seems that they have recovered particles that we suspect are viruses from many of the specimens that you sent."

Dr. Marten answered in a very reserved and subtle tone of voice. "It must be a Coxsackie virus."

Dr. Chen was a little disappointed that Dr. Marten had taken this new information so lightly and also that he indeed had chosen the correct virus group. "Yes, you are correct. There is evidence that the recovered virus is of the Coxsackie virus group. But, Coxsackie viruses cause most viral myocardial problems.

"Most, but not all," replied Dr. Marten.

Dr. Chen continued talking. "We are in the process of typing the virus. I do not have the report in hand, but we hope to be able to give you more information in the near future."

"Type A Coxsackie viruses are most commonly associated with myocardial complications, and in recent years the A-9, 15 and 17 have been the most frequently seen whenever myocardial problems arise. I suspect that this will be the case with CM Disease. However, we may be dealing with an entirely new entity, a new virus in the sense that we have not found it before; it could be a mutant of an already known virus type. And we still must speculate that CM Disease might not be caused by a virus at all."

"What you say indeed has merit, Dr. Marten. But I can tell you that the Center for Infectious Diseases in Atlanta has cultured particles that appear to be viruses. But, I also must report to you that they are having great difficulty in their culture processes for some unknown reason."

"What are your plans for us now?" inquired Dr. McKay.

"I was just about to come to that," replied Dr. Chen "I would like for Dr. Marten and Jim Street to go to the NIH. We have tentatively made arrangements for him to fly with us this evening by government transportation as soon as we leave here. It would be beneficial for the people at the NIH to confer with Dr. Marten and Jim Street, exchange data and ideas with them, and then develop a tentative plan as to how to handle CM Disease in communities in the future. At the same time, we would like to hold another conference here with Dr. McKay and Mrs. Clarke in the morning and exchange what knowledge we have on the clinical aspects of CM Disease."

Jim Street did not look happy. "We have our suitcases at our hotel."

"Don't worry about your hotel. We can pick up your luggage on the way to the airport."

Jim Street looked at his watch. "If those are your plans, then we had better get started."

Dr. Marten made an attempt to back out of going to the NIH. He would have preferred to go home, even that night. Dr. Chen insisted that his input would be valuable at the NIH.

After Dr. Chen had made the appropriate phone calls, Jim Street and Dr. Marten were on their way to the airport with Dr. Cathy Chen and her group.

Steve and Lisa sat facing each other across the small table in a dim, candle lit corner in the French cafe where they had gone for dinner. Steve sipped from the wineglass that he had been gingerly fondling and smiled at Lisa.

Lisa smiled back. "It has been a beautiful evening, Steve. I really needed this."

Steve smiled easily as his and Lisa's eyes met and exchanged glances of love. "It has been a long time since we have had an evening together."

"You really have been busy these past weeks, Steve. We have not only not had time to have an evening together, but we have hardly had time to spend any time together."

"You know," Steve began, "I miss you when I do not see you at least once a day. It is getting to be more and more difficult to be without you, Lisa. I have become more and more frustrated, and yet, I am not sure that the time is now for us to make a final decision as to when we will dissolve our marriages so that we can get married."

"It will have to be a final decision when we do make that choice, Steve. There will be no turning back. And I am not at all sure that now is not the right time. And I really cannot anticipate David's reaction. There are times when he doesn't seem to care about our marriage, and then there are times when I think that he does. It will not be easy, or pleasant, for either of us."

"When we return home?" Before Lisa could answer Steve answered his own question. "No, Not now. CM Disease comes first."

Lisa became teary eyed, withdrew her hand from Steve's and said, "I love you, Steve. But it is so difficult to face what must come with the dissolution of a marriage. Lawyers, court, and hard feelings. If only I could just go home and say, 'David, it is all over.... I am leaving, with Steve.'"

There was a time of silence that seemed like an eternity. Lisa still teary eyed, smiled and said, "I'm sorry, Steve. I shouldn't cry like this. I know that it bothers you and you have so many other things to worry about."

Steve took Lisa's hand again. "You have no reason to be sorry. I should not have brought up the matter tonight. I am in love with you like I have never been in love before. Nothing will ever change that. We will find a way. When, I don't know, but we will find a way."

Then they retreated to Lisa's room and made love…three times that night.

Chapter 11

After Diane Vaughan had died of CM Disease, two more staff people at Good Samaritan came down with the disease and died. Jim Street and his nursing office did everything possible to keep the hospital in operation. They held meetings with all personnel, urging them to stay on the job. They played on devotion to duty of health care dispensers to try to stimulate the staff to continue to report for work. Their fortunes wavered between success and failure, depending on whose friend or relative came down with the disease and died. The administration was able to manage to keep the hospital in operation, although there were days when there were more patients than could be roomed, fed, bathed, and medicated adequately and efficiently. Everyone was just plain scared.

The business and shopping areas of the town were deserted much of the time. People kept to themselves and visits, even among very close friends, seemed to be a vanishing pastime. Schools were open and operating, but absenteeism among both the students and the teachers was high. Industry managed to remain in operation albeit with skeleton forces part of the time.

After its initial fiasco of throwing the city into panic, the newspaper had done a magnificent job in doing its part to alleviate the fears and speculation of the population. It ran a series of articles by the medical society and the hospital administration explaining the situation as it was, and pointing out that although the epidemic was serious, it was by no means hopeless; and that the statistical chances of any one individual person contracting CM Disease was minimal. Still, few people viewed with relish the possibility of becoming a statistic when it meant having your name on the obituary page and your body lying in a casket in a grave somewhere. Everyone was hoping and praying for a miracle. But hope was turning to despair as prayers went unanswered and deaths from CM Disease continued to rise at an alarming rate. Dr. McKay's fears of an epidemic rivaling the Black Plague of the Middle Ages seemed to be turning to reality.

Dr. McKay stood in front of Bernie's desk in Jim Street's outer office. "I was so sorry to hear about your brother's death, Bernie. If there is anything that I can do…" Steve hesitated, feeling uncomfortable in the role that he was playing.

"Thanks," said Bernie, "But I'll be O.K. He lived in L.A., and I just got back last night."

"I know. You should have taken more time off." Steve bent over and kissed Bernie on the forehead. "Is Jim in his office?"

"Yes he is. He has been overwhelmed with all kinds of problems and is badly in need of a few days off himself. Maybe you can talk him into it."

Bernie announced to Jim Street that Dr. McKay wanted to see him.

"Send him right in."

Steve took his usual seat in front of the desk. "You look awfully tired, Jim. You should take a few days off."

"Sure, take a few days off. And who in the hell is going to take care of all this crap. Look at that pile of papers that have to be checked over and answered." He picked up another sheaf of papers, "And these stacks are phone calls that I have to make…before noon."

"Sorry, just a thought. But if it will make you feel any better, I'll take some time off with you. That way you won't feel like you are abandoning ship. Jacque took a few days off after Diane died. He was really feeling stressed out. And, that is very unusual for him." Steve drew a deep breath and wrinkled his forehead. "And I think the rest really did him a lot of good."

"Fine. If you and I leave, everyone will think that we know something that no one else does and that we are leaving to avoid the final disaster, whatever that might be."

"Where's the coffee?" asked Steve as he looked around the room. "You are not your usual gracious host."

Steve had barely finished speaking when the door opened and Bernie brought in the tray with the hot coffee and bagels with No Fat cream cheese.

"Sorry, Jim."

"You have Bernie trained better than I do," replied Jim Street.

Steve began on a bagel. "I really don't need this," he said as he pointed to the bagel then downed a gulp of coffee.

"You have been here once with your usual daily report of how we are doing in our battle with CM Disease, so this must be something different, and important," said Jim Street.

"How much money can you get for Jacque and me?"

Jim Street half way pointed his coffee cup at Steve. "For what?"

"Research."

Jim Street took a big slug of coffee, then refilled his cup. "What in the hell kind of research are you going to do? You are not the research kind of person, so why come here with an asinine request like that?"

"For Jacque."

"Why doesn't Jacque come himself and ask for money? He is a big boy now."

"He did, once, and you refused him."

"Where in the hell am I going to get money for him to play around with white mice? It just ain't there, Steve."

" Jim, you can find it somewhere in your budget. We are in a very unusual situation. Jacque has milked his department budget for all he could so that he could carry out the research that is necessary in trying to find out something, anything, about CM Disease. He has even used a lot of his own money."

Jim Street was unmoved. "We are not a research institution."

Steve spoke demandingly, "Now, let's get something straight, Jim. Jacque needs money to continue research in CM Disease. Now it is up to you to get it for him. He needs forty thousand now, and maybe more later."

"Get a Grant from somewhere," Jim Street replied. "He knows a lot of people in the right places."

"No, Jim, you get the grant. You know the people in the right places, and you are good at Grantsmanship. Get it for Jacque."

Jim Street remained quiet for awhile. Then he said, "I'll ask the Board at the next meeting. Then later I'll work on a Grant."

"The Board, when do they meet?"

"You are in luck. The next meeting is tomorrow night."

Steve and Lisa drove out to Old Town for lunch where they stopped at their favorite eating establishment, "Jeans."

"We'll have the French onion soup, a chunk of your house cheese, the French bread, and iced tea."

The tight-skirted waitress left with the order. "How do you think I would look in one of those outfits, Steve?"

"Your legs are not that shapely."

"You have noticed."

"A long time ago."

"Your mood has been terrible today, Steve. I would have stayed home if I knew you were this grumpy. You were not even nice to the waitress when you gave her your order."

"Things are getting worse, not better, Lisa."

"You really did not expect the relationship with your wife to improve, did you?"

"No, but I cannot help it if we have an epidemic on hand and I am stuck taking care of a lot of people. I know that it would be nice for me to be able to spend more time at home, but I just can't."

"You could be home today, having lunch with your..."

"Come on, Lisa. I never did go home for lunch. If I were not here with you, then I would be lunching at the hospital or somewhere else. And besides Carole is gone for the day."

"You are rationalizing."

"It has just been a bad week for me."

"At home or at the hospital?"

"Both."

"What's going on at home to throw you into this terrible, nasty state of mind? Most of the time you don't let those things bother you. Maybe I shouldn't ask."

"I just do not like cocktail parties, and I can't help it if I can't be home all the time."

"Cocktail parties can be fun. I'll bet you would like them if I were there with you."

Steve grinned a little, "Maybe."

"I don't think that you are very nice to your wife."

"She is not very nice to me, either."

"Well, if you are not nice to your present wife, maybe you would not be nice to me either if I were your wife."

"You are different."

"All of us are 'different,' until we become someone's wife."

"Listen, you could handle me, anytime. I get grumpy and you tell me I'm grumpy. I like that. I tell people exactly how I feel, and I expect them to do the same for me. Carole doesn't do that. She just pouts and I don't know why. Hard to live that way."

Lisa bit her lip and shook her head, then smiled and said, "I don't think that that is what's bothering you today."

"The O'Neal girl died early this morning."

"CM Disease?"

"What else do people die from these days?"

"She wasn't very old."

All was quiet for awhile. Lisa and Steve were served their food and ate with only an inconsequential comment every now and then. When they were almost finished, Lisa reopened the conversation. "You should not take these deaths personally, Steve."

"It shows, doesn't it?"

"Yes. You always get irritable when things are not going right, or when you lose a patient that you think should not have died. But you might just as well face it. CM Disease will be with us for a long time."

"Thanks," said Steve. "I need that kind of encouragement."

The conversation stopped to get reorganized. Then Lisa said with a smile, "I forgot to tell you something today, Steve." Lisa leaned forward and whispered, "I love you."

Steve finally smiled. "Now, that kind of encouragement I can use. I thought that you may have changed your mind about me."

"I was just teasing to see how long you could go without asking," replied Lisa.

"I have never asked, yet," said Steve kiddingly.

"If you are saying that you have never asked if I love you, no, you have not," replied Lisa. "But you have asked."

"It is written in the Bible, 'Ask and ye shall receive,'" interjected Steve. "And I have received, more than I deserve."

"And that is what I like about you, Steve, your honesty. But I think that it is me who is receiving and it is you who is doing the giving."

Steve grimaced at Lisa. "Ah! So it is settled. We both give and receive. What a delicious arrangement." Steve leaned forward and asked very quietly. "Now, when can we get together for the serious part of our affair?"

"This is serious enough for me," said Lisa with a smile.

"And I shall ask once again. When can we get together for the serious part of our affair?"

"Tomorrow night," said Lisa.

"Sorry, but I have an important meeting to attend," replied Steve.

"Who is she?" asked Lisa.

"You still do not trust me, do you? I wish that I were as good as my reputation. If I have been in bed with as many women as I get credit for, I would be showing the fatigue of a marathon runner right after a race."

"You do," said Lisa.

"You are quite athletic in bed yourself," replied Steve.

"If tomorrow night is out, then we will have to play the waiting game," said Lisa.

"That is what we've been doing for five years," said Steve,

Lisa checked the time. "We should really be going. You have to get back to the office and I have an appointment with my hairdresser at twothirty."

"It has been an enchanting lunch, Lisa. You have a way of raising my spirits when they are down. Let's plan on lunch next Wednesday."

"You have a date."

*

Steve casually entered Dr. Marten's office. The Pathologist was busy peering into his microscope and dictating notes. "I was not expecting you until later, Steve. Sit down. I will be done with this slide in a minute."

Dr. Marten finished dictating his notes, then migrated to the chair behind his desk. "Thank you for putting in a good word for me. Jim Street called this morning and said that the Board had approved the twenty thousand dollars to be used by me, or us, for research. How did you get him to get the entire amount that I thought we might need?"

"We only got half of what I asked for," said Steve.

Jacque replied, "Jim is still putting in for the Grant and we will have to repay the money that the Board is giving us if we do get the Grant."

"That seems fair enough. We have the money and the hell with the Grant," said Steve.

Dr. Marten leaned back in his chair. "I have made some interesting observations in the past few days, Steve."

"That sounds encouraging," replied Steve.

"In some of the last cases of CM Disease on which we have done post-mortems, I have noticed some changes in the myocardium."

"For the better, or for the worst?"

"For the better, I think," replied Dr. Marten. "I have noticed that the myocardium showed definite areas of healing. Here, let me show you."

Dr. Marten took Steve over to his microscope and showed him some of the slides that he had been studying. He pointed out areas where the myocardium showed evidence of a definite decrease in the inflammation. "These areas are healing. And there are a lot of other areas of myocardium that are actually healed already. And the myocardium has healed without any appreciable residual damage or scaring."

"What do you make of this, Jacque?" asked Steve.

"I really can't say, yet. Give me a little more time to study some more slides and to think about it."

"Maybe I was correct then," said Steve. "If there is evidence of substantial healing as you have indicated, then, if we could get the patients through that crucial stage where they develop the asystole, then maybe some of these patients would live."

"Exactly," answered Dr. Marten. "But even more interesting is the fact that all of the slides that I have shown you were made from specimens taken from different victims of CM Disease. No two were taken from the same patient. And that is just a small sample. I have re-examined about fifty slides and they all show the same findings...areas of healing with some areas of complete healing. Some of the slides were specimens from patients who have recently died from CM Disease, and some were taken from patients who were among the first victims of the disease."

"Then what you have seen is not merely a chance finding," said Steve.

Dr. Marten continued. "The healing is a natural part of the disease process. Conceivably the virus, or whatever the causitive organism is, has an affinity for the conduction tissues of the heart. Or, perhaps the myocardium surrounding the conduction fibers is so afflicted that in some unknown way it interferes with the conduction of the electrical impulses of the heart. Or, there could be some toxin or immunilogical process at work that we don't know about that is affecting the conduction system."

"Have you notified the CDC of your new findings?"

"No, not yet. I want to do a little more work and more thinking about the meaning of these observations."

"It could mean that we have been on the wrong track altogether," said Steve.

"I'm not sure what you mean," said Dr. Marten.

"I'm not sure what I mean either," replied Steve. "But we'll have to think about some of the things you have shown me. I'll sleep on it."

Jim Street was not happy to see Winston Welsch sitting in his office. But, Winston was there, so Jim Street knew that he would have to hear him out.

"It is my understanding, Jim, that the Board has allowed a significant amount of funds to be diverted to Dr. Marten for research. On CM Disease I presume."

"Your understanding is correct, Winston. The Board has approved Dr. Marten's request and at the same time we are going to apply for a Grant, and if we do get a grant, then the money given to Dr. Marten will be returned to the general hospital fund. So what we are really doing is giving Dr. Marten a loan, gambling on the probability of his coming up with some positive results and using the Grant money to repay the Board."

"And if the Grant is not allowed?" asked Dr. Welsch."

"Then the hospital will absorb the cost. We can afford it. I think that it is appropriate for the Board to loan or provide money for research in CM Disease. Do you agree?"

"Not agreeing would be like voting against chocolate ice cream and sex. But BMI would be happy to allow Dr. Marten to use its facilities so that he might do his research. They would also furnish him with the necessary materials and funds."

"You will have to talk to Dr Marten about that."

"I have. I myself have done research in the BMI laboratories. They have outstanding facilities, and equipment."

"I thought that they were engaged in the development of instrumentation for research," said Jim Street. "I did not know that they were engaged in research themselves."

"They develop and manufacture instruments for research, but they furnish materials for industry, government, hospitals, and anyone who might need such materials. And they do have a research facility."

"That is very interesting, Winston, but if you want to discuss the matter further, please talk to Dr. Marten. The research project is his, not mine."

"I may do just that," answered Winston.

The two sat in silence. Jim Street was waiting for Dr. Welsch to take the initiative to leave. Finally, Dr. Welsch spoke again. "But there is one other small item that I would like to discuss with you, Jim."

Jim Street looked at his watch in a gesture that he hoped would speed Dr. Welsch's discussion. "Go right ahead, but I hope that it will not take too long. I have an important meeting soon, and I don't want to be late."

"This will take only a moment; it concerns Dr. McKay and Mrs. Clarke."

Jim Street noted that Winston Welsch emphasized the Mrs. in Clarke. "What about Dr. McKay and Mrs. Clark?"

"There have been rumors about them. It is almost certain that they are having an affair. And with both of them being married, well, that could be embarrassing to the hospital, and to the medical staff, and perhaps to you as well, Jim."

Jim Street had to struggle hard to keep his violent temper from flaring. "What Dr. McKay and Lisa Clarke do on their own time is their own goddamn business. If you have any evidence that they are disrupting hospital activities, or if whatever you say they are doing interferes with their work in the hospital, then come and talk to me. Otherwise, don't talk to me about rumors concerning personal conduct of anybody."

"Then you at least agree with me that they are having some kind of an affair."

"I did not say that, and I really don't know, and I don't give a goddamn whether or not they are. It is none of my business what they do in private, and none of yours."

"I am surprised that you take such a serious matter so lightly. It is imperative that we maintain the integrity of the medical staff and that of hospital personnel. But if you feel the way you do about such matters, I can accept that, even though I do not agree with you. I just hope that it does not come back to haunt you sometime in the future, and it very well could do just that."

"I'll take that chance," replied Jim Street.

"I have some patients to see, so I will leave so you can get to your meeting," said Dr. Welsch.

As Dr. Welsch was walking out the door, Jim Street stopped him. "Winston!"

Winston Welsch stopped and slowly turned around until he was facing Jim Street.

"No one is perfect, Winston, not even you."

The face of Winston Welsch was soon covered with what Jim Street often times referred to as Winston Welsch's silly ass grin.

"Thanks," said Winston. Then he left.

That same afternoon, Jim Street had another visitor, Dr. McKay. "Jacque is doing some excellent research on CM Disease, Jim, and I do not think that the Board will be sorry that they furnished him the money for research, even if the grant does not come through."

"You know damn well that I would have given him the money. You just can't make it too easy for those goddamn researchers to get money or else they are on your front porch looking for a handout every time you turn around."

"Jacque is different."

"Maybe, but I treat everyone alike."

Steve settled in a chair before he began. "I have spoken with a lot of the members of the medical staff, and I think that I have been able to mend a lot of the fences that Welsch tore apart at the last staff meeting. If he will only keep his mouth shut for awhile I believe that we can make some headway in orienting the staff for a more concentrated effort on the CM problem."

"I don't think that he is finished with you, Steve. He wounded you at the last staff meeting, but he did not stab you deep enough. Steve, you are wielding too much influence, and he does not like that. He has been the grizzly bear around here for too long and he does not want anyone, especially you, trespassing on his domain."

"The CM Disease debate is a dead issue. Everyone is convinced that we must have a concentrated effort with a unified staff to make things happen. Everyone is not yet in the circle, but it won't be long until they are," replied Steve."

"You're right, Steve. Winston is not going to challenge you or Jacque on the CM issue anymore. He is too smart for that. It would be foolish, and he would have no way of winning that one now."

"I'm not going to let Winston disrupt us again," said Steve.

"No?" quizzed Jim Street.

"I think that even he knows that this is no time to cause a major disturbance in staff relations."

Jim Street spun around on his chair. "Shit! You are so goddamn naive that it isn't funny. Or maybe it is. Winston Welsch wants your ass tied high in a tree and he won't stop till he sees it there, for everyone to see. Don't underestimate him, Steve."

"What is he going to do? There are no other major problems glaring at us now. The plague of CM Disease will keep us busy for a while. By the time something else comes up I will no longer be Chief-of-Staff, only a former Chief. And like all the other former Chiefs-of-Staff, I will remain in the shadows of the younger men who are making their way up the ladder. No, Jim, after this term I will only want to be a plain staff member. I have no further ambitions regarding staff leadership."

"You may not be planning on any, but you have gained enough stature with the staff that you will remain a major influence, whether you like it or not. And knowing you, you will not be able to disassociate yourself from the important problems that will continue to pop up in the hospital. And Winston knows this, and that is why he wants to discredit you as much as possible. Winston is very vindictive and he still is not satisfied with the trouble that he has caused you at the staff meeting. He weakened you, Steve, but he did not destroy you. But he will try again, and maybe soon."

"You sound as if you know something that I should know."

"Winston was in my office today and he mentioned the relationship between you and Mrs. Clarke, and he emphasized the Mrs."

"That is hardly hospital business."

"I just want to warn you. What you do with your own time is your own business, and not mine. But Winston thinks that it is his business. Frankly, I don't give a damn what your relationship is to Lisa Clarke."

"We are friends, close friends. Maybe I screw her once in awhile, but so what."

"Goddamn it, Steve, get serious; you could be ruined by all this."

"What do you want, Jim? A true confession series for the hospital newsletter?"

"I just want you to be careful, Steve."

"I'm not sure what I can do to stop a rumor, and I am not even going to try."

Jim Street knew Steve very well, professionally and personally. He liked Steve and he would do his best to protect him from any difficulty created by someone like Winston Welsch. "Just be careful, Steve. He could cause you a lot of trouble."

Two days later Steve was in Dr. Marten's laboratory once again. It was late at night, and both were very tired, but they had so many things to discuss and just had not been able to find time to meet sooner. Steve was pouring the strong, freshly brewed coffee and Dr. Marten was going over some of his data.

"Cream?" asked Steve.

"A little," replied Jacque.

Steve settled in a chair next to the large table where Dr. Marten had his papers strewn about in haphazard fashion. Steve sipped at the coffee and asked, "How do you make heads or tails out of that mess of papers that you have scattered all over the table?"

"Just don't touch anything. I know exactly where everything is."

"The original, indefatigable, unerring calculator…your brain," said Steve.

"Thanks. I have been reviewing a lot of our past work and I think that I am coming up with something. With what, I don't know. Some things don't add up."

"Like what?" asked Steve.

" Like, no one has yet come up with an organism that could be the cause of CM Disease."

"I thought that the Center for Infectious Disease in Atlanta came up with some positive virus cultures."

"They thought that they did. But I received a letter from them this week. They are having problems. They have been able to grow something, but they are not sure now that what they are growing are viruses. They have found particles that resemble viruses, but that's all there is, a resemblance. Whatever we are dealing with is acting erratically, and the CDC is having difficulty in typing and classifying the particles as a virus."

"Which makes you think that maybe it is not a virus after all," added Steve.

"They have thought about that too, and they are pursuing that avenue of thought."

"You know a lot more about things like that than me, Jacque. I am a clinical doctor. All of that research stuff buries me in no time."

"I still want and need your input. You may not be able to follow through with the actual research, but you come up with some good ideas for researchers to pursue."

"Thanks for the compliment. Have another cup of coffee. How is that for a good idea?"

"Excellent. You put just the right amount of cream in the first. Do the same with this one."

Dr. Jacque Marten stopped working on his papers. He took a swallow of coffee, then sat back in his chair so that he could devote his full attention to Steve. "We have to dig a little deeper into trying to find the method of spread of CM Disease. We really do not know much about that, and it is important. If we can find how it is spread, that might give us a clue to etiology. I have some people working on some of the early cases of CM Disease that we had at the hospital. They are reviewing the records in minute detail. We want to know where all of these people lived, where they worked, what they ate, what they did in their spare time.... Anything and everything about them. As soon as we have all of that data collected, we'll put it in the computer and see what we can come up with. You and I can go over the data and see if we can pick up some kind of emerging pattern or trend. We can try to find a clue as to the spread of the disease as it is reflected in the patients who had it."

"Sounds like a lot of work to me."

"Putting it in the computer is the hardest part. But Jim has given me the use of his computer firm, and they are good."

Steve emptied his cup and yawned as he looked at his watch. Three A.M. Time to go to bed. "If you do not have anything else on the agenda, I am going to head for home. Five-thirty is going to come pretty fast."

"Just one moment," interrupted Jacque. "I have something that I want to show you."

Jacque walked over to a locked file cabinet. He dialed the combination and pulled open the drawer. He flipped through the files until he came to a large, brown, manila envelope. He brought it to the table and took out a sheet of paper and laid it down, upside down. "Steve, I want you to read this, but I must insist that the content of the letter go no further than this room. I am confiding in you because I trust you, and because you have been so close to the problem of CM Disease." He gave the sheet to Steve to read.

Steve carefully read the communication. It was from the CDC, addressed to Dr. Marten and labeled STRICTLY CONFIDENTIAL. Steve finished reading the communiqué, then looked up at Dr. Marten. "Can this be right? Can it be accurate?" Dr. Marten nodded his head in the affirmative. "I have no reason to doubt its content." Dr. McKay re-read a portion of the communiqué:

> ...Interpolating from our statistics, within two years, one quarter of the population of the United States could be dead, victims of CM

> Disease. The number could very well be one third of the population if the present trend of increasing virulence of the etiological agent prevails. It is therefore imperative that an all-out effort be made to establish the etiology of CM Disease, its method of spread, and if possible, a treatment.

Steve handed the paper back to Dr. Marten. Jacque locked the document back in his file. He returned to the table where Steve was now standing. Steve was silent. He was only thinking about the scourge of the Black Death in the Middle Ages and the new scourge, CM Disease.

Dr. Marten said, "We have a lot of work to do, Steve. Either we find some way to stop this damn thing, or I'll be doing a hell of a lot of autopsies."

Chapter 12

It was two a.m. when Steve had stopped at Lisa's house. He had spent the night at the hospital taking care of two very ill patients. He was dead tired and he was depressed over the death of Dr. Hillary. Steve wanted to talk to someone, so he turned to Lisa, the one person in the world whom he trusted without reservation. Lisa was the only person to whom Dr. Steve McKay had ever revealed his most private thoughts and emotions. Steve presented himself to the world as an image of granite-like stability, a man in complete control of his own destiny, and a man with complete and unerring control over his emotions. Deep down, however, Steve McKay was a very emotional person, a person with great empathy for the needs of others. He was a very kind person, and he was always ready to comfort and to assist, but always without visible emotional involvement. It was Lisa Clarke who, over the years, had been able to prompt Steve McKay to reveal himself to her, and more importantly, to himself.

David was away on one of his frequent out-of-town business trips. Steve and Lisa were alone in the big, rambling, ranch style house, and they just sat and talked for a long time. Dr Hillary's death had affected Steve very deeply. He somchow felt that the Almighty had betrayed them when he struck down a doctor with the disease that the doctor was fighting. Dr. Steve McKay was also angry. He was angry because he was so helpless in his battle against the now dreaded killer. He wanted so badly to be able to do something, any little thing at all, to stem the tide of the scourge that was striking down the people around him. And although he would never admit it, he was scared. He was frightened that the dreadnought would strike even closer to him than it had. He harbored no great fear for his own life, but he did fear for the lives of those close to him.

After talking for over an hour, Lisa could see that Steve was exhausted and badly in need of sleep. She offered him one of her famous relaxing back rubs. He consented and as he was dozing off to sleep, she promised to awaken him in two hours. Lisa did not keep her promise. She allowed Steve to sleep for four hours before she awakened him.

Lisa shook Steve, very gently. He moved a little and Lisa touched him again. Steve looked up and found himself staring into Lisa's ocean blue eyes. Lisa leaned over and kissed him gently on the lips. Steve smiled, pulled Lisa closer to him and pressed his lips tightly to hers. "I love you," he said.

"And I love you. But it is time for you to get up. I have some fresh coffee, and I have biscuits in the oven. I'll fix a complete breakfast if you want - the works."

Steve rubbed the sleep from his eyes. "You know that I rarely eat breakfast. Biscuits and coffee are fine."

"Want to shower?" asked Lisa.

"Is that an invitation?" replied Steve with a playful look on his face.

"An invitation for you, and I do mean you, to take a shower. I have too many things to do and you have a very busy morning."

"You can't blame a guy for trying," said Steve. "But I think that I had better go home to shower, shave and do all of that kind of stuff." Steve looked at his watch and then at Lisa. He was glad that Lisa had let him sleep longer than he had planned. He really needed the extra rest, and it gave him a reprieve from the exhausting pace of the prior thirty-six hours.

"It looks as if I am going to start the day playing catch up," said Steve. After a moment of thinking he added, "No, I would have to say that starting the day with you puts me way ahead."

Jim Street shivered in the early morning cold when he stepped off the porch of his home and walked towards his garage. His car sputtered a few times before it finally took hold. It was still dark as Jim Street drove slowly down the nearly deserted street. The sky was overcast, and a snow was predicted for later that day. Jim Street drove to the hospital where there was plenty of work waiting for him. It seemed that with each passing week the workload became heavier and heavier and more and more complicated than the last. He wondered if the Ferris wheel of divergent daily activities would ever slow down. Jim Street had been working long hours, getting less than a normal amount of sleep, and he was getting more hassle from all of those to whom he had to answer...the Hospital Board of Directors, the Medical Staff and now, even the press. His years of experience had taught him to expect nursing staff and ancillary staff problems to land on his desk every day. He could handle the Medical Staff and the Board of Directors even though he sometimes came out on the losing end of the confrontations that he had with them. But now he felt like telling the whole goddamn bunch to shove it, but he could not afford to do that. He needed the job.

Jim Street parked the Cadillac in his private parking space in the employee parking lot. As he left the warmth of his car the chill of the outside air hit him and he cursed and wished that it were summer. The hospital employees were surprised to see their chief executive officer in the hospital so early in the morning. It was common for Jim Street to be at the hospital by seven and to leave late, but this day's arrival was earlier than usual. Important matters that needed his immediate attention were waiting for him, and he wanted to get an early start to begin work on them. They were difficult, as well as delicate matters, and Jim Street wanted some time, alone, so that he could put them in proper perspective. He stopped off at the Emergency Room and poured a cup of hot coffee. He chatted briefly with the Emergency Room doctor and the nurses, then headed for his office.

Jim Street sat at his desk, his brain mired in deep thought, still groggy from lack of sleep. Four crushed pieces of paper lay in the wastebasket, testimony to the memos that Jim Street had begun, then discarded. Dr. Charles Hillary, the very likable and talented family physician, had died the day before...of CM Disease. Young Dr. Hillary left a wife and three small children behind. Jim Street had to compose a note of sympathy to send to the family and he was not good at that sort of thing even though he possessed more empathy than he allowed himself to reveal to others or even to himself. He leaned over, wrote three lines, read them over, then crushed the paper into a tight clump that made a loud thump as it hit the bottom of the waste basket. He threw down the pen and headed for the Emergency Room and another cup of coffee and another chance to talk to someone. Jim Street did not like being alone at times like this. "Anyway, Bernie is much better than I am at composing sympathy letters," he said to himself.

It was late in the afternoon when Steve McKay walked leisurely into the Pathology Office. "I want to talk to the Chief Pathologist, right way," said Steve in a gruff, demanding tone of voice to the young secretary.

"Yes, Dr. McKay. Dr. Marten is expecting you," replied the young secretary with a touch of fright in her voice.

The Pathologist was hunched over his microscope dictating as he examined each slide and made his diagnosis. "Sit down, Steve, I am just finishing with this slide."

In a minute Jacque Marten had spun his chair around and was facing Steve. "I tried to get to you early this morning, but I could not find you."

"I was dead tired and slept in late," said Steve.

"It did not matter, really," said Jacque. "It was just that Winston Welsch was busy arranging Dr. Hillary's funeral."

"What in the hell does he have to do with that?"

"You know Welsch. He likes to be a part of everything of any importance that is going on, invited or not."

Steve said, "I had an appointment to see Jim Street, but by the time I arrived at his office it was closed. There was a note on the door telling me to see you."

"You are planning to go to the funeral tomorrow, aren't you?" asked Dr. Marten.

"Yes, of course," answered Steve.

"Well, Winston has arranged a big affair. He talked to the Monsignor at the parish and there will be at least five priests con-celebrating the Mass, including the Catholic chaplain and the Protestant chaplain from the hospital."

"The Protestant chaplain can't con-celebrate Mass with them, Jacque."

"I know that, Steve. The Protestant chaplain is just going to be there, maybe give a little eulogy. Welch thought that it would be a nice gesture, so he arranged it."

"For once I would have to agree with Welch. It is a nice gesture," said Steve.

"Winston also thought that it would be a nice gesture if somebody from the medical staff gave a eulogy as well."

"It sounds as if this will be a really big affair," said Steve. "I wonder if Winston would do that much for me if I died."

"And that is what Jim Street wanted to talk to you about," said Jacque.

"About me dying?" asked Steve.

"Get with it, Steve," said Jacque. "I am just trying to get the message to you, that's all. I am just Jim Street's messenger."

"Where is he anyway? This is too early for him to leave the hospital."

"He is out helping Mrs. Hillary make the funeral arrangements. He and Bernie went to help pick out the casket and anything else that needs to be done. Mrs. Hillary has no family nearby, and she was very upset and did not know where to turn, so Bernie volunteered the services of Jim."

"I'll bet he liked that," said Steve.

"He didn't mind too much, as long as Bernie went along," replied Jacque.

"Sometimes I think that if we let Jim go, Bernie could run the hospital," said Steve.

Jacque smiled. "I think that you are right." Jacque looked at Steve. "They think that you should be the one to give the eulogy."

"No, not me, Jacque," said Steve. "I hate to say this, but Winston would be good at that sort of thing."

"I think that he would have liked to have done it, but he was so busy making arrangements that everyone agreed that you should be the one," said Dr. Marten.

"I don't even go to church very often anymore, Jacque."

"Neither do I," replied Jacque.

Steve continued. "The Monsignor and I don't always see eye to eye, either. He still thinks that the Vatican should run the Church. Maybe you can get someone else. Maybe even Jim could do it."

"It is too late. Your name has already been given to the paper. If you were available earlier in the day, maybe you could have gotten out of it," added Jacque.

"What should I say?" asked Steve.

"You will have to figure that out yourself. You are rarely at a loss for words and I am sure that you will do a decent job. You are a good speaker, and that is one reason why they chose you."

"Well, I guess I don't have much choice since the decision has already been made."

"You are to call the Monsignor tonight and let him know that you are going to speak."

"I'll call him as soon as I get home," said Steve.

"I hate to change the subject," said Jacque, "But I received a communication from CDC today."

"Something new about CM Disease?"

"They think that they have identified the virus. They are going to be in touch as soon as they learn more details," replied Dr. Marten.

"We need and deserve a big break somewhere, and soon."

"And I need to break away from this place." Dr. Marten rose from his chair and took off his lab coat. "I am going home. It has been a long day and we have a funeral to go to tomorrow."

The doctors both left for home, not looking forward to having to attend Dr. Hillary's funeral the next day.

It was a cold day for Dr. Hillary's funeral. The church was overflowing and a pall of disaster hung over the congregation. The scepter of CM Disease was alive in the church and not locked up in the casket with Dr. Hillary. Five priests con-celebrated the Mass. Both the Catholic and the Protestant chaplains delivered a homily and then, before the cortège left the Church, Dr. Steve McKay delivered his short eulogy.

Dr. McKay expressed his sympathy to the family on behalf of the medical staff, and noted that Dr. Hillary's presence would be sorely missed at Good Samaritan Hospital and in the community. He hit briefly on the problem of CM Disease and brought to the attention of the congregation that perhaps Dr.

Hillary's death could become a rallying point for the medical community to close ranks so that they could do their utmost to combat the scourge that was plaguing them. They could best do this by continuing to perform their duties as members of the health care system. He ended with a prayer asking God to take cognizance of their plight and to help them to find an answer to the problem of CM Disease.

After Dr. McKay finished the eulogy the funeral service was completed and the body of Dr. Hillary was taken to the cemetery for burial. Hospital personnel returned to their assignments at Good Samaritan, hoping that the scythe of CM Disease would pass, leaving them and the members of their families untouched.

It was now over a month since the death of Dr. Hillary. CM Disease was still striking down people in the community and reaching into the ranks of hospital personnel.

Dr. McKay was busy researching some articles over the Internet in the Hospital library. He printed some articles from THE CHEMISTRY OF DRUGS and put them with the other articles in the pile in front of him. He folded them neatly, and put them in the pocket of his white lab coat. Then he left to meet with Dr. Marten.

Steve walked into Dr. Marten's office unannounced. "How are things going, Jacque? Have you heard anything more from CDC?

"They now are not sure about the organism they isolated and identified as a virus that could be the cause of CM Disease."

Steve pulled the papers from his pocket and unfolded them and put them on the desk. "I think that I may have something."

"What is your something?" asked Jacque.

"I have done a lot of thinking about the death process in CM Disease. It is invariably cardiac asystole. The heart simply stops beating. Obviously there is an electrical dysfunction in the heart's ventricles. The cardiac muscles that pump the blood fail to react to the electrical impulses that come from above, from the S-A node. The electrical impulses get to the ventricles, but they fail to contract and the heart is unable to pump the blood through the body. What we are seeing is electrical failure of the ventricular muscles of the heart."

Jacque leaned back in his chair. "I think that we have talked about all of this and discussed it at length, Steve. So what is new?"

"I have been thinking, Jacque. Remember the drug, Rhythodyne?"

"Sure. It has been taken off of the market... Too toxic," replied Dr. Marten.

"Toxic, yes," continued Steve. "But in what way was it toxic?"

Jacque thought for a second, then answered. "If I remember correctly, many of the patients developed ventricular fibrillation, and some of them died. Rhythodyne stimulated the electrical function of the pacing system of the heart, but it also stimulated the ventricle muscle itself.... and I am beginning to see the light."

Dr. McKay spread out his notes on the desk. "I have researched Rhythodyne and chemically it appears to be just the drug that we need. It affects the calcium transfer system and alters polyrazation and depolarization of the myocardium, the heart muscle, so that the electrical conduction initiated in the S-A node will stimulate the heart muscle and make it contract. The sick myocardiurn of victims of CM Disease will be able to continue to function."

Jacque shrugged his shoulders. "It would be worth a try, but where are you going to get the stuff? It has been off the market for over six months now. And besides that, if you want to use it, you should really get an experimental drug permit."

"No time for that," said Steve in a blunt, matter-of-fact reply.

"You are taking a chance if you don't, and you will have a difficult time finding any Rhythodyne," said Jacque.

"I have found some," answered Steve as he collected his papers.

"Where?" Jacque was surprised to hear that Steve had been fortunate enough to find any of the drug.

"Our pharmacist here at the hospital," replied Steve.

"I thought that all of the drug that was in stock was supposed to have been returned to the manufacturer for disposition," said Dr. Marten.

"It was. But our pharmacy just has not gotten around to doing that. They were waiting for the time that they had a big order to give to the drug salesman, then they were going to return it for credit. There is nothing strange about that. It is done that way all of the time with drugs."

"Steve, the pharmacist will not give it to you.... Or will he?" asked Jacque, hopefully.

"Yes and no. No one knows that the pharmacy is in possession of the drug. I went over all of these papers with our chief pharmacist and convinced him that this shows promise for the treatment of the arrhythmia that develops in CM Disease. Then, I just happened to find a dozen twenty c.c. vials of Rhythodyne in my box in Medical Records this morning."

"I did not hear you say that, Steve. But I have to admit that the information from the articles you've shown me does present a good case for the use of Rhythodyne, and I'm going to prepare a communication to send to

CDC regarding the use of the drug."

Steve's jaw dropped in surprise. "Now wait a minute, Jacque. I thought that we might agree not to go through CDC with this project."

Jacque Marten's face was painted with a large grin. "Just checking to see if you were paying attention. Steve, this conversation never took place. No official records unless this works. And sometimes I am not good at keeping records."

"You had me worried for a minute. I thought that you were losing it." Steve thought for a minute, then continued. "The only thing about the whole matter is that we will practically have to live with the patients receiving the drug. We can't officially make notes on the chart that we are using Rhythodyne and we cannot expect the nurses to give it. We will have to administer it by the intravenous route, ourselves."

"We? And we means you and who?" asked Jacque.

"You and I." Steve smiled and left the room before Jacque could object.

Dr. Steve McKay stood over the patient in ICU. Lisa stood nearby, nervously watching every move that Steve was making. Steve looked up at the EKG monitor. The heart rate had picked up. "Sixty-five beats per minute now. Check his blood pressure again," said Steve.

As Lisa was checking the blood pressure, Dr. Marten came into the room and stood next to Steve.

"How is it going?" asked Jacque.

Steve McKay did not look at Dr. Marten, but continued watching the monitor. "So far, so good. His heart rate has increased, his blood pressure is rising, and his chest is clearing. He is more alert and answering questions coherently now."

"Looks encouraging," said Dr. Marten. Then he walked over to the nurse's desk to check the patient's chart.

"Pressure still one-eighteen over eighty. It has remained stable for over an hour," said Lisa.

Dr. McKay placed his stethoscope on the patient's chest. The young man watched as Steve moved the bell of the scope over the chest wall and listened intently as he stopped at each position. Then Dr. McKay asked the patient to sit up. Steve listened carefully to the chest. "Much improved," he said to the young man. "Maybe we'll beat this yet." Steve then walked over to where Dr. Marten was reading the chart.

"Steve, this patient was pretty sick before you started the Rhythodyne. His bradycardia has improved. That should help his heart failure. How much have you given him so far?"

"A total of six milligrams," answered Steve.

"Are you ready to leave?" asked Dr. Marten.

"Yes, but let me scribble a few notes on the chart first."

Lisa winked at Dr. Marten. "He is not kidding when he says scribble. He is the world's worst writer."

Steve handed the chart to Lisa and was leaving with Dr. Marten. "Just one second, Doctor McKay. Let me check your orders before you leave. Sometimes I have difficulty interpreting them," said Lisa.

"Incompetent help," mumbled Dr. McKay.

Lisa quickly went over the notes and orders. "You may leave, Doctors. I can read them all."

As Steve and Dr. Marten walked down the hall, Jacque said, "I want to talk to you, Steve, in private."

Steve stopped. "How about right here in the head nurse's office. Lisa will not be back for awhile." Steve and Dr. Marten sat down and made themselves comfortable.

"Steve, what in the hell is the matter with you?"

"What do you mean?" questioned a surprised Dr. McKay.

"That is Dr. Welsch's patient on whom you are experimenting with Rhythodyne."

"It is also my patient, Jacque. Dr. Welsch asked me to see the patient in consultation with him. He told me to do whatever I wanted. He has been gone for two days and he won't be back until tomorrow evening."

"Jesus Christ," exclaimed Dr. Marten. "Sometimes you just don't think, Steve. What if something goes wrong with your using Rhythodyne? Welsch will be on you in no time."

"What can he say? The guy was going to die if we did nothing, and he was going to die even if we did everything that we have been doing with CM Disease patients. CM is a fatal disease, remember?"

"Steve, don't be that trusting all of your life. If something goes wrong, well, you are just giving Welsch a chance to hang you, but good."

"It is a fifty-fifty chance. Welsch should know that if Rhythodyne works, it was his patient on whom we tried it and he will get half the credit. He would like that."

"He will take half the credit, but not half the blame. Does he know that you are using Rhythodyne?" asked Dr. Marten.

"No. He left town before I decided to use it on this patient."

"You should have told him," exclaimed Jacque.

"Too late now. We have committed ourselves." Steve stood and put his hands in his pockets. "Look, Jacque, that guy was dead. That is one of the reasons why I chose him. He was near death and I waited as long as I dared. I did not want to make any mistakes when using Rhythodyne. Not on the first patient at least. This patient had an arrhythmia that was getting worse. He developed a bradycaradia and his heart almost stopped beating completely. He was very close to dying. But the Rhythodyne is working."

"Yes, it is working, and for your sake I hope that it continues to work."

"For our sake, remember."

"Yeah, for our sake," repeated Dr. Marten, grudgingly. As he turned to leave he mumbled sarcastically, "But I didn't realize that I was working with an idiot."

Dr. Welsch jauntily walked into the Intensive Care Unit. "Good morning, Mrs. Clarke."

"Good morning, Dr. Welsch. It is good to see you back."

"I had a patient here before I left.... CM Disease. I left him under the care of Dr. McKay who was seeing him with me. Has the patient died yet?"

"No, in fact he is improved. He is over there."

"That is a change, but a delightful one," answered Dr. Welsch. Dr. Welsch walked over to the bed and carefully examined his patient. He was utterly surprised that the patient looked so good and was doing so well. He walked back to the nurse's desk and picked up the chart. He read the progress notes of Dr. McKay and saw that the patient had been showing continued improvement over the past two days. Then he noticed the special sheet that was stuffed in the back of the regular chart…the unofficial sheet that Dr. McKay had been using to document his treatment with Rhythodyne.

Dr. Welsch called Lisa over to the desk. "Rhythodyne. Is Dr. McKay using Rhythodyne on this patient?"

"I am not sure. You will have to talk to him about that. He has handled part of the therapy all by himself. The nursing staff has had nothing to do with it. Dr. McKay will not allow any of us to give some of the medicines or to make notes on it."

"Rhythodyne has not been used for months. It is off the market," said Dr. Welsch. "There were a lot of complications, and a few patients died after we used it on them. Is that all you know about this?" asked Dr. Welsch.

"That is all. If you have any further questions, I would suggest that you speak to Dr. McKay." Then she added, "But the patient is much improved. So whatever Dr. McKay is doing, it seems to be working."

"Do you know where I can find Dr. McKay?"

"No. He said that he would be back to check the patient at ten. I can call you when he arrives," said Lisa.

"I want to talk to him about this," said Dr. Welsch. "And do not give any more Rhythodyne to this patient until I have talked to Dr. McKay."

"We do not give it. We do not even have it on the floor."

"Very well. But be sure to call me when Dr. McKay arrives."

Dr. McKay arrived at Intensive Care precisely at ten. He did not have to page Dr. Welsch. Dr. Welsch was waiting for him.

"Hello, Winston," said Steve. "It is good to have you back."

"I want to talk to you, Dr. McKay, alone."

Lisa was standing next to the two doctors and could not help but hear them. "You can use my private office if you wish. It is just down the hall," she said.

Steve and Dr. Welsch both felt a little uncomfortable. Dr. Welsch spoke first. "I saw the patient and he looks a lot better."

"Yes," replied Dr. McKay. "He has improved in the past twenty-four hours."

"I understand that you are using Rhythodyne on him. I thought that the drug was not to be used anymore," said Dr. Welsch.

Steve then explained his theory of electrical failure in patients with CM Disease and why he thought that Rhythodyne was a choice drug for the treatment of the bradycardia of CM Disease. He took great pains to carefully explain to Winston Welsch the chemical and electrical reasons of why the drug should work in this particular situation.

Dr. Welsch was not wholly convinced, but he did have to admit that the patient had improved.

Dr. McKay waited for a commitment from Dr. Welsch to use the Rhythodyne in his patient. But none was forthcoming.

"Since I have been out-of-town for a few days, and since you have been caring for the patient this long, you might just as well continue, Steve. I will sign off of the case."

Steve was not too happy about that, but he could not press the point. If he did, then Welsch could justifiably ask him to stop treatment with Rhythodyne. And worse yet, he might start asking questions as to where Steve had obtained the drug and as to whether he had been in contact with CDC regarding the use of the drug in CM Disease patients.

The two doctors left the room. Dr. McKay headed back to ICU so that he could give the patient another dose of Rhythodyne.

It was now twenty-four hours later. Dr. McKay was in sole attendance of the young victim of CM Disease. Dr. Welsch still came to see the patient to see how the treatment was progressing, or digressing, as the case might be. Everyone was amazed as to how well the patient was doing. Patients with

CM Disease had always taken a rapid downhill course once the heart slowed down to low levels and congestive heart failure developed. But this time the congestive heart failure had been controlled and the bradycardia that had developed a few days earlier was completely absent. The heart rate of the patient was a steady eighty beats per minute and regular. The lungs of the patient were clear of the fluid that had flooded them just a few days before. The nursing staff was elated at the progress that the patient was making, and Dr. McKay was beginning to voice a cautious optimism.

Dr. Marten frequently came to the Intensive Care Unit to check on the patient. But he had taken a wait and see attitude. He was a pragmatist and optimism was not a part of his emotional makeup. He walked over to the nursing desk where Lisa was busy writing notes on patients. "I see that the patient is doing very well," he said.

"Dr. McKay thinks that the patient has stabilized. So far he has not shown any signs of reverting to bradycardia," said Lisa.

"How long do you think that it will be before we will know if the patient will fully recover?" asked Dr. Marten.

"I should be asking you that question, Doctor. I am just a nurse."

"Lisa, you are not just a nurse. I respect your judgement. You have seen so many of these cases that your experience is invaluable in judging the progress being made in a case like this," replied Dr. Marten.

"If you insist on an answer, Doctor, then I would say that in twenty four hours we should know as to whether this patient is going to survive," replied Lisa.

Dr. Marten checked the chart once again, scrutinizing every bit of information that was there. He paid special attention to the private notes that Dr. McKay had made in the back of the chart. Dr. Marten then left to go back to his office to begin preparing the papers for application for the use of experimental drugs, for Rhythodyne.... Just in case.

Blood pressure stable at 120/80; apical heart rate 92 and holding; respirations sixteen and not labored; the patient's skin warm and dry; his mind clear and his sensorium alert. Dr. McKay was reviewing the patient notes that he had just made. He was beginning to feel that finally after so many months they were finally getting a break in their battle against CM Disease. Steve walked over to the patient, spoke to him briefly, evaluated his heart and lung function, and watched the EKG monitor for awhile and then went back to the desk where Lisa was waiting for him. "Looks good. Keep your fingers crossed."

"Care for some hot tea or coffee?" asked Lisa.

"Tea will be fine, decaffeinated."

Lisa poured the hot water over the tea bags in the cups. "Sugar?" she asked.

"I prefer a sweetener."

"You got it," said Lisa as she reached into a box of envelopes of artificial sweetener and handed a couple to Steve. "What do you think his chances are now?" asked Lisa.

"Fifty-fifty…at best," answered Steve.

"Why do you say that?" Lisa looked at Steve inquisitively. "I thought that you may be ready to roll out the victory flags. He has been so stable it is unbelievable. Everybody around here is afraid to say anything about it thinking they might place a hex on the whole business and bring defeat out of the clutches of victory. I hope that Rhythodyne is the answer to CM Disease deaths."

"I hope so, too," said Steve as he sipped tea.

Steve and Lisa drank hot tea and talked for a while. Then Steve left for home, hopefully to get some sleep.

It was 2:30 a.m. when Dr. Steve McKay was awakened by his phone ringing. "This is Intensive Care, Dr. McKay. Your patient is developing a bradycardia and some PVC's. His blood pressure has dropped and he is in and out of coma."

Steve was at the hospital in unbelievable short time; three red lights, five stop signs, three near accidents. The head nurse met him as he stepped through the doors of ICU. "He is worse than when I called you, Dr. McKay. His heart rate is down to twenty-four, his blood pressure is down to seventy. I think that he is going to die."

Dr. McKay quickly examined his patient. His condition was not good. "We will give him more Rhythodyne and see."

"His next dose is not due for three more hours," said the nurse.

"I know," replied Dr. McKay, "but this is not a time for protocol."

Dr. McKay drew up four milligrams of Rhythodyne and quickly put in into the young man's veins. For about fifteen minutes it appeared that the patient would rally. His pulse rose to sixty, his blood pressure hit one hundred, and the PVC's became less frequent.

Then the bottom dropped out, quickly and disastrously. The heart rate slowed to thirty, the blood pressure plunged to rock bottom, and the monitor flashed and flickered with the ominous PVC's…the same old precursors of death that Dr. McKay had seen so often before. Dr. McKay grabbed for the vial of Rhythodyne in desperation, withdrew five milligrams of the drug, and injected it quickly into the dying man's vein. One minute later the EKG monitor was alive with multiple premature ventricular contractions. Then the monitor face was covered with a wild array of electrical impulses, rapid ventricular tachycardia...Not good. Steve tried to counter the death dealing rhythm with drugs - Lidocaine, Disopyramide, and Procainamide – and a few others. They delivered shock after electrical shock in an effort to convert the heart back to a normal rhythm. But the wild heart rhythm continued at over two hundred beats per minute. Blood pressure was undetectable. Steve intubated the patient by placing the plastic tube into the patient's trachea. Still the heart ran wild. Finally the ventricular tachycardia, a deadly rhythm, digressed to ventricular fibrillation, a rhythm incompatible with life. Steve defibrillated the patient ten times. But each time the effects of the defibrillation lasted only a minute or so before the heart reverted back to the completely dysfunctional ventricular fibrillation. More drugs; more defibrillation shocks and still no response. The staff had been delivering CPR to circulate the blood and deliver oxygen to the stalled heart, and still there was no response. Finally after one more electrical shock, the heart stopped completely. No electrical activity whatsoever-a straight line on the EKG monitor. The patient was dead. CM Disease had won again.

Chapter 13

The icy cold fingers of an early March storm that swept over the Good Samaritan medical community were not as cold as the icy fingers of death that came wrapped in the cloak of CM Disease. People did not even stop to look anymore at the daily funeral corteges that crept through the city. The community was beginning to wonder where they would find enough space to bury the dead. Four more personnel from Good Samaritan Hospital had been laid to rest, victims of CM Disease. Two of those were nurses. The medical community was awe-struck when another physician, a talented young surgeon, became a victim of CM Disease. Everyone was past the stage of panic, and the community rested subtly in its terror, waiting patiently to see who would be the next victim, and hoping that it would not be them.

Dr. Winston Welsch stepped out of his Mercedes and made his way through the parking lot and into the hospital. He left his coat in the doctor's lounge on the first floor then went straight to Jim Street's office. Bernie was on the phone when Dr. Welsch entered. She politely held her call when she saw Dr. Welsch. "Mr. Street will be a little late. You may wait here, or if you have other things to do, I can page you when Mr. Street comes in."

"I'll wait, thank you." Winston Welsch had waited for Jim Street's page for him in the past, and sometimes the page did not come for a long time. He picked up a TIME magazine that was on the table and began reading.

It was not long before Jim Street poked his head into the outer office where Winston was still reading. "Sorry to be late, Winston, but you may come right in."

Winston closed the door gently behind him. Jim Street sat down in the big chair behind his desk. "What can I do for you today, Winston?"

"I'm not quite sure, Jim. It appears as if Dr. McKay and possibly Dr. Marten have overstepped their bounds in treating one of my patients."

"How is that, Winston?"

"Dr. McKay used Rhythodyne in treating the patient."

"I don't know what in the hell you are talking about, Winston. And what in the hell is Rhythodyne, and what patient are you talking about?"

"Rhythodyne is a drug that has been taken off the market by the FDA. It was found to be too toxic to be used clinically,"

Jim Street leaned back in his chair. "I still do not know what you are talking about, Winston."

"Let me start from the beginning," said Dr. Welsch.

"That is a good idea." Jim Street looked at his watch. "I hope this won't take too long. I have to meet with some members of the press in a little while…a very important meeting."

"I'll be as brief as I can," said Winston. "We can talk about the details later. I want to discuss the matter with Dr. McKay and Dr. Marten anyway before any decisions are made. But I am surprised that they did not inform you that they were using a drug experimentally."

"Hell, Winston. I am sure that Dr. Marten and Dr. McKay know what they are doing."

"I hope so because if they do not, then Dr. Marten, Dr. McKay, you, the hospital, and possibly I, could be in deep trouble."

What Dr. Welsch said had gotten Jim Street's attention. He suddenly became very interested in what Dr.Welsch had to say. "Go ahead, Winston. Tell me what this is all about."

"I had a patient who apparently had developed CM Disease. I was leaving town so I signed the patient to the care of Dr. McKay...with the patient's and Dr. McKay's consent, of course. When I returned I discovered that Dr. McKay was using Rhythodyne to treat the patient, apparently with the consent of Dr. Marten. I do not know whether they received consent from the patient. I also do not know where they got the Rhythodyne, but I certainly hope that it was not from your pharmacy."

Jim Street winced at the thought.

"After I returned from my trip and talked to Dr. McKay. I was not sure as to the propriety of using the drug, but since it had already been started I saw no reason to disturb those involved, especially the patient, by making a fuss over the matter. I simply signed off of the case and allowed Dr. McKay to continue with his unorthodox treatment."

"And the patient?" quizzed Jim Street.

"He died," said Winston.

"Just like every other patient who has had CM Disease," rapidly replied Jim Street. "So what else is new, Winston? I don't see what in the hell the problem is that is bothering you."

"You don't use drugs experimentally without getting permission from the FDA, even in a case like this. You must also get consent from the patient and fill out the necessary forms."

"Okay, Winston. I will check into the matter with Dr. McKay and Dr. Marten."

"I think that you should, and I am going to talk to them myself. I'm not sure what steps should be taken in the future, but I believe that we are putting ourselves in an impossible position by using an unorthodox treatment, even in the treatment of CM Disease. I think that we are especially vulnerable when we are using a drug that has been taken off of the market because it had been labeled as being too dangerous for clinical use."

"I will look into the matter and get back with you as soon as soon as I can," repeated Jim Street.

"I know that you will look into it, Jim, because if you don't, then I will," threatened Winston.

Dr. Welsch had put Dr. Marten on notice the day before that he wanted to see him on a very important matter, so Jacque's secretary was not at all surprised when Dr Welsch made his appearance. "I would like to see Dr. Marten," said Dr. Welsch in a demanding tone of voice.

"I believe that he is expecting you." The secretary rang up Dr. Marten's office on the intercom. After a short exchange, the secretary put down the receiver and said, "You may go right in, Dr. Welsch. Dr. Marten can see you right now."

"Thank you," replied Dr. Welsch as he opened the door to the private office of Dr. Marten.

"Sit down, Winston. And what is on your mind?"

"I just came from Jim Street's office."

"You didn't have to get an appointment to tell me that," said Dr. Marten.

"I told him about the experiment that you and Dr. McKay had performed on my patient. Whose idea was it to use the Rhythodyne, Jacque, yours or Dr. McKay's?"

"His, but I concurred," replied Dr. Marten, unhesitatingly.

"Sort of out of context for you to do such a thing. You are usually a stickler for proper protocol," said Winston.

"We did nothing that was too much out of the ordinary. We are dealing with a fatal disease, and anything that we try would have to be considered experimental. Anything that we can do to improve our death rate, which is one-hundred percent as you are well aware, is worth the effort."

"But you know the rules regarding experimentation, Jacque,"

"We kept good records, and if Rhythodyne works out, I will send in the application request that we be allowed to continue to experiment using

Rhythodyne. In fact, I have already filled out the preliminary papers."

"Have you sent them in?" asked Winston.

"Not yet," replied Dr. Marten.

"Then this is an illegal experiment," blurted out Dr. Welsch.

"In a sense," said Jacque Marten, unruffled.

"Not in a sense, Jacque, it is an illegal experiment... period!" exclaimed Dr. Welsch.

"It is how you interpret it, Winston. I have worked with the FDA long enough to know that they can overlook certain matters, if need be."

"But you are putting the hospital, and in this case, me, in jeopardy."

"You signed off the case, remember. But I have to admit that I was not happy to hear that Steve had begun using Rhythodyne without your permission. I believe that was a mistake. But on the other hand, you signed the patient over to him and you were out-of-town. Steve had no way of asking your permission to try the drug. He did not think that you would mind. The boy was dying. There was no hope for survival. Using Rhythodyne was a last minute attempt to save a life. I doubt that there would be much criticism against Dr. McKay, unless somebody pushed the alert button somewhere."

"I would not be too upset if Dr. McKay had used some orthodox method of treatment, or even an unorthodox method. But using Rhythodyne, a drug that has been taken off of the market because of explicit side reactions that have been known to have caused death in some patients, well, that is too much even for me to accept."

"But you don't understand, Winston. It is just that particular side reaction, the one that was the cause of death of patients in the past, that Dr. McKay thought might save the lives of patients with CM Disease."

"I know all about that. Dr. McKay has talked to me about his ideas on the subject, and I have done a lot of research in the library these past few days. I have learned a lot about Rhythodyne." Dr. Welsch leaned across the desk. "Do you know the cause of death of that young man?"

"Yes. I did the post. He had CM Disease." Dr. Marten pointed an accusing finger at Dr. Welsch. "And this time there is no doubt about that. You can send the pathological slides of the heart to any pathologist in the country and I am confident that they will all, without exception, make that diagnosis."

"That is not what I mean, Dr. Marten. I am talking about the immediate cause of death. Why did he actually die?"

"Cardiomyopathy, and like all of the others, cardiac arrhythmia."

"Precisely, Doctor. And what kind of an arrhythmia?" asked Winston.

"I really don't remember," answered Dr. Marten. "But I suspect that the patient died of cardiac aystole, like all the rest." Jacque Marten stood now, and placed his hands in his laboratory coat pockets. "For God's sake Winston, all of the people with CM Disease die of asystole. Their hearts quit beating. The electrical system fails."

"Not this one, Jacque."

For one of the few times in his life Dr. Jacque Marten was caught speechless, and he did not know what to say. He stood staring at Dr. Welsch, his eyes begging for an answer.

"This patient did not have cardiac asystole, Jacque. The electrical system of his heart did not stop, like all of the rest of the patients with CM Disease. This patient's heart went into ventricular fibrillation. The electrical system was working, but inappropriately. He went into ventricular fibrillation, and that is what happened with a lot of other patients who had been given Rhythodyne in the past. That is the reason that it was taken off of the market. Rhythodyne can cause ventricular fibrillation and kill people. And Rhythodyne was given to this patient, and he went into ventricular fibrillation, and he died."

"Winston, what difference did it make? That patient would have died anyway. He had CM Disease. And all patients with CM Disease die. What difference did it make whether he died of ventricular standstill or ventricular fibrillation?"

"The big difference is that CM Disease would be the cause of death in one case, and Dr. McKay would be the cause in the other."

"Winston," began Dr. Marten in a quiet tone of voice that bled with desperation, and rarely for Dr. Marten, emotion. "For God's sake, Steve tried something to try to save a life. Can't you understand that it did not work. The patient was moribund when he began treating him. The patient rallied for a while. For about twenty-four hours he lived with CM Disease, then he died. This is only one case. Rhythodyne may have been the immediate cause of death in this patient, but I still would like for you to think about this. This is no time to make waves. We are in a desperate storm and shipping water faster than we can bail out. We are sinking, slowly sinking in a sea of CM Disease. And if we do not find an answer soon, we may all be drowned in that sea." Dr. Marten now turned grim and angry. "Now get this through your head. We have got to find a cure for CM Disease, and soon, or a lot of people are going to die. Now get the hell out of here. I have too many important things to attend to."

Winston Welsch remained stoic. As he was about to leave he turned around and stood silent for a moment, then said, "I am not easily intimidated,

Dr. Marten." Then he left, slamming the door behind him.

It was a little after five in the afternoon and the late winter sun was reaching for the horizon in a dark, cloudy sky. The air was brisk with cold, and snow flurries had peppered the day from time to time without any noticeable accumulation. The streets were busy with people going home from work, and the bus with the high school basketball team just pulled out of the school parking lot on its way to that night's game. Lisa became a little edgy as the heavy traffic slowed her down. She waited impatiently for the traffic signal to change, then darted away with a jerk. In minutes she was nosing her compact car into the private parking area in the rear of Dr. Steve McKay's office. She met Dr. McKay's nurse as she was leaving the office through the back door. "Hi, Lisa. Dr. McKay is doing some dictating in his private office. He is waiting for you. I put on the water for some hot tea or chocolate." The nurse left in a hurry. It was rare that she was able to leave the office this early any more and she wanted to take full advantage of the situation.

Lisa closed the door quietly behind her, then walked toward Steve's office.

"I thought I heard you talking," said Steve as Lisa entered the room.

Steve could not help but notice the worrisome look on Lisa's face. He stopped dictating and wrinkled his forehead and asked, "What is wrong?"

Lisa made herself comfortable in one of the side chairs and busied herself unbuttoning her coat. But she said nothing.

Steve sensed the feeling of aloofness that filled the room. He smiled as best he could and said, "You look chilled. How about some hot tea ....a cup of hot chocolate?"

Lisa smiled back. "I'd like some hot chocolate. But I'll help you fix it."

Steve and Lisa went to the laboratory-part-time kitchen. Steve poured hot water to make tea for himself and put some milk in the microwave to warm for hot chocolate for Lisa. After some quiet, casual conversation, Steve said, "Let's make ourselves more comfortable, in my office."

The phone rang and Steve answered the call regarding a patient in the hospital. When he was finished his attention returned to Lisa who was lazily paging through one of Steve's medical journals.

Steve sat down and enjoyed the picture of Lisa, looking all the part of the beautiful mistress. Her hair was more meticulously set than usual. She had just been to her hairdresser. Her face was radiant. The winter had painted her cheeks with a pale pink that enhanced her already lovely features. Steve noticed the leather Ainje jacket thrown against the back of the chair; the red, silky, small print blouse with the wide tie; the navy wool boucle blazer, the winter white, wool flannel skirt. He noticed that she was wearing her Ainje sandals, the small curve earrings with diamonds and sapphires, the gold road runner pin with sapphire eyes pinned to her jacket. She was wearing his favorite perfume. He sat back as a touch of nostalgia struck him....everything that Lisa was wearing had been given to her by him. "We must be going some place special. You look beautiful, enchanting." Steve paused a second, then added, "And I love you."

Lisa bit her lower lip as she often did when she was in deep thought. "I had a few things to do this afternoon."

"It must have been something important."

She bit her lip again. "I dressed especially for you."

Steve smiled. "Thank you."

"Steve, I had a long talk with David last night."

Steve said nothing, but he had a strange feeling, a feeling of abandon, a feeling that he was about to be dispossessed of the one thing that he had learned to live for... Lisa.

"David and I had a long talk, Steve."

"Did you tell him about us, or did he already know?"

Lisa's eyes turned downward. "Neither, really. I am not sure. We talked about us, David and I, that is. And we talked about us, you and I." Lisa's eyes looked up and at Steve. "I don't know whether he cares about us or not. Someone told him about your car being at the house very late one night…the weekend that he was gone. What seemed to bother him more than the fact that you were there was that someone knew about it. He was concerned to think that someone knew that you were at the house so late at night with him not being home."

"Does he love you?" asked Steve.

"I don't know that either. He hinted at it, but he never said it." Lisa looked sad as she stared at Steve. "I am so confused, Steve. I do not know what to do. I do not know what to believe, about David."

"And you. How do you feel about David?"

"I love you, Steve."

Steve pierced Lisa with his eyes. "Do you love him, Lisa?"

"No," replied Lisa immediately and without hesitation.

"Then what do you want to do? If you think that this is the time, I will face my wife with the inevitable, no matter how difficult that might be for myself."

Lisa sipped from the cup of hot chocolate. Then she broke eye contact with Steve as she spoke. "David does not want a divorce. He does not want to end our marriage."

"How do you know?" asked Steve.

"He said so, in so many words," answered Lisa.

"And us," continued Steve, "He surely must know."

"Yes, I am sure that he does. I have been aware that he knew about us for some time, but I have not been ready to admit it to myself." Lisa peered directly into Steve's eyes. "But he just seems to ignore it. He acts as if it were not there. He is happy to live in the façade of our life as it is."

"We do not have many choices, Lisa, and all of them are associated with a lot of unpleasantness."

Lisa and Steve were now both standing, facing each other. Lisa threw her arms around Steve and looked deeply into his eyes. "Steve, I am frightened. I am so afraid that I will lose you."

"You won't ever lose me, Lisa. I want you, very badly. I want you for my own. I don't want to share you with David or anyone else. I am jealous of him. I can hardly bare the thought that you would ever be with anyone else. I am selfish. I want you totally." He planted a kiss on her eager and desirous lips. They embraced and kissed hard and deep.

Tears welled up in Lisa's eyes. "I am worried that last night was just the beginning of an eventual ultimatum. I don't think that we can go on like this forever. We will be forced to make a decision."

They embraced and kissed... and made love, as if it were for the last time.

Dr. Welsch had forced the meeting. Neither Dr. Marten or Steve or Jim Street wanted it, but Winston Welsch kept insisting and threatening. So Jim Street finally relented and set a time for Drs. Marten, McKay, and Winston Welsch to meet with him to discuss the decision of Dr. McKay to use Rhythodyne on Dr. Welsch's patient. And more importantly they had to decide as to whether they should use Rhythodyne on any patients in the future. It was a late night meeting in Jim Street's office. Jim wanted as little exposure as possible regarding the meeting. The fewer people who knew about it the better. It was an awkward situation and any decision made that night could have far reaching consequences on the treatment of CM Disease by Dr. McKay as well as on the treatment of CM Disease by anyone in the immediate future.

Jim Street had the coffee and hot tea ready for the small group by the time they gathered in his office. After appropriate pouring and sipping Jim Street opened the discussion. "I believe that you all know why we are here. Dr. Welsch is quite concerned, and rightly so, about the use of certain drugs in this hospital. I am asking all of you to maintain an aura of objectivity in relation to the consequences that could be ushered in by the decision that we may make tonight regarding that drug."

"The drug is Rhythodyne," said Steve.

"Okay then, Rhythodyne. But can somebody tell me what the FDA has to say about using drugs on an experimental basis?"

Everybody, including Dr. Welsch, automatically looked to Dr. Marten for the answer. He was the unofficial, and sometimes official, expert in almost everything concerning medicine at Good Samaritan Hospital. Jacque Marten took the cue and answered Jim Street's question. "I am not going to go into any great detail about the requirements for experimental use of any drug. Simply put, if someone wants to use a new drug on an experimental basis, then proper application is made to the FDA together with appropriate documentation regarding the drug. The FDA will then allow experimental use of that drug, or they will deny the experiment. It may in any case ask for further information and clarification about the use of the drug. All of this takes time, sometimes a lot of time, like months. There are rigid guidelines that bind the experimenter to preset protocols that must be met and followed. It is also necessary for the patients on whom the new drug is being used to give proper consent after being informed that the drug is of an experimental nature and may have unknown side effects that could be detrimental, and sometimes disastrous. The procedure is complicated and rigid."

"Damn governmental bureaucracy; that's what it is," noted Dr. Welsch.

"Damn governmental bureaucracy, yes," answered Dr. Marten, "But the drug experimental program of the FDA was designed to protect the patient. I realize that the restrictions are at times most prohibitive for honest experimental investigation by conscientious, reliable researchers, but at the same time it does hinder the helter-skelter experimentation by some unethical investigators.

"There are very few of them," said Dr. Welsch.

"Very few, but enough to make the laws as rigid as they are," replied Dr. Marten.

Jim Street asked, "But this Rhythodyne that you guys have been using is not even a new drug. Why all of the flak?"

"The fact that it is not a new drug is not the problem," said Dr. Marten. "The problem lies in the fact that the drug has been on the market before, and that it has been found to have side effects that have been deleterious to the well being of some patients. Rhythodyne has been removed from the market for that reason."

"Why don't you say it in clear terms, Jacque. Rhythodyne has killed patients," commented Dr. Welsch.

"You are begging the question, Winston," said Steve. "Rhythodyne has caused ventricular fibrillation in patients in the past, but in entirely different situations. We are not using Rhythodyne in any ordinary cardiac situation. We are using it in cases where the patient is going to die anyway. I still think that Rhythodyne has the potential to reverse the asystole in patients with CM Disease, and I think that we should use it on a few more patients."

Winston Welsch spoke again. "I am not denying that. I am not denying that at all, Steve. What I am saying is that if we are going to use it, then we should apply through the FDA to use it for this purpose."

"Let me get this straight," said Jim Street. "You all agree that this Rhythodyne may have the potential to treat CM Disease. Is that correct?"

Dr. Marten acknowledged that the three doctors were in agreement on the use of Rhythodyne.

"Then what in the hell is the problem? Why don't you just apply to the FDA and get permission to use Rhythodyne experimentally in cases of CM Disease. I am sure that you will not have any trouble getting permission from patients to use it."

"It's like this, Jim," continued Steve. "We can apply for permission from the FDA to use Rhythodyne, and we might get permission very quickly, and in fact we could get permission by phone the very day that they get the application. They might put it in the Orphan Drug category. But, and this is the big question mark, the application just might get hung up in somebody's office, maybe for weeks, even months. It could be a long time before we got proper clearance. Like anything else in a bureaucracy like the FDA, it depends on who reads the application first. If the idea strikes that individual positively, Bingo!, we are in business. But if it doesn't, then the application gets shuffled around for a long time before any action is taken."

"But right now Dr. Marten and Dr. McKay are doing unethical experimentation," chided Dr. Welsch.

Steve quickly answered, "Theoretically we are breaking the law, but we are not doing anything unethical. We have excellent information to show that Rhythodyne could be effective in treating CM Disease. And I think that it is more unethical not to use it. We have nothing to lose. The patient has nothing to lose. The patient is going to die anyway." Steve now spoke with a dash of anger in his voice. "And come off that ethical stuff, Winston. I think that it would be more unethical not to try it again."

"Well, what do you think, Jim?" asked Jacque.

Jim Street was a practical man. "I have to agree with all of you. You all have made some good points. Personally I am for continuing the use of Rhythodyne if you can assure me that the hospital will not get in trouble with the FDA. I sure as hell would hate for the hospital to lose its license over something like this. And I could lose my job and have a difficult time getting another. And I have a family to raise and send to college."

Winston Welsch spoke up. "I am curious about one thing, Dr. McKay. Where did you get the Rhythodyne anyway? It has all been recalled."

"None of your business," replied Steve.

"Not a good answer," said Winston. "But I will not press the issue. That could be an embarrassing problem if the Rhythodyne came from the pharmacy in this hospital."

"It sure could," replied Dr. Marten.

"All of you keep your damn mouths shut," said Jim Street. "I don't want to know where you got the goddamn stuff. In fact I don't want to know anything about this." Jim Street got off his chair. "Goddamn it. You have got me all confused. You say that we are using Rhythodyne illegally ...not unethically. Let's say that this drug, this Rhythodyne, or whatever it is, works. Then what? You tell the FDA about it and they say, 'Why in the hell didn't you apply for an experimental license to use it.' Then we still are in deep trouble."

"No, I don't think so," said Dr. Marten. "They can overlook a lot of things in a case like this. I have the application made out and we just tell them that we could not wait for official clearance. If we use it on, let's say, four or five patients and get positive results, then they are not going to say much. They couldn't. The public would be on them in no time flat. Success will help them to overlook a lot of things, but failure could stir a hornet's nest at the FDA if they found out that we were using Rhythodyne, even for the ever fatal CM Disease."

Jim Street spoke. "I don't see how in the hell the FDA will find out about it. There are not too many people who know about what you are doing, and those who do really don't know the ins and outs of drug experimentation. I sure as hell am not going to spread the word."

Steve and Jacque shook their head in agreement. It was obvious that they would not say anything and they were glad that Jim Street was on their side. They all looked at Dr. Welsch.

"Well, Winston," said Jim Street half angrily. "What in the hell are you going to do, phone the FDA tonight?"

"I don't think that your sarcasm is warranted Jim. I am just looking out for the welfare of the hospital and the patients we are treating. Remember, I am involved in this first case on which Rhythodyne was used, and I am culpable and liable if some question should arise concerning its use. I am not against experimentation; I am just against experimentation not performed in the proper setting and with the proper controls, and done in respect to existing rules and laws."

"I want to use Rhythodyne again and soon," said Steve. "I think that one of the reasons that we failed the first time is that we waited too long and we did not titrate the dose accurately enough. There is a very critical gray area between a dose that will cause the heart to maintain its electrical stimulation potential and a dose that is toxic and will cause the heart to go into ventricular fibrillation. We will just have to adjust and readjust the dose in patients until we find one that will give us the effect that we want without the side effects. Ordinarily this type of procedure would be done in animals prior to usage in humans, but we don't have time for that, and we don't have enough Rhythodyne. We just have to go on a hit and miss basis and see what happens."

"And what about the poor victims who die from Rhythodyne?" asked Dr. Welsch.

"I suppose that we could give patients with CM Disease the choice of dying from cardiac standstill or ventricular fibrillation," added Dr. Marten.

"Your sarcasm is again unappreciated, Dr. Marten," said Winston. "I believe that you should go ahead and make an application to the FDA for the use of Rhythodyne."

"And what are we going to tell them if they ask where we are getting the Rhythodyne, or do you intend to get the Rhythodyne for us?" asked Steve.

Dr. Welsch added, "Clandestine appropriation of the drug only makes the whole situation worse. Surely they must have some way of getting Rhythodyne for you. I may look into that."

"We are getting nowhere, and fast," added Jim Street. "When do you intend to use Rhythodyne again, Steve?"

"Can't really say," answered Steve. "I have to find the right patient. We must have an unequivocal diagnosis that the patient has CM Disease."

"And you, Jacque, how long will it take to fill out the proper application for us to use Rhythodyne?"

"I have already begun to fill out the appropriate forms. It may be a couple more weeks if we are going to do it right. The forms are quite voluminous, and again, what makes all of this more difficult is that we are talking about a drug that has been proven to cause fatalities in patients. It will take a lot of information to prove to them that Rhythodyne is the drug of choice to use in CM Disease. It may appear obvious to us that it is a logical drug to use, but logic is not part of a bureaucracy. Only facts and qualified information are going to make any dent in their thinking."

Jim Street spoke again. "Well, go ahead with preparing the proper application forms. I am leaving now and that is my last, but unofficial word on the matter. I don't want to know anything about your using the damn stuff anymore, do you understand, Steve?"

"Jim, I probably won't use it any more anyway," said Steve.

"I have given a lot of thought about what you said," said Jacque. "I am sure that Steve will not use Rhythodyne anymore. And I will keep a close watch on him to see that he does not use it."

"Your word is good enough for me," said Jim Street as he got up to leave. "And I hope that it works next time."

The three doctors sat in silence until Jim Street was well down the hall. "I am sorry, gentlemen," began Winston Welsch, "But I must warn you that if you use Rhythodyne before getting proper clearance with the FDA, then I cannot promise that I will not make your use of the drug known to the proper authorities."

"You are an asshole, Winston," said Dr. Marten.

"I appreciate your bluntness, Jacque. But let me just put it this way. If Steve uses Rhythodyne and it fails to accomplish the desired effect, you cannot hold me responsible if the authorities are notified of the inappropriate use of the drug." Winston Welsch looked sharply at Steve. "It had better work the next time you use it."

There was another long silence. Dr. Welsch reopened the conversation. "Steve, this evening I admitted a patient whom I am sure has developed CM Disease. I would like for you to see the patient in consultation with me, if you don't mind."

Steve heaved a sigh and stood, hands in pockets, his mind in deep thought. Then he spoke quietly. "I appreciate your trust in asking me to see your patient, Winston, but I would like to beg off the case, if you don't mind. I don't harbor any ill feelings toward you or anything like that, but I think that the time has come where it is not necessary for me to see every patient who comes into the hospital with CM Disease. It is getting too hard for me psychologically to have to keep meeting families and telling them that one of their loved ones is going to die. Anyway, Winston, you can do as well as I can with patients with CM Disease." He was looking directly at Dr. Welsch. "This is not the first case that I have begged off seeing, Winston. I have done the same a number of times this past week with other doctors."

Dr. Welsch answered. "I don't harbor any ill feelings either, and I can understand your frustrations. Maybe in a few days you might feel differently again. We need for you to continue seeing these cases, Steve. We have to have someone who is deeply involved in the problem to help us make important decisions when questions arise concerning CM Disease."

Winston Welsch prepared to leave. "I thought that this might be a good patient for you to use Rhythodyne, if you intended to try the drug again. This fellow is a derelict, an alcoholic. He is not a regular patient of mine, and as far as I can determine he has no family. He is sort of a transient, a musician, and he moves frequently from city to city. He would be an ideal patient on whom to try Rhythodyne. But do as you wish. I just thought that I would ask." Dr. Welsch looked at his watch. "It is getting late now, so I'll be leaving. Good luck to you in whatever your decision might be regarding Rhythodyne."

Jacque and Steve looked at the empty doorway where Winston had just stood. Steve shook his head. "Some days I would like to give him a good, swift kick in the ass."

Dr. Marten rubbed his sleepy eyes. "Tomorrow is almost here and it will be another impossible day. Let's go home and get some sleep."

And so they did, with the specter of CM Disease still hovering over their heads.

Chapter 14

Charlie (The Trumpet) Teringo had been sick for a week, maybe a little longer, before he finally presented himself in the Emergency Department at Good Samaritan Hospital. Sometimes it was difficult for Charlie to tell whether he was sick because he had caught some "bug," or that he was sick because he had drank too much. Drinking too much was common for Charlie, but being sick with some illness was not. In fact, Charlie had never been seriously ill in the past, except for the attack of appendicitis that he had as a child that his grandmother attributed to his eating too many raspberries with seeds in them. So, when Charlie developed the "flu" with its achiness, fever, and loss of appetite, Charlie did not pay too much attention. He did not feel like going to work, but he did anyway, and he figured that in a few days he would be as good as new. He even quit drinking so that he could get well quicker. But Charlie did not get better. In fact his condition relentlessly worsened, insidiously at first, then with an overt increase in his signs and symptoms. He stayed in bed for two days, but even Charlie could see that his aspirin and castor oil treatment was not going to cure him, so he dragged himself out of bed and took a cab to Good Samaritan.

Winston Welsch was the staff physician on call that week for new patients who did not have their own doctor, so Dr. Winston Welsch and Charlie (The Trumpet) Teringo were cemented into a doctor-patient relationship that neither had freely chosen.

Dr. Welsch sat down at the nurse's desk in Intensive Care. He had Charlie (The Trumpet) Teringo's chart in front of him:

NAME: Teringo, Charlie
ADDRESS: #304 4511 Grandeur (Local is 235 Bright St.) St. Louis, Mo.
AGE: 46 **OCCUPATION:** Musician, trumpet player
INSURANCE: None
EMPLOYER: Various (right now Tilfers Jazz Emporium)
DOCTOR: W. Welsch
ADMITTING DIAGNOSIS: Flu (Possible CM Disease)

The charge nurse in ICU was watching as Dr. Welsch reviewed the chart. Dr. Welsch did not look up as he spoke. "The temperature has gone up a little, but his blood pressure and pulse rate have been stable for three days now. That is at least one encouraging sign." Dr. Welsch looked at the nurse. "Let's go over and see how Charlie 'The Trumpet' is doing today."

The nurse led Dr. Welsch to Charlie's bed. Charlie was still and quiet, but he was awake and seemed to be alert and well aware of his surroundings. His gray-black, straight hair was unkempt and he had heavy stubble on his face. He looked flushed, his skin was moist and his eyes had a glassy look. Charlie looked every bit the part of the sick alcoholic.

"How do you feel today?" asked Dr. Welsch.

"I've felt better, Doc," answered Charlie.

"Is there anything special that bothers you today, Charlie? Like a headache, or do you feel sick to your stomach...or maybe you feel dizzy or light headed?"

"All of the above," said Charlie. "I just ain't feelin' good at all. All my bones hurt and I threw up after supper last night, so I didn't eat nuthin' this morning."

"Have you been short of breath?" asked Dr. Welsch.

"When I lay down I get short of wind, Doc. I'm okay when I am sitting up like this. I have not been out of bed, but I don't think I would have the strength to get out, and I don't think that I could do very much walking even if I did get up. I'd be too much out of wind."

Dr. Welsch proceeded with his examination. He noted that Charlie still was well hydrated so he assumed Charlie was drinking enough fluids. Dr. Welsch did notice a slight tinge of jaundice in the sclera of Charlie's eyes. The neck veins were distended and emptied poorly, indicating that Charlie was developing some degree of heart failure. Winston Welsch also noted the heart rate…90 beats per minute, a little faster than the day before. The chest was filled with crackling rales and some wheezes, an indication that the lungs were beginning to fill with fluid. They were becoming congested. Dr. Welsch could feel Charlie's liver below the ribs and Charlie winced a little when Dr. Welsch pressed down on it. An enlarged, tender liver thought Dr. Welsch, another indication of congestive heart failure. Finally Winston Welsch saw that Charlie's ankles were swollen… still another telltale sign that Charlie's heart was failing. Dr. Welsch exchanged a few niceties with Charlie "The Trumpet," then he went back to the desk with the nurse to evaluate all of his findings.

"He really has done pretty well considering that he has CM Disease," said Dr. Welsch. "But all of the signs and symptoms point to the development of congestive heart failure and you know what that means."

"Yes," said the nurse. "It means that it will not be too long before he dies."

"I have no doubt but that you are correct in the estimation of his condition. We will treat him in the usual way and I will be seeing him when I can. I am afraid that it is only a matter of time, exactly how much time I don't know."

"That is too bad," said the nurse. "He is an excellent musician, an outstanding jazz player."

"And a derelict," added Dr. Welsch.

"An excellent derelict musician," said the nurse.

"How do you know so much about his musical abilities?" asked Dr. Welsch.

The nurse blushed. "I have heard him play at Tilfer's." She then wished that she had not been so free in her remarks.

"It must be nice to be young," said Dr. Welsch, surprised that he should have made that kind of remark. "But let me see his X-rays, the ones that were taken of his chest today."

The nurse collected the films and placed them on the viewing box so that Dr. Welsch could study them. "The heart is a little enlarged now. It was not that way on the first X-ray of his chest that we took when he was admitted to the hospital. And look at the vasculature, distended and prominent. Congestive heart failure."

"That only confirms what you have already suspected from your clinical examination," replied the nurse.

"Yes, precisely," said Dr. Welsch. "I believe that we will get an echocardiogram for completeness. I really don't think that it is necessary and it will add to the cost of his hospitalization and not tell us anything that we do not already know. But let's get it anyway."

"You have been getting Echocardiograms on all of these patients, so I guess that you might just as well get one on Charlie," said the nurse.

Dr. Welsch replied, "Yes, but most of the other patients could afford it."

Dr. Welsch checked Charlie's EKG monitor. "Still stable at 90 beats per minute. No PVC's, yet, and outside of the moderately increased heart rate, the monitor looks pretty decent. Take him down for the Echo and call me when it is finished. I will either be here in the hospital or at my office. Call me if he takes a turn for the worse."

Two days later Dr. McKay was in Dr. Marten's office. The topic of conversation was a discussion as to whether Steve should or should not continue to use Rhythodyne in treating patients with CM Disease.

"Maybe I should have consulted on Winston's new patient with CM Disease. It would have given me the opportunity to use Rhythodyne again. Then Winston would have been involved and he could not have been too critical."

Jacque shook his head. "I would not trust Winston under any circumstances. That patient is an itinerant alcoholic and Winston is not interested in him as a person, but as a case." Jacque leaned back in his chair. "But you may be right. Maybe you should have consulted with Winston on this particular case."

"Let me ask you bluntly, Jacque. If you were me, would you pursue using Rhythodyne before submitting the proper application to the FDA?"

"I don't know, I really don't know. And I cannot say whether you should or should not use Rhythodyne, Steve. Ordinarily I would give you an unequivocal yes, but with Winston Welsch in the picture, I just find it difficult to say. It is impossible to predict just what his reaction would be in varying circumstances. He is too unpredictable. It would mean a lot of unnecessary trouble if he should leak information to the FDA as to what we are doing." Jacque took a drink of tea from the cup that he had been holding in his hand. "Steve, I have done a lot of thinking about this in the past few days. In fact, I have even lost sleep thinking about it. As much as I hate to say it, I think that perhaps you should cool it with Rhythodyne, at least for now. I do not want you to get yourself into a lot of hot water. You do not have the academic credentials that could carry you through a crisis in case a serious conflict should arise with the FDA regarding Rhythodyne. A lot of researchers could get away with it, but I do not think that you could. I would help you as much as possible, but that might not be enough in a tight squeeze."

"I know what you mean. I have thought about it since our meeting with Winston and I had halfway decided that I probably would not wait for you to submit the application to the FDA. But after talking with you, I think that I will stonewall it for now. I hate to do it, but that seems to be in the best interest of everybody involved." Steve slouched down in his chair a little more. "I don't have anyone right now on whom I could use it anyway, unless I asked Winston if I could use it on his patient."

"Play it smart, Steve. Stay away from Winston and his patients when you decide to use Rhythodyne."

The soft voice of Jacque's secretary came over the intercom. "Dr. Welsch is here and would like to talk to you, Dr. Marten."

Dr. Marten looked at Steve, frowned and shrugged his shoulders. He answered the intercom, "Send him right in."

"Do you want me to leave, Jacque?"

"Nah. I don't know what he wants. It might prove interesting. Who knows?"

Dr. Welsch was surprised to see Dr. McKay in the office, but it did not disturb him. "Good afternoon, Steve. I did not expect to see you here."

"I'll leave if you prefer, Winston."

"No, you don't have to leave on my account," answered Winston. "I just want to ask Jacque a few things about my patient."

"Go ahead and ask," answered Jacque.

"The patient with CM Disease, you know the one, Steve, the one who I asked for you to see in consultation. Well, so far he is still alive. He is not doing too badly. What I want you to do, Jacque, is to collect samples of blood on a day to day basis. Keep the serum refrigerated, or even frozen if you prefer. I have some information that there are some research studies evaluating rising titers on patients with CM Disease. I want to send the specimens into CDC for their evaluation."

"No problem, Winston. It sounds as if you are referring to the studies that Warrington and Smith are doing. They are just in the preliminary stages of their research, but your idea is a good one. I will make sure that we get samples every twelve hours."

"It might be a good idea to do that with all patients with CM Disease," added Steve.

Dr. Marten laughed lightly. "And where in the hell are we going to store all of that blood, the freezer at the IGA down the street?"

"There, or Winston's wine cellar," said Steve.

"No thank you," replied Winston "Just collect the samples on my patients and you do what you want with the others. I will keep you in touch as to how the patient is progressing."

"Or digressing," replied Dr. Marten.

"Maybe he won't die," said Dr. Welsch with a coy smile as he closed the door behind him.

Steve waited until the door was closed and Winston would be out of the outer office. "You don't think that he is using Rhythodyne and not telling us, do you?"

"I would not put it past him. Rhythodyne does look good on paper and the person who finds anything that will improve the mortality with CM Disease is going to be famous, and Dr. Welsch would like to be famous."

"But where would he get the Rhythodyne?" asked Steve.

"I don't have the slightest idea," replied Jacque. "But I would not be surprised at anything Winston Welsch would, or could, do."

Then they both went back to their work.

It was midnight when Lisa Clarke looked up from her desk as Dr. Welsch entered. "Good evening, Doctor Welsch. It is rather late for you to be here, isn't it?"

"It is late, but I was on my way home and I thought that I would drop in to see how Charlie is doing."

Lisa handed the chart to Dr. Welsch. "His condition has remained stable. However, his heart rate is up to 120 tonight. He is having a little more difficulty in breathing than he had yesterday. His temperature is onehundred, the same as it has been the past few days." Then Lisa said, "Dr. Welsch, I just don't know about Charlie. He should be getting worse, and he is, but not as rapidly as patients with CM Disease usually do."

Dr. Welsch was reading the chart as Lisa was talking. Then the two of them went over to Charlie's bedside. Charlie's lungs were rattling with more congestion now and the rapid heartbeat was fainter than it should have been. Charlie was not as bright as he had been when Dr. Welsch saw him last, and he had to be roused from a deep sleep. After Dr. Welsch completed his examination, he and Lisa went back to the desk.

"What do you think about him now?" asked Lisa.

"He is getting worse alright. We will have to begin a more aggressive approach to treating him." I want to put in a Swan-Ganz catheter by the subclavian route so that we can monitor him better and so that we can do a myocardial biopsy."

Lisa had not expected Dr. Welsch to be that aggressive in the treatment of Charlie, especially since he had not done that much for his other patients. "I can get the patient prepared for the catheter insertion and all, but I am not so sure about the myocardial biopsy."

"I have the necessary equipment in surgery and if you call down there they can send it to you."

"Are you sure you want to do the procedure here in ICU?" asked Lisa.

"Yes. We will have Radiology bring the portable fluoroscope for the procedure. I'll do the myocardial biopsy, and then we will leave the catheter in place for fluid delivery and monitoring of the pulmonary wedge pressure. That will allow us to more accurately measure how much fluid we can give Charlie."

"I am not questioning your ability to perform the biopsy or your reasoning. I am just surprised that you are doing this since you have not been doing biopsies on any of your other cases," said Lisa.

"That is not entirely true," retorted Dr. Welsch, "We have done biopsies on patients with CM Disease for awhile, but then we gave it up since it really did not add anything to our ability to treat them. But this is a very special case for me. I am trying to collect as much information on him as possible. We are collecting multiple blood specimens that we will send to the CDC later. I thought that the biopsy might be helpful."

Lisa helped Dr. Welsch place the subclavian catheter in Charlie in ICU. Dr. Welsch did the myocardial biopsy by threading the long wire-like biopsy instrument through the plastic catheter into Charlie's heart. The procedure was uneventful and uncomplicated.

"I have written orders to increase the diuretic and the Digoxin. Let's get another chest X-ray early tomorrow morning, and get blood gases, too. Call me tonight if Charlie gets worse." Dr. Welsch then left the hospital, leaving his patient in the hands of the ICU Department.

Late in the afternoon Dr. McKay dropped by to talk to Dr. Marten before he had a chance to go home. "Just dropped in to say hello, nothing more," said Steve. "No new problems, no new exciting developments, and for once, I did not even have one patient, not a single one, in the hospital with CM Disease."

Jacque did not say anything, but kept working, examining the slide under his microscope.

Steve continued. "If that is the way you feel, Jacque, I will never again come into your office with good news. Bad news only from now on."

Jacque lifted his head and swung his chair around. "What is Winston up to?"

"What do you mean?" asked Steve.

"He sent down a myocardial biopsy specimen from his patient with CM Disease," replied Jacque.

"I think that he is qualified to do myocardial biopsies. He took the course at the University and I have seen him do one or two. He does a pretty decent job. But then, they are not really that difficult to master."

"But I wonder why he did it on this patient?" quizzed Jacque.

"We have done myocardial biopsies on a number of patients with CM Disease before," said Steve. "Some centers are doing them on almost all patients with CM Disease. That is okay if you are doing research, but it does not help us in treating the patient."

"I know, and that is why I wonder why Winston did it on this patient," said Jacque. "We are not a research center, and you could see clinically that the patient has CM Disease."

"Maybe he had nothing else to do," replied Steve. "Or maybe Winston wanted the practice and he thought that Charlie is a good patient on whom to practice."

"He did it late last night," said Jacque.

"Well maybe he had nothing to do last night." Steve plopped into a chair. "Jacque, I don't know why Winston does a lot of things, and sometimes I think that he doesn't know either. And I don't see what difference it makes."

"Neither do I," said Jacque. "But it still makes me wonder."

There was a knock on the door and the pretty secretary came into the office, collected the day's reports, and then left. Steve watched the young secretary very closely as she moved about the room. Steve waited until she had left and closed the door before speaking. "That gal has got a real, honest-to-goodness female body that would rev up any man's motor, even mine." Steve got out of his chair. "Your secretary just reminded me of something that I forgot to do last night."

"At your age..."

Steve interrupted Jacque; "At my age a reminder now and then does help."

Steve said goodbye and left.

Charlie "The Trumpet" was still alive. He had CM Disease, but he was battling the dreadnought of the Disease to a degree that was not to be expected from a decrepit, alcoholic derelict. Charlie was hanging on. Lisa Clarke checked the oscilloscopes and saw that Charlie's EKG pattern was within normal limits, but she also noted that his heart had slowed down over the past few hours from a high of 130 beats per minute down to a steady 80 beats per minute. That would be a good sign for most patients with congestive heart failure. It would indicate that the drugs that the patient was being given were working and were being effective. But in the patient with CM Disease that might not be the case. When a patient with CM Disease developed a bradycardia, that usually was the precursor of the eventual heart stoppage that would prove to be inevitably irreversible.

Lisa's mind was fixed on evaluating Charlie's EKG monitor pattern and she did not notice Dr. Welsch come into ICU. She was startled out of her concentration when Dr. Welsch greeted her. "How is my patient doing, Mrs. Clarke?"

Lisa turned quickly and looked up at Dr. Welsch. "I'm sorry, Doctor. I was not expecting you at this time of the night." Lisa turned toward Charlie Teringo's bed. "I am not sure what to think about his condition. You have literally blasted him with Digoxin and diuretics, and he seems to be stable.

He still has difficulty in breathing, but it has not gotten any worse. I did not hear any more congestion in his lungs tonight than I did last night, but his heart rate worries me. The heart rate has been steadily slowing over the past twelve hours and it is now down to 70 beats per minute, and slowing. That is the same trend that we have found in all patients with CM Disease shortly before they die. I am worried about him. I don't think that he will be with us very much longer."

"I respect your assessment very highly, Mrs. Clarke. You have seen a great number of these patients and I am sure that you have learned what to expect, and when. Why don't you come with me while I examine him."

The two walked over to the bed where Charlie was half-sitting, halflying. He was not very coherent and responded poorly when Dr. Welsch asked him any questions. Dr. Welsch found that Lisa was correct in her evaluation of Charlie's condition. Charlie was still short of breath, but no worse than he had been the last time that Dr. Welsch had examined him. His heart rate was 60 beats per minute, even slower than when Lisa had checked it a short time before. The ankles were still swollen and the only thing that Dr. Welsch noticed that was different about this patient was that Charlie now appeared to be somewhat more jaundiced. Dr. Welsch attributed the jaundice to Charlie's alcoholism that was now complicated by his now terminal illness. Dr. Welsch completed his examination and then walked back to the nurse's desk to write his notes.

Dr. Welsch completed his notations and then looked up at Lisa. "Mrs. Clarke," he began, "When Dr. McKay began treatment of his patient with the drug Rhythodyne, was the patient in about the same stage as my patient is in at the present time?"

Lisa felt a little uncomfortable answering the question. "I really don't like to talk about that particular situation. And Dr. McKay asked that we not discuss the matter with anyone."

"I was just a little curious, that's all. But, again, do you think that his patient was sicker? And how about the heart rate?"

Lisa felt still more uncomfortable, but she could see that Dr. Welsch was determined to get whatever information he wanted for whatever reason, so she decided to be coy in her answers without being incriminating. "No, I do not think that your patient is quite as ill as the patient that Dr. McKay treated with Rhythodyne."

"What was the patient's heart rate when he began treatment?"

"About thirty beats a minute, and there were some PVC's developing," answered Lisa.

"And the patient's general condition?" continued Dr. Welsch.

"Poor, very poor," replied Lisa. "His blood pressure was zilch and his pulse was barely perceptible. He was unresponsive."

"As I understand it, the patient rallied for a period of time," added Dr. Welsch.

"That is correct. He did well for a few days, and then one night the bottom dropped out." Lisa hesitated and thought that she had already said too much so she continued. "I would rather not talk about it, Dr. Welsch. I am sure that Dr. McKay or Dr. Marten would be glad to answer any of your questions about the patient if you would just ask them."

"I have asked them, and as you say, they were very willing to talk about it. In fact, it was my patient who Dr. McKay was treating, so I had complete access to the records. But I was just trying to get it clear in my mind that if Dr. McKay had begun treatment with Rhythodyne sooner, the patient might have survived."

"That is pure speculation, Doctor," said Lisa.

"It might be speculation, but it is important." Dr. Welsch paused for a moment in deep thought. Then he blurted out, "I understand that you are very close to Dr. McKay."

"Dr. McKay and I are very close friends." Lisa could feel the redness burning her cheeks as she wondered just what Dr. Welsch was driving for, and more so, what he knew about her and Steve.

"Do you know where he acquired the Rhythodyne that he used on the patient?"

Lisa thought that it was time to bring the inquisition to a halt. "Doctor Welsch, let us get one thing straight right now. I know nothing about the drug, where it came from, or why it was used in that particular situation. I asked no questions and was given no information. None of the nurses were given any information regarding the drug. Dr. McKay and Dr. Marten had full and complete control of giving the drug. They personally brought the Rhythodyne into the Intensive Care Unit and they personally gave the drug. They made all the notes regarding the delivery of the drug themselves. They asked the nursing staff not to make any notes. We all complied. And I would like to end the conversation there, if you don't mind, Doctor."

"I understand. I did not mean to put you in an unnecessarily difficult position, but I thought that perhaps Rhythodyne might be used on this patient."

"Then you should talk to Dr. McKay about it," said Lisa.

"I stand corrected," said Dr. Welsch. As he was about to leave he turned to Lisa. "And I would appreciate it if you told no one about our conversation tonight, even Dr. McKay."

Lisa acknowledged that she would not tell anyone, even Steve, and Lisa was faithful to her word.

Chapter 15

Monday, the second week of June…Lisa squirmed a little in horniness as Steve locked his lips on hers. Steve's arms surrounded Lisa with a gentle fierceness that anticipated his burning desire to devastate her with a ravishing act of love. As Lisa felt the rising crescendo of fire on her bare thigh she dug her fingers deep into Steve's back, locking him into a position from which he could hardly escape, a position which would facilitate the love making that they both desired. Steve's skin dampened as Lisa's kisses became fiery and triggered an escape of adrenaline that added fuel to an already overheated love furnace. The two grabbed at each other so that they became a single mass of flesh and passion as they twisted on the carpeted floor. Lisa moaned a little as sensuous touches in erotic areas brought her to a shaking orgasm even before its time. She grasped Steve hard, her fingers digging themselves even deeper into Steve's back and bringing him even closer to her, an impossible thought a moment before. Steve buried his tongue into Lisa's mouth sending love electricity racing through Lisa that gave rise to a galvanic excitement that Lisa could feel as tingles cruising through her body. Steve slowly and gently positioned himself. He could feel the warmth of Lisa's breasts against his bare chest, hardening him as if he were eighteen again. Love flowed across lips that were locked as tongues searched, and found, a delightful sensation with every tiny movement that was delivered with exacting precision by lovers who knew how to tantalize. They found themselves totally into each other as raptures like a thunderstorm deluged them. Then Steve exploded inside of her, sending another wave of lovely orgasm spiriting through them both. The two lovers lay quiet... spiritually exhausted from the ritual of love that they had just enacted.

They lay still for a long time, Steve gently stroking her hair. "I am glad that we are still lovers," said Lisa in a near whisper.

Steve shifted a little, and with his eyes still closed, said, "And so am I."

Then they talked of intimate things after their experience of absolute intimacy had brought them together in a way that even the gods would envy. Finally they closed their eyes and lay close together in the holy silence of love.

Lisa broke the spell when she quietly said, "You need a rest, Steve. Why don't you try to sleep for a little while."

"I can't," replied Steve. "I have to get back to the hospital."

"You really need some time off. Just a day or two will help."

"You need the time off as much as I do. So we both need some time off." Steve opened his eyes and looked at Lisa. "We can fly to Puerto Rico or some place."

"Dreamer."

"We have been living in dreams for years, so we might just as well continue." Steve sat up a little, leaning on his elbows. He spoke with a far away look in his eyes, as if he were looking beyond the universe. "Without dreams we could never have come as far as we have."

"Do dreams come true?"

"Only if you make them come true. Nothing happens to us. We make things happen. We are all architects of our own destiny."

Lisa spoke sleepily. "It looks like we need new architects."

The head nurse in ICU watched Dr. Welsch as he examined his patient, Charlie Teringo. Dr. Welsch was surprised to see that Charlie was still alive. He had expected Charlie to be dead long ago. The nurse looked at Dr. Welsch. "It appears to me that Charlie is going into DT's. He is very restless, and he has the shakes. He does not have a fever that could account for some of that."

"He is on the Chlordiazopoxide for his alcoholism."

"I was just thinking," the nurse's voice faded into nothingness.

Dr. Welsch waited for the nurse to finish. She didn't, so Dr. Welsch said, "You were thinking of what?"

The nurse answered. "I was just thinking that it might be a nice gesture to give Charlie some booze to help his DT's. We have nothing to lose. He is going to die anyway, so he might just as well die happy. Giving him alcohol to control his DT's is better than the Chlordiazopoxide anyway."

"You know, you may be right." Dr. Welsch picked up the chart and paged through it. "I think that I will transfer Charlie to another floor. There is nothing that we can do for him here in ICU and we might just as well let him die peacefully."

"A lot of the other doctors have been transferring their patients lately," said the nurse. "I personally think that it is a good idea. Charlie's heart rate dropped down to 40 beats per minute once last night, but since then it has been slowly rising and it is now up to 60."

"The lull before the storm," replied Dr. Welsch.

Charlie was transferred to another floor that afternoon. That evening Dr. Welsch returned to the hospital with a bottle of twelve-year-old scotch for Charlie. He handed the bottle to the nurse "Stop the Chlordiazopoxide and give Charlie a shot every three to four hours, or more often if he wants. If you run out of Scotch, I'll bring him another bottle. That should stop his DT's and make him happy."

Jacque and Steve were sitting in the Pathologist's office waiting for Jim Street. Steve poured the boiling water into Jacque's special teapot, the one that his laboratory staff gave him one year for Christmas. Steve put the lid in place and checked the time on his watch. "Earl Gray had to be steeped for five minutes, no more, no less." Steve spoke as he watched the speck of steam rise from the tiny port in the lid of the teapot. "Maybe we should not give that information to Jim. He overreacts sometimes."

"I am not sure either," acknowledged Jacque. "But I think that he is entitled to the information and I am sure that we can trust him not to divulge it to anyone else." Jacque was referring to the latest report that he had received from CDC that indicated that there was no sign of lessening of the CM Disease epidemic, and that CDC would be shortly advising all hospitals to brace themselves for a developing new crisis in the battle with the disease. The CDC and the NIH confidential report predicted there would be, within the next six months, a dramatic rise in the number of persons who would be afflicted with the deadly disease.

Jim Street knocked but walked in even before Jacque Marten could get to the door. "Sorry to be late, but I was just notified that we have had another doctor from our medical staff die of CM Disease."

"That had to be Krider. That is too bad. I really liked him." Steve watched the teapot with eyes that were seeing the laughing face of Dr. Krider etched on the steam that rose from the spigot. "We are going to have a hard time finding another neurologist of his caliber. We'll miss him."

"I wish that they had not taken him to University Hospital," said Dr. Marten. "He would have been a good candidate for another trial of Rhythodyne."

"The family wanted the best," added Jim Street.

"There is no best with CM Disease," said Steve.

Steve poured tea into two cups, one for himself, one for Jacque. Jim Street, as usual, would have coffee. Steve spoke as he poured. "Jacque has something to talk to you about, Jim."

"Sounds ominous," said Jim Street.

"It is," said Jacque as he sipped the hot tea.

"Well, dammit," said Jim Street. "Go ahead, talk. I have not had any good news in so long a time that I don't believe there is any good news in the world anymore."

Jacque went on to explain the joint report he received from CDC and NIH, the one that he had shown to Dr. McKay. Jim Street listened carefully, then he said, "That is a very ominous report. How accurate is that information, Jacque?"

"Very accurate, I would say. They would not dare to make a mistake in a matter so important as this; there is just too much at stake." Jacque gave his next words a good think before he spoke. He measured his words carefully. "So far CM Disease has not followed the usual pattern of an epidemic as we have known them to be in the past. Most epidemics will die of their own accord after a certain number of people have contracted the disease. But CM Disease has not shown that trend. From the projections that the CDC is making from the computer analysis that they have made, one fourth of the population of the United States could easily be dead within the next two years."

Jim Street spoke softly. "That means that in two years one of us here in this room will be dead."

"Maybe all of us," said Jacque in a tone of voice that sounded like he really meant it.

"Is the report available to all hospitals?" asked Jim Street.

"No. Only a few select individuals have received the report. CDC and NIH want to get a feel of the reaction that it will generate before it is put out for general publication. The biggest fear that NIH has is that it will be leaked to the press before it should be, and in that case there is a good chance that panic would take control of the population. If that happens there is no telling what might take place."

"Were you advised that you could give the report to me?" asked Jim Street.

"No," replied Jacque. "It is a confidential report, and we were advised not to divulge its contents to anyone."

"Then why in the hell are you telling me about it?" asked Jim Street.

Jacque smiled. "Because I need more money, for research. And I want you to get it for me, from the Board."

"Jesus Christ, Jacque!" yelled Jim Street. Then he looked around the room. "Where in the hell do you keep the coffee?"

"Try some tea," said Steve.

"I don't like tea," snorted Jim Street.

"The coffee is in the other room," replied Jacque.

"I'll get it," said Steve as he motioned for Jim Street to sit down again.

"Cream?" asked Steve.

"No, make it black," said Jim Street. "Now where in the hell were we?"

"You had just called upon the Lord," said Jacque.

"Yah!" began Jim Street. "What in the hell did you do with the money that we gave you before?"

"It is not completely gone, but it will be soon. I have some pregnant ideas as to what course we might pursue in tracing down something that might control CM Disease." Jacque refilled his cup. "That is why I told you about the communiqué. I thought that it might impress on you the urgency for the need for money for further research."

Steve handed the cup of coffee to Jim Street. Jim took a hard swallow and looked at Jacque. "I don't know if the Board will give me any more money for research. They think that the Universities and the CDC should be doing that sort of thing. They feel that our duty as a community hospital is to take care of sick people." Jim Street took another hard swallow of the hot coffee. "And I sure as hell am not going to reveal that report to them just to get the money."

"Good thinking, Jim," said Steve. "But Jacque needs that money. You can get it for him."

Then Steve looked at Jacque. "Jacque, why don't we take Jim into the basement and you can give him some idea of the kind of work that you are doing."

Jacque looked at Jim Street. "Come on, Jim. Steve is right. You should have some idea as to where your money has gone, so far anyway. Then you can report to the Board."

Jim Street shook his head and emptied his cup. "Sure, I'll go with you."

The three went to the sub-basement of the hospital. It was gloomy and damp. At one time it had been used to store a portable field hospital and supplies that were to be available in time of a disaster. It was an archaic residuum of the 1960's when the country was preparing for the possibility of an atomic attack by the Russians. The supplies had long been outdated and removed from the area, but the field hospital was still carefully stored in one corner of the room.

Steve and Jim Street followed Jacque over to one side of basement where a hundred small cages were carefully stacked and occupied by varying numbers of white mice. Ventilation in the sub-basement was poor and a noticeable stench hung in the air.

"You need a ventilation fan down here badly," remarked Jim Street.

"You noticed. But we can't afford one," answered Jacque.

"Have maintenance get down here and devise some kind of a ventilation system tomorrow. The hospital will pay for it."

"Thanks," replied Jacque.

"That is the work area," said Steve as he pointed to another corner of the basement. "It doesn't look like much, but it is a very functional area."

"Well, what in the hell do you need more money for? Do you want a new laboratory?"

"No, nothing like that," said Jacque. "But let me explain. We are not doing any basic research. We are not trying to grow viruses or anything that sophisticated. Our approach is strictly clinical. We are using homogenized tissue material and blood specimens to inoculate the animals in order to try to demonstrate some type of antibody reaction that might be effective against the disease, but so far, nothing. We need the money for mice and men: mice on which to do the experiment, men to collect the data and put it into the computer. We need a lot of clerical help to sort out the information and put it into some meaningful and organized pattern. That takes money."

"Do you think that you are whistling Dixie, or do you think that you might be on to something that could bear fruit?" asked Jim Street.

"I don't know," said Jacque. "I really do not know; but you read the bulletin. Somebody has to find something that will work, or the whole world may be desolate in ten years."

"Do you really believe that?" asked Jim Street skeptically.

"Yes we do," interrupted Steve. "We have never said this to you so bluntly before. We are scared, Jim. This thing is something different, something that the modern world and medical science has never had to face before. We have good scientific tools at our disposal, Jim. And even with all of our sophisticated equipment and tools, we have not been in the least bit successful against CM Disease. It has us by the balls, Jim."

The presence of the specter of CM Disease could be felt in the silence of the sub-basement. The three men stood motionless, each engrossed in his thoughts. Finally Jim Street said, "I'll try to get you ten thousand dollars."

"Twenty," said Steve.

"Fifteen and no more," replied Jim Street.

"I'll take it," said Dr. Marten.

"You bastards," said Jim Street as he moved slowly toward the elevator. "I have no idea how in the hell I am going to talk the Board into giving you guys twenty thousand dollars, but I'll try."

"You will not only try, Jim," said Steve, "You will do it."

*

Lisa could not believe it. She had reported for work in ICU that night and the A.M. crew told her that Charlie "The Trumpet" was still alive and looking better all the time, half intoxicated, but looking and feeling better. In fact, the P.M. Crew told Lisa that Charlie had been up in a chair most of the day and was even threatening to leave the hospital. Lisa had to see for herself. She headed for the third floor where Charlie had gone after his transfer from ICU.

When Lisa walked into the room she saw Charlie sitting up in bed. He had a half-empty glass in his hand, and he talked with a slurred speech. "Hi there, nurse." Charlie fixed his eyes on Lisa and studied her very carefully. "I think that I know you, don't I?" he blabbered.

"Yes. I'm Lisa and I helped take care of you when you were in ICU."

"Well, what in the hell do you want? I got some extra Scotch somewheres, but they is starting to ration it. Maybe they will give you some."

"I just wanted to check on you and see how you are getting along," said Lisa.

Charlie put the glass on the table at the side of the bed. "Go ahead and check, but there ain't nuthin wrong with me, and I am leaving this place tomorrow. I have a playing engagement to take care of."

Lisa carefully assessed Charlie. His apical heart rate was a good, strong, 73 beats per minute, with an occasional extra beat. His blood pressure was 112/70, normal. His chest was clear with an occasional wheeze that Lisa attributed to Charlie's heavy smoking. Lisa did notice a bit of jaundice in Charlie's eyes and she could palpate the liver below the lower margin of the ribs. Charlie had an enlarged liver and with the jaundice, that added up to a case of early cirrhosis. Charlie's heavy drinking over the years was beginning to take its toll.

Lisa walked to the nurse's desk and read Charlie's chart. It was true. Charlie was getting better. But why should Charlie of all people be one who did not die from CM Disease as he was supposed to?

As Lisa was leaving the floor she noted the bottle of Chivas Regal on the medicine shelf at the back of the nurse's station. "Are you girls having a party tonight?" she asked.

"Oh, no," replied one of the nurses. "That belongs to Charlie. Dr. Welsch brought it for him. That is his third bottle and at the rate that Charlie is downing it, it will not last through the night."

Lisa left the floor, shaking her head in disbelief.

*

"How could he let him go?" Dr. Marten spoke with dismay and disgust.

Dr. McKay had just arrived at the sub-basement where Jacque was working. It was a little past midnight. "I did not find out about it till just a few minutes ago. I came right down so that we can plan some strategy for us to follow."

"Tell me what happened," said Dr. Marten.

"I came to the hospital late tonight to see a patient in ICU. Lisa was waiting for me. She said that Charlie had gone home, signed himself out AMA, (Against Medical Advice). She said that she saw him the night before and that he was improving, but she never dreamed that he was well enough to leave the hospital."

"Why didn't Welsch stop him?" blurted Dr. Marten.

"When Charlie threatened to leave, the nurses called Welsch, but he just told them to tell him to stay. I guess Charlie had a snoot full and insisted on leaving."

"But Welsch could have stopped him," said Jacque.

"Yes and no," answered Steve. "Legally, Charlie had every right to leave. But I'm sure he could have been persuaded to stay."

"With Chevas Regal?" asked Jacque.

"Why not. That was probably the best stuff Charlie has had in years. Welsch should have come out and talked to him." Steve stuffed his hands into his pockets. "I wish the nursing staff would have said something."

"Nursing staff," exclaimed Jacque. "I wish that Welsch would have said something. If he did not want to come out himself he could have asked me. I would have gone up to talk to Charlie," commented Jacque.

Steve continued. "Welsch did not refuse to come out. He just said that it would be a little while before he could make it. But Charlie got belligerent and the nursing staff thought for a while that they would have to call security. They called Welsch back and he said that if Charlie went home, then he would have to report to him in his office in a few days. He even promised Charlie that there would be a bottle waiting for him as a reward, and that he would take care of him."

"Maybe Charlie will show up in Welsch's office on Friday," said Jacque, hoping that his statement would come true.

"I doubt it," said Steve. "Now we have to figure out whether we should try to trace Charlie tonight."

"No. It is too late to do anything tonight. We will start first thing in the morning," said Jacque.

"Maybe Welsch can help us." Steve banged his hand on the table in a gesture of frustration. "A patient with CM Disease recovers, and Welsch loses him."

"We think that Charlie had CM Disease and recovered, but we do not know that for sure," commented Dr. Marten. "He may still die, or, maybe he did not have CM Disease after all."

With that, Steve left Jacque and went up to ICU to talk to Lisa for a while before he left for home and a few hours of sleep. He wanted to get back to the hospital early in the morning so that they could start tracing Charlie "The Trumpet."

It was near noon the following day and Jacque, Steve and Jim Street were in the Administrator's office. The newspapers had already been leaked the information that a patient who had CM Disease had lived and left the hospital alive. The news media had retrieved only scattered details of the incident and Jim Street was not about to admit publicly that they did not know where the patient was. Steve and Jacque had checked at Charlie's local address and they found out that Charlie had reported to his landlady that he had returned, but when the landlady asked Charlie for his rent Charlie told her that he had to go to the bank to get the money. Charlie never returned. He took with him his trumpet and a few odds and ends. The St. Louis address that he had given to the hospital, 4511 Grandeur, did not exist.

"That goddamn son-of-a-bitch. That stupid ass." Jim Street was painting a word picture of Dr. Winston Welsch with his own kind of colors. Jim threw the pencil on his desk. "What in the hell am I supposed to tell the newspapers? That phone has been ringing off the hook."

"All we can do is put a tracer on 'The Trumpet,'" said Steve. "He is bound to show up at some offbeat nightclub. He is going to need money, and he is bound to do what he knows best, play the trumpet in a band." Steve threw out his hand in a motion that called for a calming of tensions. "Let's keep our cool. If we don't, we might end up doing something very foolish."

Bernie's voice came over the intercom. "Dr. Welsch is here to see you, Mr. Street. Do you want him to come right into your office?"

"Shit head is here," commented Jim Street. He pushed hard on the intercom button and said, "Dr. Welsch can come right in."

Dr. Welsch entered, a bright smile beaming across his face. "Good morning, gentlemen. I am glad that you are all gathered here. We have a lot of planning to do."

Jim Street replied with a confused look on his face. "Er....Ah...." Then he rubbed his hand across his mouth as he thought of the right words to say.

"And what in the hell are you so happy about? A patient with CM Disease is cured, and we can't find the bastard. You let the son-of-a-bitch go."

"Now look here, Jim, that is pretty strong language…"

"You're goddamn right it is strong language. The newspaper has been all over me this morning about this thing. I hope that you have a good explanation of why you let that alcoholic bastard leave."

"I came here with all the intentions of discussing this sudden turn of events, and I am greeted with foul discourtesy." Winston Welsch was talking almost with a shout. "And I have already talked to the newspapers."

"You know goddamn well that all hospital reports are to come out of this office, and this office only."

Steve interrupted. "Okay, now both of you, cool it. Sit down, then we can get this worked out. Shouting and accusations will get us nowhere."

"He is right," added Jacque. "Let's all cool down and collect as much of the information that we have at our disposal. Then we can map out a plan of action."

Steve continued, "Now, Winston, can you tell us where you stand on this?"

"Certainly," said Winston. "Each of you is aware that Charlie Teringo, the patient, threatened to leave AMA. There is nothing that I, nor anyone else, could do about that. If the patient wants to leave, he is free to do so. We would almost have to get a court injunction to keep him in the hospital against his will."

"He has a point there," said Jacque as he looked at Jim Street who shook his head in reluctant agreement.

Winston continued. "Seeing that I could not keep the patient in the hospital, then I did the next best thing. I gave him an appointment to come to my office, and, I made it worth his while to keep that appointment by bribing him with some good whiskey. He likes Scotch. I also offered to assist him with his monetary problems while he is in town. I think that he will return."

"I hope so," said Steve pessimistically.

"But what about the newspapers?" asked Jim Street.

"When I talked to them," said Winston, "I told them that we would give them full information as soon as we could be sure that we did indeed have a patient who had CM Disease and whom I cured."

"We are not too sure that you cured him," said Jacque.

"What do you mean?" asked Winston, surprised by Jacque's remark.

"Just that we do not know for sure that he has not died. We have no proof that he is not lying in a gutter somewhere, dead or dying. We also are not absolutely sure that he had CM Disease."

"He had CM Disease alright," said Winston with confidence. "We did the myocardial biopsy, remember? He had all the signs and symptoms of CM Disease, and he lived. Now what we have to do is go over his case record very carefully and see what I did differently that affected a cure."

"Chivas Regal?" asked Steve.

"That remark cannot be discounted, gentlemen. Perhaps alcohol did have something to do with his survival." Winston got up from his chair. "I will review his record with a fine tooth comb, and I would like to discuss it with Dr. Marten and Dr. McKay. Then, when he comes into my office, we will do further tests and evaluations. I will offer Mr. Teringo a 'stipend' to stay in town so that we can study him further. I will make the fund available personally."

"Very good, Winston. I just hope that he shows up in your office," said Jim Street whose emotive storm had finally blown away.

"Okay, Winston, give us a call when Charlie comes into your office," said Steve.

"Don't hold your breath," said Jim Street sarcastically.

Winston Welsch was almost out the door when Steve beckoned him. "Winston, tell us one thing. Did you use Rhythodyne on Charlie?"

Winston Welsch smiled. "No. But I would have if I had been able to obtain any." Then he left.

Almost three days had gone by. Charlie "The Trumpet" did not show up in Dr. Welsch's office, and there was a low-key search in progress for him. The administration did not want any more publicity on the matter than was absolutely necessary. Dr. Welsch was still studying Charlie's hospital records, convinced that something he had done, or not done, that contributed to Charlie Teringo's recovery from CM Disease.

Jim Street felt as if he were sitting on an atomic bomb that was ready to explode to create a devastating catastrophe. The pessimistic NIH/CDC report was bound to be revealed soon, with unpredictable consequences. Charlie's disappearance was still an enigma. The newspapers were not hounding Jim Street, but they were not letting him alone either.

If Charlie had CM Disease, and recovered, then a new dimension would have been added to the annals of CM Disease. CM Disease had been, up to that time, universally fatal. The revelation of the discovery of a cure could serve as the impetus to avert the worldwide panic that the specter of a CM Disease epidemic could create. Charlie's proven recovery would give hope where there had been no hope. But right now, no one knew where Charlie was, or even if he was still living. It was indeed possible that Charlie was dead, and if he were, then premature publicity of his recovery from CM Disease with the ultimate acknowledgment of his death would serve no useful purpose. Jim Street was not sleeping well at night.

Steve found Dr. Marten in his makeshift laboratory in the sub-basement. Jacque was devoting more and more of his time to his research project.

"Your office secretary contacted my office and said that you wanted to see me, Jacque."

Jacque continued transferring blood samples to the centrifuge tubes. "Find a chair and sit down, Steve."

Steve looked around and finally found a stool near one of the counters that Jacque had devised for his work. "I don't have much time, Jacque. I don't mean to rush, but I have to make rounds this evening, and then I have a meeting to attend."

"Oh, yes. You and Jim Street are meeting with the press tonight. Good luck," said Jacque as he continued to work.

"You should be there," said Steve.

"Jim asked me but I have too many other things to do," replied Jacque.

"We all have too many other things to do, Jacque. I suppose that you are aware that Winston Welsch will be there."

"No, I was not aware of that," said Jacque.

"Jim has Winston up in his office now, advising him as to what and what not to say," said Steve.

Jacque continued working as he spoke. "I spent some time with Winston last week. I think that we have him cued into what is important to say and what facts should not be divulged at this time. I have tried to play on his ego by telling him that, since he has the only cure so far in a patient with CM Disease, then we had better not break the story until we have all of the facts and details in good order. I think that he will do all right. If he doesn't, all hell could break loose."

"That is what I'm afraid of," said Steve.

"What I called you about is that I want you to know that there is no doubt that Charlie Teringo did have CM Disease."

"How can you be so sure?" asked Steve.

"We had drawn a load of blood samples from him and we sent a lot of them to the CDC for study. The rise in his titers match exactly with those of many other patients who have had CM Disease."

"I knew that the CDC was doing work with rising antibody titers in CM Disease, but I was not aware that they had been successful in determining CM antibody titers with any degree of certainty."

Jacque placed the tubes in the centrifuge, started the motor, and washed his hands. "The work is just being published. Titer studies will be available for general use within the next few weeks. I am not sure that CDC will be able to handle the case load when they do announce the availability of antibody testing, but they intend to try."

"Then they can accurately determine whether a person definitely has contracted CM Disease prior to the autopsy," said Steve.

"Yes, for what that might be worth. At least it is one step in the right direction, and it could lead to other discoveries," said Jacque.

Steve rose from his chair. "And what are you doing now? You have been spending a lot of time here in your dungeon lately. If you are not careful the sunlight will burn your eyes when you surface into the daylight."

The two doctors started walking toward the elevator. "I have some interesting ideas that I have been working on in these past few weeks," said Jacque. "I have been inoculating the mice with homogenized cardiac muscle and I have invariably been able to produce the myopathy similar to that caused by CM Disease in humans. I am becoming more and more convinced that the myopathy is a toxic manifestation of some kind. But, to determine the kind of toxin and how it is produced is another matter. That would take a rather sophisticated laboratory and we just do not have that kind of money. So, we will have to be satisfied with clinical research rather than basic research." Jacque turned toward Steve, "And I'm using some of the protocols that you developed, Steve. I have found them to be very helpful.

Steve pressed the elevator button. "Since Charlie Teringo is the only known survivor of CM Disease, maybe we ought to do some research with his serum. You should have enough blood to at least get you started."

"I have thought about that already, Steve. In fact, that is what I was doing when you arrived. And it also makes it even more imperative that we find Charlie, dead or alive."

Steve got off the elevator and headed for home; Jacque returned to his work in his research laboratory, hating every minute of it. He would rather be out on his farm working in the field on his tractor.

It was now late afternoon on the following day. Steve walked over to Lisa. "How long has he been ill, Lisa?"

"I really don't know, Steve. David is the type of person who does not like to be sick. He goes to a doctor on very rare occasions. In fact, the only time that I know that he has been sick enough to go to a doctor was when he had a Strep throat infection."

"He does not look good, Lisa. He has a low-grade temperature, and he is very pale. I thought that I detected some rales in his chest, but I could not be sure." Steve stopped talking, allowing Lisa to absorb what he was saying.

"Do you think that it is the flu?" asked Lisa.

"It could be," answered Steve. But then it could be something more serious."

"I think I know what you mean, Steve." Lisa looked Steve straight in the eye as she continued speaking. "We don't have to play games Steve. You think that he may have CM Disease, don't you?"

"Yes," said Steve. "I think that is a distinct possibility." Steve tried to be as professional as he could. David, Lisa's husband, was a patient, and Lisa was at that moment just another relative.

"Are you going to put him in ICU?" asked Lisa.

"Not yet. He should be all right in a regular room on third. If he gets worse, then we can transfer him," said Steve.

"I was not expecting this," said Lisa. "But then again, I guess that I was, at least for the past two days." Lisa looked up at Steve with a pathetic look on her face. "Maybe I should have brought him in sooner."

"Why?" asked Steve.

"I don't know, Steve." Lisa broke down and cried. Steve held her closely. They stood holding each other for what seemed like an eternity of time.

Then Steve lifted Lisa's head and looked at her, his piercing eyes penetrating Lisa with sympathy. "It may not be all that bad, Lisa. We will just have to wait and see. And we'll do our best for him."

"I know that you will," said Lisa.

"Come on," said Steve, "Let's go and talk to David and get him admitted, and hope for the best."

Chapter 16

David Clarke had been in the hospital for two days and his condition had remained relatively stable. He developed a mild degree of congestive heart failure, but Steve had been able to control that with Digoxin and a diuretic agent that helped to rid the body of excess salt and water, two major components contributing to the development of cardiac failure. After admitting David to the hospital, Steve had second thoughts as to whether or not he should be the doctor in charge of David's case because of his relationship with Lisa. It was an unspoken recognition in the hospital that he and Lisa were having an affair, even though few people knew with absolute certainty that the affair was real. Lisa insisted that Steve stay on the case and David also trusted Dr.McKay's ability as a physician without question. He would not even think of having any other physician see him, regardless of what his personal feelings may have been. Steve stayed on the case.

Late in the afternoon Steve walked into Dr. Marten's office, unannounced and uninvited. He flopped into a chair without saying a word.

Jacque swung around in his chair. He took a long, hard look at Steve. "You look awfully tired, Steve."

Steve leaned his head back against the chair and closed his eyes. "I am."

Jacque spoke, softly, articulately. "If you think that I can give you advice, Steve, I can't. You will have to make those decisions by yourself."

"I know," said Steve, his head still thrown back, his eyes still closed. "I don't expect you to do that." Steve settled into quiescence, his mind submerged in his problems. Suddenly he opened his eyes and sat up with a jerk. "Jacque, don't let me do anything stupid. Promise me that you will be honest with me and that you will tell me if you think that at any time I am doing the wrong thing. I am trying to keep my emotions out of my decisions, but sometimes that is difficult."

Jacque answered, "I promise." Then he leaned back in his big chair. "How is David doing?"

"He is stable," said Steve. "David has mild congestive heart failure, but that has not been a problem. We have been able to satisfactorily control that.

Up to this time his heart rate and rhythm have been normal." Steve nervously shifted in his chair. "But we all know that it is only a matter of time."

"What are your plans Steve?"

"First of all I must be sure that David does have CM Disease." Steve's eyes bore into Jacque. "How long will it take to get titers back from CDC?"

Jacque shrugged his shoulders and wrinkled his mouth in a manner that telegraphed his uncertainty. "I can't say for sure; a week, maybe two. Maybe even more?"

"That is not good enough," said Steve angrily. "I want to find out just as soon as you can. I must know for certain David has CM Disease."

Jacque remained silent. He was a very close personal friend of Steve's, and he could empathize with him. "I'll try. I can make no promises, Steve, but I will try."

"Call them tomorrow... call them every day." Steve pleaded in a loud voice. "I have to know, Jacque, as soon as possible."

Jacque drew a deep breath. He could read the frustration in Steve's voice. He rose from the chair; his voice was now filled with his own anger and frustration. "Okay…okay," he yelled. "What difference does it make anyway? If he has CM Disease he is going to die, period." Jacque spoke directly into Steve's face. "And there is not a thing that you can do about it, Dr. McKay, not a thing." Jacque turned his back to Steve and stood silently, his shoulders slouched, his head hanging down.

Steve's voice was now very soft and quiet as he spoke. "I have to know, Jacque. If he does have it I am going to use Rhythodyne on him. It is our only chance."

Jacque turned around slowly. "Go ahead, Steve, use it. I will back you as much as I am able. I am with you, all the way, Steve. Just don't say anything about this to anyone else; not to Welsch, not to Jim Street."

It was late that same night when Steve came back to the hospital to see David. Steve still had not transferred David to ICU. Steve could have the heart beat monitored by telemetry since he did not necessarily want to put David in ICU. Steve read David's chart, then he walked slowly and deliberately to David's room. Every time that he had made that trip he wished that he had chosen another career, anything but being a doctor. He greeted Lisa, then he asked her out of courtesy if she would leave the room while he examined David.

Lisa anxiously waited for Steve at the nurse's station. The head nurse offered to get her some coffee or tea, but she refused. Lisa checked her watch every minute, thinking that it had been ten every time she did. Finally Steve came out of David's room and Lisa met him half way down the hall. Lisa drew a deep breath, not knowing what to say, and expecting the worse from Steve. "How is he?" she finally managed to say through parched lips.

Steve's eyes were puffy from lack of sleep, his hair was ruffled, and his tie was unknotted and hanging haphazardly. He grabbed Lisa's arm and the two walked toward the nurses' station. Steve put the chart on the counter and said to the charge nurse, "Can you get us some coffee or tea and then can we go to your office where we can talk alone?"

"Of course. No problem. Sugar, cream, whatever?"

Lisa and Steve both opted for black coffee and headed for the head nurse's office. "I do not think that he is doing as well tonight, Lisa."

The look on Lisa's face was a combination of regret, worry and hopelessness. She looked directly at Steve. "Level with me, Steve. All the way. I want to know the truth."

The charge nurse put the coffee on the desk then left the room, closing the door behind her. Steve took a gulp of the hot coffee and spoke. "Don't panic yet, Lisa. I said that David is worse, but not that much worse. I detected a worsening of his congestive heart failure and he is more lethargic, but his blood pressure is still stable and his heart is still at 90 beats a minute, and regular.

"Ninety beats a minute, a little fast, isn't it?" said Lisa.

"Yes," replied Steve." But that goes along with his heart failure. He is young and his myocaradium can stand a tachycardia for a long time without undue damage. It is when the heart muscle begins to wear out and the heart rate begins to slow down that we have to worry."

"I know, Steve." Lisa sipped at her coffee. She broke the silence that had enveloped them. "Steve..."

Steve waited, but Lisa remained silent. "What is it, Lisa?"

Lisa looked up. "Steve, are you thinking about using Rhythodyne on David?"

Steve did not answer immediately. Then he said, "Yes, I have thought about that. But we have not had confirmation yet that David has CM Disease. The blood titer report that could tell us for sure is not back from the CDC."

"I want you to use it, Steve. David wants you to try it. We have talked about it."

Steve reached out and touched Lisa's hand. He said with a confidence that he fabricated, "As soon as Jacque can get the blood titer report from CDC, then we will use Rhythodyne."

Steve sent Lisa back to David's room, and then he went back to ICU to check the EKG oscilloscope that was monitoring David's heart action. He had not told Lisa everything. The condition of David's heart had definitely deteriorated. Although the heart rate was still satisfactory, Steve had detected an irregularity and a faint friction rub. Both were ominous signs that David's heart was developing a severe Myocarditis. Steve watched the EKG monitor for a full five minutes. He followed the tracing as the heart rate would slow for a few seconds, then speed up again. He noted an occasional PVC, an extra heartbeat. From his past experience with CM Disease, Steve knew that these signs were the forerunners of the deadly arrhythmia that would strike David in the days to come. He headed for home and another sleepless night.

Steve was back at the hospital early the next morning. He made rounds on his patients, then he headed up to ICU to check David's EKG monitor. The head nurse greeted him at the door. "I was hoping that you would come in early, Dr. McKay. I was about to have you paged if you did not come soon. David Clarke's EKG is deteriorating. His heart rate is down to 56 beats per minute and dropping about 5 beats every hour. I am worried about him."

Steve walked over to the EKG monitor. The rate was now 50 per minute, and irregular. Steve noted an occasional pre-ventricular contraction; an extra heart beat. Steve took one last look at the EKG, and then he rushed off for Pathology.

Jacque was busy studying slides when Steve burst into his office. "Jacque, I want you to call CDC and find out about the titer on David. He is getting worse by the hour."

Jacque looked up. "Calm down, Steve. The morning mail is not in yet." Jacque got up from his chair. "Have you had your morning coffee yet?" he asked.

"No. Jacque, I want to know about that titer on David. They can FAX or e-mail it to you, or you can call." Steve was frantic and out of control...very unusual for him.

Jacque pushed down on the intercom button. "Two coffees, and bring some cream." Then he looked at Steve again. "Steve, sit down and pull yourself together."

Steve nervously shuffled on the floor, then he sat down in his favorite chair as the secretary brought in the coffee. It was one of the rare times that Steve did not notice her.

Jacque stirred some cream into his cup. "Cream in yours, Steve, or do you want it black?"

"Cream, please," answered Steve. He continued. "I'm sorry Jacque, but I am just on edge."

"I understand." Jacque pushed the button on the intercom again. "Get me Dr. Chen at CDC, right away!"

"Thanks, Jacque." Steve took a couple of hard swigs at the coffee. "He is getting worse, Jacque. His EKG is going to hell. I have not talked to him or examined him yet today, and I'm afraid to. I'm afraid to face Lisa. He is going to die, Jacque, unless we can do something."

Jacque took a deep breath. "Steve, why don't you go upstairs and see David. It will give you a better evaluation of his condition rather than just going on EKG findings alone. Come on back down after you are finished and by that time we should know about the antibody titer."

Steve drained the coffee from the cup. "Sure. That sounds reasonable. Again, I am sorry, Jacque. I just have not been getting very much sleep lately. I know that you are doing all that you can." Steve then headed for the third floor, and David's room.

Steve had it pretty well put together by the time that he went to see David. He was calm and he had his emotions under rein. He had to; David and Lisa were depending on him. At this time Steve McKay took the part of Dr. McKay, Physician, not Steve McKay the friend. "Good morning, David. Good morning, Lisa."

Steve read from the chart as he walked slowly to David's bed. Steve made a few mental notes, handed the chart to Lisa and began talking to David. David was still awake, but he was very lethargic, and his breathing was labored. Intravenous fluids were running into his left arm, and David was breathing oxygen through a mask. Steve concentrated his examination on David's heart and lungs. There was more congestion in the lungs now than there was the night before. The heart rate had slowed to 50 beats per minute and again Steve noted some skipped beats and extra beats together with a friction rub. The Cardiomyopathy was getting worse, and it would be a rapid downhill course from now on. Steve grabbed David's hand. "Your heart is a little worse, David. We will have to give you more drugs to help it to beat stronger and to keep your lungs from filling with fluid. You will be able to breathe easier."

David managed a faint smile. He spoke with his eyes closed. "Are you going to use that new drug that Lisa told me about?"

Lisa walked over to the bed and spoke to Steve. "He means Rhythodyne, Steve. Like I told you last night, we have talked about it. But David does not want you to use it if it is going to get you into trouble."

Steve stood thinking, trying to find the right words to say. Finally he squeezed David's hand with assurance. "Sure, David. We'll be using Rhythodyne, soon."

Steve found himself in Dr. Marten's office again. "Have you heard from CDC yet?"

"Yes," said Jacque, "They just called a few minutes ago."

Steve smiled. "I knew that you could do it, Jacque."

Jacque remained grim. "They don't have the titer."

Steve slumped into a chair. "And we don't have time to do a myocardial biopsy." Steve grimaced and looked out the window. "Damn, we should have gotten one right away. But I thought that we would have a titer."

"They said that they are swamped with requests for CMD titer level evaluations from all over the country. They have not even started to run the tests on David's blood."

"And how long will it be before we have it?" Asked Steve.

"I spoke to Dr. Chen personally," said Jacque. "I can't go much higher than that in the CDC hierarchy. She is personally going to make sure that it is done as soon as possible."

"What does that mean, Jacque? Will it take less time to get an answer from CDC if Dr. Chen is involved?" asked Steve impatiently.

"They will have to track down the sample," said Jacque. "Dr. Chen does not know how long that will take. After that they will have to perform the antibody titer test. Dr. Chen will personally telephone the results to me as soon as she receives them." Jacque sat down in his chair.

"How long, Jacque?" Steve asked. "How long?" repeated Steve. "I have to know."

"If we are lucky we could have the results late tonight. It could take as long as three days," mumbled Jacque, knowing that Steve would be disappointed by his answer.

"I can't wait, Jacque. David is not doing well. His congestive heart failure is getting worse by the hour and his heart is slowing precipitously. He is developing an arrhythmia. I will have to start Rhythodyne, now!"

"Without the titer confirmation that David has CM Disease?" asked Jacque.

"I have no choice. If I wait till he is moribund, the Rhythodyne may not work. The reason that we failed the last time we tried Rhythodyne was that we waited too long before we started using the drug." Steve ran his fingers through his hair. "And anyway, I do not think that there is any doubt about the diagnosis of CM Disease."

"In the past I have said that I would not give you any advice as to what you should do, and that all of the decisions would be yours," said Jacque. "I will stick to that, but if you do use Rhythodyne, and it should turn out that David does not have CM Disease, then you may kill him with Rhythodyne. You are treading on thin ice, Steve. You could be putting your whole career in jeopardy."

"Right now my career is the least of the problems that is on my mind." Steve crossed his arms over his chest and gazed out the window toward the horizon as he spoke. "David is on the third floor, in a private room. I think that I will keep him there. The fewer people who know about this, the better. We can follow his progress on third almost as well as if he were in ICU. I'll just monitor him in his room."

Nursing care will not be as intense on third, Steve, " said Jacque.

"Lisa will be with him most of the time and I'm sure that the girls from ICU will volunteer to do private duty, for Lisa's sake. It will work out."

Jacque stopped Steve as he was walking out of the office. "Good luck, Steve."

"Thanks. I'll need it."

One day later, Dr. Winston Welsch was in Jim Street's office. "The people at CDC asked me to fly to Atlanta with them concerning my case of CM disease. They are very interested in studying all of the records and in trying to determine what I did that had made the difference in his survival. We were fortunate in that I had Dr. Marten draw frequent blood samples all through Charlie's illness."

"I heard that they wanted to talk to you, Winston," said Jim Street as he leaned back in his chair.

"They wanted Jacque to come along since he has been on top of CM Disease ever since the epidemic started. Unfortunately, Jacque had to decline. With Lisa's husband ill with CM Disease, Jacque did not feel that he wanted to leave right now. He may change his mind in a few days."

Jim Street rocked in his chair. "Has Charlie shown up at your office, Winston?"

"No, he has not, but I am still confident that he will, in due time. He is not very dependable, but I made it worth his time for him to return. When he gets hungry enough, he'll show up."

"Winston," began Jim Street, "Are NIH or CDC aware that you do not know where Charlie is?"

"I believe so. Jacque has been in contact with them about the case," said Winston.

"Are you doing anything to help find Charlie?" asked Jim Street.

"No, not personally. I believe that Jacque has taken care of the details with the NIH and CDC. They have a low-key search going on for Charlie. They don't want to generate too much publicity at the present time. I have confined my association with the case to reviewing Charlie's medical record and in preparing a report for the CDC. All of that has taken up much of my time. Anyway, you said that you would take care of all of the other details. I believe that kind of thing is part of your job."

"Yes it is," said Jim Street with a smile on his face. He had indeed told Winston not to become involved in the matter outside of making his own report. But Jim had been afraid that perhaps Winston would forget their prior conversation and Jim's admonition, and that Winston would indiscreetly take some action that would put the search in jeopardy.

Jim Street continued. "Just continue working on your part of the problem, Winston, and I will take care of my part. Everyone will be better off if we do it that way."

Winston continued the conversation. "Do you think that you might talk to Jacque about going to the NIH with me? He knows his way around there, and I think that he could add a lot to what I will have to say."

"I don't think that he will go," said Jim Street. "Jacque is tied down with too many things here at Good Samaritan."

"If he should change his mind I would appreciate your letting me know," said Winston.

"You can trust me to do that, Winston. Now, if there is nothing else to discuss, I have a lot of work to do and I'm sure that you do, too, with your report and all." Jim Street could take only so much of Winston Welsch in one serving and the cup was already overflowing.

Winston hesitated, shuffling his feet in a nervous pantomime. "Yes, Jim, there is one more thing." Winston walked over to the front of Jim Street's desk. "Are you aware that Dr. McKay is using Rhythodyne on David Clarke?"

"No, I am not aware of that, Winston, and you should not be aware of that either. That is a very private matter, so let it remain a private matter."

"That is difficult to do, Jim. It is my understanding that Dr. McKay began treating David even before he had antibody titers that would have proved that David has CM Disease."

Jim Street was irritated. "I do not think that is any of your business, Winston. Just go back to your report on the case of CM Disease that you have cured and let Steve alone."

"If it should turn out that the antibody titers come back negative, then that could spell trouble, Jim. Dr. McKay may have killed the last patient on whom he tried Rhythodyne."

Jim Street's fuse was lit and burning. His face was red from the adrenaline that poured into his veins. He bit his lip and his knuckles were aching as he crushed his hands together.

Winston Welsch continued. "I suspect that that is one reason why Jacque did not want to leave at this time."

Jim Street was fighting it, but he managed to keep his cool. He said, "Yes, if Dr. McKay is using Rhythodyne, then I would suspect that Jacque will want to be here to give Steve all the support that he can give in a rather tense situation."

"Tense, but convenient," said Winston Welsch. "I wonder what Steve would do with his wife if David should die."

Jim Street exploded. He jumped from his chair and almost leaped upon the desk as he yelled at Winston, "Get your ass out of here, Winston."

The frightening look on Jim Street's face hurried Winston to the door and the fiery look in Jim's eyes pushed Winston out the door, in a hurry.

Steve had just given David another dose of Rythodyne. He waited for the usual thirty minutes to see that there were no reactions from the drug. Then he re-examined David once more before leaving. David was more alert, less lethargic, and his pulse rate was good; a strong 80 beats a minute. There still was an occasional extra beat, but Steve was not worried about them. If David continued to make progress, Steve planned to have him up in a chair the following day, at least for a while. Steve talked to Lisa for a short while, and then he headed for Pathology to talk to Dr. Marten. Jacque had left a message for Steve to come see him as soon as he had some free time.

"Hello, Jacque," said Steve as he walked briskly into Jacques office. "I have just given David another dose of Rhythodyne and it appears that it is having an efficacious effect. I plan to...." Steve stopped in the middle of his sentence when he saw the uninterested, but worried look on Jacque's face. "What is the matter, Jacque?"

"Dr. Chen from the CDC just called. The antibody titer on David for CM Disease was negative."

"But that can't be right, Jacque. He has all of the signs and symptoms. I know that he has it," said Steve.

"There is no doubt in my mind about it either," said Jacque. "I know that he has CM Disease. But the titer was still negative."

Steve rubbed his hand through his hair. "How accurate is the test, Jacque?"

"It is a new test and the accuracy percentage is not known.

"There have not been any false positives reported to date, but we do not know yet how many false negatives we are getting." Jacque took off his lab coat and hung it up in the corner. "There is always the chance that his titer was not high enough when we drew the first specimen, and we will be sending another specimen today. This one could very well be positive."

"Thanks for the report, Jacque." Steve spoke in a low of voice now. "And I would appreciate it if you did not tell anyone about this."

"I won't tell anyone…but," Jacque's flow of words stopped.

"But what?" asked Steve.

"What about the Rhythodyne?" asked Jacque.

"I am going to continue to use it. I have to. If I don't David, is going to die."

"If that is your decision, I will go along with it. But you must realize that if anything happens…"

Steve interrupted Jacque. "You mean, if David dies."

"Yes," continued Jacque. "If David dies; even if he dies from CM Disease, then you could be in deep trouble. You could lose your medical license."

"I know. But a man's life is at stake. I believe that David's only chance, his only chance to live, is for us to use Rhythodyne."

"One more thing, Steve. I will be blunt and honest. Jim Street had a conversation with Winston Welsch, and Winston has made insinuations about your relationship with Lisa, and about your treating David with a dangerous drug. He insinuated that your treatment could very well be the cause of David's death."

Steve shrugged his shoulders. "I can't worry about that, Jacque." Steve looked at his watch. "Thanks for the information and I have to get home so I can get back to the hospital in time to give David's next dose of Rhythodyne."

The next morning Steve was at the hospital early. He went to check David, but David was still asleep. David had spent a comfortable, uneventful night, so Steve gently shook Lisa who was asleep in a chair in one corner of the room. "Lisa, David is still sleeping. I won't wake him now. I have to talk to you."

Lisa rubbed the night from her eyes, gave her hair a quick brush with her hand, and then the both of them were on the elevator on their way to the cafeteria. They found an out-of-the-way table so they could talk privately. "David is doing better," said Steve.

"He did have a comfortable night," said Lisa. "I believe that the Rhythodyne is working."

"So far," said Steve. Steve took a gulp of the strong tea that he had ordered, wiped his lips with the paper napkin, then he leaned forward as he spoke. "Lisa, we have gotten the CM Disease titer report on David from the CDC."

"They were a little late in coming but that makes no difference," said Lisa.

"They were negative, Lisa. The antibody titers for CM Disease on David were negative."

Lisa stopped put down her cup. "What does that mean, Steve? Are you telling me that David does not have CM Disease? If you are, that is the best news that I have heard in a long time."

"I wish that were true," said Steve. "I still think that David has CM Disease, and so does Jacque. We think that the titer studies are not accurate. Clinically, David has CM Disease."

"But how can the CDC be wrong?" asked Lisa with frustration painting her words.

"Jacque and I both think that the blood that we drew may have been drawn too early in the disease process to show up positive. The study of CMD antibody titers is new and I do not think that CDC has it all sorted out yet."

Lisa's early hope had grown into disappointment. "Then you are still sure that David has CM Disease?" said Lisa.

"Yes. Both Jacque and I are convinced without a question that David has CM Disease."

"Then why are you telling me all of this?" asked Lisa.

"Because I want to continue to use Rhythodyne on David."

"And if he does not have CM Disease and you continue to use Rhythodyne?" asked Lisa.

"Lisa, you know the drug as well as I do. It has side effects that could be lethal. I just want you to know where we are on all this."

"You are putting me in a tight corner, Steve. Do you want me to make the decision as to whether you should continue to use Rhythodyne? Do you want me to talk to David about it?"

"No, Lisa. I will take full responsibility. But I just wanted you to know." Steve drank some tea. He put down the cup. "You realize that he may die whatever we do. It is an awkward position for both of us, Lisa."

"I know. But we will have to do the best we can under difficult circumstances."

Steve and Lisa returned to the third floor and David's room. David was sitting up in his bed, eating a light breakfast. He was very alert and a smile crossed his lips as he saw Steve and Lisa enter the room. David took a sip of juice, then reached for the cup of tea. "I slept like a baby last night, Doctor, and I am not short of breath this morning."

Steve carefully examined David. The heart rate had remained stable at 70 beats per minute, and Steve could hear only an occasional extra beat. The chest was almost completely cleared of fluid. Steve could not hear the friction rub that he had heard over David's heart the day before. David was definitely improving. The Rhythodyne was working. Steve reached for the vial so that he could give the next dose of Rhythodyne to David.

Chapter 17

David Clarke's condition had remained stable. His heart rate had varied from a low of 60 beats per minute to a high of 95 beats per minute, but his blood pressure had remained stable at 120/80 and he was breathing without difficulty. Dr. McKay had returned to the hospital twice that afternoon in order to give David his intravenous injection of Rhythodyne. David continued to improve. He had sat up in a chair for forty-five minutes in the morning, then he sat up for an hour and a half in the afternoon. He had eaten a good lunch and he had felt strong enough to take a short walk around the room with the aid of a nurse. At three p.m. David returned to his bed complaining of fatigue after his day of relatively heavy activity. At four p.m. the nurse checked the EKG leads. She had noted that David's monitor oscilloscope was showing some irregularity and some abnormal looking heart beats and his heart rate had dropped to 60 beats per minute. The nurse checked David and consulted with Dr. McKay by telephone. They concluded that they would treat the patient, not the electrocardiogram, and since David was holding his own, no new treatment was ordered or contemplated for the immediate future.

Lisa had gone home about noon so that she could freshen up, get some rest, and attend to some necessary chores that had been left undone since David had become ill. When she returned to the hospital after supper, David was less alert and more restless than he had been. Both David and Lisa blamed the fatigue and agitation on David's busy day.

Steve returned to the hospital at seven in the evening. He assessed David's condition once again. His heart rate was down to 52 beats per minute, but his chest remained clear of any rales or noises that might suggest that the congestion in his lungs was getting worse. Steve studied David's EKG pattern on the monitor and reviewed the hard copy EKG strips taken at hourly intervals through the day. David's heartbeat was still 52 beats per minute, but Steve became a little worried when he saw the steadily increasing number of premature ventricular contractions that were appearing in the strips and on the monitor. They were not yet frequent enough to cause Steve to panic, but they were there and there were enough of them to make Steve uneasy. The premature beats, the slowing of the heart rate, the recent friction rub...all of these signs were enough to put Dr. McKay on his guard and expecting the worst.

Steve did not know why but he rechecked David's pulse and listened to his chest once again. Maybe Steve was hoping for a miracle to happen. Maybe David had been made well. Maybe Steve was just stalling for time. David was due to receive another dose of the dangerous Rhythodyne. Dr. McKay reached for the vial. He decided to give David two c.c.'s of the drug instead of the usual one c.c. he had been giving. He injected the Rhythodyne into David's vein, waited for the usual thirty minutes to elapse to see whether any untoward reaction developed, and then he and Lisa went downstairs for coffee and a talk before Steve left for home.

3 a.m. Steve received an urgent call from the hospital. David's heartbeat had dropped to 40 beats per minute and his heart was throwing premature contractions. Steve hurried to the hospital and quickly gave David another intravenous injection of Rhythodyne, even though the next dose was not due for two more hours. After he administered the Rhythodyne, Steve waited at David's bedside for one hour. David's heart rate increased to 80 beats per minute, but the number of premature ventricular contractions also increased. David's condition was very unstable and wavering.

Steve asked Lisa to go with him to the head nurse's office where Lisa drank the heavy, old, black coffee. "We are in trouble. I can tell by the look on your face," said Lisa.

"No, Lisa, we are not in trouble, but David is in trouble. He is entering a critical period. The Rhythodyne is maintaining an adequate heart rate, but it is also making the heart muscle very irritable. A big problem, Lisa." Steve took a long draught of the coffee and winced at the bitter taste. "I cannot promise what is going to happen within the next few hours, Lisa." Steve thought awhile before he spoke again. "Maybe I am a Don Quiote fighting windmills. Maybe Rhythodyne is not an answer to the slowing of the heart beat of CM Disease."

"What is the answer then?" asked Lisa, her eyes looking into the distance.

"I don't know," said Steve, "But I wish that I did." Steve emptied his cup, then refilled it from the steaming pot of old coffee on the hot plate. "Why am I doing this, Lisa? If David does not have CM Disease, then I could very well kill him with Rhythodyne. Maybe in my subconscious that is what I want to happen. These are crazy thoughts Lisa, but I can't help it. They keep coming back to me. I like David and he is my patient, and he is very ill, and I want to cure him. But he is also your husband; I am in love with you and I want you for my own." Steve took a big slug of the coffee, and then he slammed the cup on the table. "God, I want to do the right thing, Lisa. Most of all, I do not want to do anything that would hurt David, or you."

"Steve you are doing the right thing. I trust you. David trusts you. David and I both know that you are doing what you think is best for David and we trust that you will continue to do that. We both know the dangers that we face if you treat David with Rhythodyne. Simply, David could die." Lisa's face turned grim. "David has CM Disease, Steve. I know that he has it. You know that he has it. And I don't care what CDC says. If you do not give him the Rhythodyne, David will die. I love you, Steve, and I always will, no matter what happens to David, or to you, or to the both of you. But I also want David to live. I do not want him to die. And, if you do not want to continue giving the Rhythodyne to David, then I will try to find someone who will." Lisa looked up at Steve with begging eyes. "Steve, it is our only chance to save David's life. I have been around CM Disease long enough to know that your treatment is doing something positive for David. It was helping your other patient before he died. I do not know what went wrong that time, but I hope and pray that it doesn't happen to David."

The nurse who broke into the room was panting from her rapid run from David's room interrupted their conversation. "David's EKG is acting up, Dr. McKay, badly."

Steve rushed to David's room with Lisa and the nurse close behind.

"Blood pressure 90/60" said the nurse at David's bedside.

Steve quickly checked David's heart. It was 150 beats per minute; very irregular. David's chest was alive with rales and wheezes, an indication that his congestive heart failure was worse. The rapid heart rate was making it impossible for the heart to effectively pump the blood through David's lungs.

"He is throwing PVC's like mad!" yelled the nurse.

Lisa was still at Steve's side. "Is it the Rhythodyne?" she asked.

"Yes," answered Steve.

"Are you going to give him any drugs or do anything?" asked Lisa anxiously.

"No, we will just wait it out and see what happens," replied Steve with more confidence than he had a right to have. Steve showed no outward sign of apprehension or foreboding. But deep inside he was scared, and his own heart rate was almost as rapid as David's.

They waited. They anxiously watched the clock tick off the minutes…ten…fifteen…twenty-five. Finally, after thirty minutes of suspense and tension, David's heart rate settled down to a respectable 80 beats per minute. There were still a lot of premature ventricular contractions, but David had passed through another crisis.

Lisa spoke softly. "He is doing better, isn't he?"

"Yes," admitted Steve. "But his next dose of Rhythodyne is due in only a few hours."

Lisa locked her eyes on Steve. "Are you going to give it to him?"

"Yes," replied Steve with a stoic look on his face. Then he led Lisa from the room, speaking as they walked. "And when I give David the Rhythodyne, he may die. But if I do not give it to him there is absolutely no hope for his survival."

Steve returned to David's room when the next dose of Rhythodyne was scheduled.

David's condition had remained good. He was alert and coherent and he was breathing easier. But his heart rate had slowed once again to 60 beats per minute. And those extra ventricular beats were still there, laughing at Steve and challenging him. With David's condition improved and stable and with the episode of tachycardia after the last dose still burning on his mind, Steve was hesitant to give the Rhythodyne right then. He left the room to think it over. He returned in forty-five minutes and found David still alert and without any breathing difficulties. But, his heart rate had continued to slow down and was now at a dangerously low of 40 beats per minute. Steve gave the Rhythodyne. He waited thirty minutes and when no untoward reaction developed, Steve left David's room and headed for the cafeteria

After a light breakfast Steve walked to Pathology to keep an appointment with Dr. Marten. Dr. Marten's secretary motioned for Steve to go right in. Steve had been such a frequent visitor lately that she was beginning to wonder who actually was the main occupant of the office.

"What bad news do you have for me this morning?" asked Steve.

"I hear that you almost killed David last night with Rhythodyne."

"Not last night…early this morning," replied Steve.

"Night, morning, whatever. It makes no difference. Death is indifferent to time." Jacque made himself comfortable in his big chair. "You know, if I had my choice, I think that I would like to die in the daytime. The evil spirits come out at night."

"I'll talk to God about it." Then Steve asked, "Has Winston been here?"

"He was and he is too nosey," said Jacque.

Steve looked poised and confident as he spoke. "I was playing a game with CM Disease last night. We were seeing who could come close to knocking David off without actually doing it."

Planning to play the game tonight?" asked Jacque.

"Might be tonight, may be sooner. Maybe not until tomorrow," said Steve.

"So you are still going to use Rhythodyne."

"I am committed to using it," replied Steve. It is the only thing that is keeping David alive."

"But you also managed to give David a ventricular tachycardia with a rate of nearly 200 beats a minute," said Jacque.

"One sixty," said Steve, and the tachycardia did not last long." Steve pulled up a chair. "But if I had not given him the Rhythodyne, David would have developed a severe bradycardia, just like all of the rest and then his heart would have stopped beating altogether."

"Would you like to know what I think about all this?" asked Jacque

"Yes, Jacque, I would like to know what you think about all this," Steve answered with mock sarcasm.

"I think that you have been very lucky so far, Steve. You have been able to control the episodes of ventricular tachycardia that you created by giving the Rhythodyne. But one of these times the tachycardia is going to degenerate into ventricular fibrillation, and then...Jacque's cupped hands came together with a loud pop. "No more David, and then maybe no more Dr. Steve McKay, Steve McKay maybe but not Dr. McKay."

"Are you trying to scare me, Jacque?" asked Steve. "If you are, you are doing a pretty good job."

"I am not trying to scare you, Steve, but I do want you to be aware of the situation as it exists. Winston Welsch is still looking for you to make a bad mistake. I would not trust him, Steve."

"I don't." Steve rose from his chair. "But you worry too much, Jacque."

The hospital page system blared out, CODE BLUE, ROOM 353…..and again, CODE BLUE, ROOM 353.

Steve shouted, "That's David's room."

The two doctors shot out of the office and ran full speed up the stairs. David's room was covered with a cloud of anxiety. David was lying still and still breathing, but he was very pale. Steve looked at the EKG monitor. "What happened?" asked Steve.

"He coded," answered the nurse.

"I know that," said Steve. "I heard the Code announced over the loud speaker. But did he experience cardiac asystole, did his heart stop beating?"

"No," answered the nurse. "He developed ventricular fibrillation. I defibrillated him, but it looks as if he may fibrillate again."

Steve continued to watch the EKG monitor with apprehension. The number of extra beats became more and more frequent and more and more erratic. "Do you have Lidocaine running?" asked Steve.

"Yes," replied the nurse. "We gave him a 100 mg. Bolus and then we started a drip at 4 mg. per minute."

"Good," said Steve as he watched the EKG tracing deteriorate. David's heart was about to go into ventricular fibrillation. Steve looked up and saw Lisa standing quietly in the corner. "Do you want to leave?" asked Steve.

Lisa shook her head in the negative. "I'll stay. I'll be alright."

Jacque Marten walked over to Lisa and whispered into her ear. He then took her by the hand and led her from the room. Steve was glad that Jacque had done that.

"V-Fib!" shouted the nurse as she instinctively put the defibrillation paddles on David's chest.

Steve turned the dial to 400-watt seconds, the highest electrical energy that the instrument could deliver.

"Go, whenever you are ready," shouted Steve.

"Stand back, everybody," yelled the nurse as she looked around to see that no one was touching the bed. The nurse pushed the buttons on the paddles. The strong electrical charge was released into David's body. David shook violently for a second, and then all was quiet.

The resuscitation group hopefully watched the EKG monitor for signs of electrical activity in David's heart. It was there, but inadequate to be compatible with life. Only one electrical impulse every ten seconds, 6 heart beats a minute. David was slowly dying.

"Start CPR," ordered Steve as he prepared the vial of Rhythodyne.

A nurse began compressing David's chest to circulate the blood through his body. One of the technicians from the Respiratory Therapy Department placed an endotrachael tube into David's windpipe and began to ventilate his lungs with oxygen. David's color remained good and pink and the pupils of his eyes remained constricted. There was no evidence of brain death.

Steve gave an IV injection of 3 cc's of Rhythodyne into David's vein. David's heart rate picked up almost immediately, but it was a very erratic heartbeat. The electrical system in David's heart was running wild. His heart was beating faster and faster with a wilder and more erratic electrical pattern by the minute.

Suddenly the nurse shouted, "He is fibrillating again."

"Shock him," ordered Steve.

The nurse put the paddles on David's chest. She pressed the discharge buttons. 400 watt-seconds of electrical energy raced through David's heart.

Steve watched the monitor. "He is still fibrillating," he mumbled.

The nurses and doctors frantically continued to administer CPR to the dying man. The nurse was busy recharging the defibrillator so that she could give David another electrical shock.

One of the nurses whispered quietly to Steve, "This is what happened the last time that you used Rhythodyne."

"I know," answered Steve in anger and frustration. "I don't need that kind of encouragement."

They shocked David's heart two more times and still he continued in ventricular fibrillation. The resuscitation team continued CPR.

"Still fibrillating, Doctor," said one of the nurses.

"I can see that," Steve shouted back at the nurse. "Get that defibrillator charged again."

"It is ready, Doctor."

The nurse carefully placed the paddles on David's chest once again. She depressed the button; the wave of electricity shot through David's heart. Everyone anxiously watched the monitor. The wavy line of ventricular fibrillation slowly ebbed away until there was nothing but a straight line on the scope. "Now he is in cardiac standstill," said Steve in anger.

Then an electrical impulse appeared on the monitor, then another, and another. In a matter of three minutes David's heart was beating with a regular rhythm at 70 beats per minute. David began to breathe on his own and he began to move his arms and legs. David was still alive. He opened his eyes.

Steve threw his white lab coat into a corner. His shirt was soaking wet with perspiration. He rapidly, but carefully, assessed his patient. The chest was relatively clear of any congestion,

A good sign; the blood pressure was 120/80, a good sign; David was breathing on his own, a good sign. David was beginning to awaken, a good sign; the heart rate was down, a bad sign.

"He is developing a bradycardia again." Steve continued to watch the EKG monitor that was announcing David's deteriorating cardiac status. "Look at that EKG. Barely 40 beats a minute."

Steve and the nurse watched the EKG pattern degenerate. 38 beats a minute…35 beats a minute…30 beats a minute.

Give me a 5 cc syringe," said Steve as he reached for the vial of Rhythodyne.

"Are you going to give him more of that?" inquired one of the nurses.

Steve looked up and said in sarcasm and anger. "Of course I am going to give it to him, unless you want to sit on your hands while we watch his heart beat go down to zero."

"I'm sorry," said the nurse "But I just thought that with the V-Fib. and all..."

"Nurses are not suppose to think," said a tired, frustrated Dr. McKay and sorry that he had said it. “We have two choices, cardiac standstill or Vfib. What do you vote for?”

The nurse said nothing.

“I vote for ventricular fibrillation.” Steve shoved down the plunger of the syringe and sent 3 c.c.s of Rhythodyne into David’s vein. At the same time he noticed that Dr. Welsch and Jacque had filtered into the room.

Steve said to the nurse, “Keep your eyes glued to that monitor and your finger on his pulse.”

Steve walked over to where Dr. Welsch and Jacque were standing. “How is Lisa doing?” asked Steve.

“As well as could be expected,” answered Jacque. “I hated to leave her alone, but some of the nurses are with her and I wanted to see how things were coming along in here.”

“David fibrillated, so we defibrillated him,” said Steve. “His heart slowed down, so we gave him Rhythodyne. Then he fibrillated again, so we defibrillated again. His heart slowed again, so I just gave him more Rhythodyne. I hope that we don’t stay on the merry-go-round for too long. I don’t have much Rhythodyne left.”

“Have you just given him more Rhythodyne?” asked Dr. Welsch.

“Affirmative,” answered Steve.

“That is precisely what causes him to go into fibrillation,” said Dr. Welsch.

“That is correct,” answered Steve.

“Dr. McKay,” said the nurse, “He is waking up.”

The three doctors went over to David’s bedside. David was coughing and gagging on the endotrachael tube. He was breathing well and he was moving his arms and legs.

Steve nearly panicked when he saw that David’s heart rate was rapidly increasing. “Not again!” Mumbled Steve.

“Rhythodyne has a tendency to do that,” said Dr. Welsh. “It causes ventricular fibrillation. That is why it is not used any more.”

Steve turned and saw Dr. Welsh standing close to him. “Shut up,” said Steve.

“He is fibrillating again,” shouted the nurse.

“Prepare to defibrillate!” said Steve.

“How high?” shouted the nurse, her finger on the energy deliver dial.

“Keep it at 400.”

The nurse put the paddles on David’s chest once again, and again she made sure that no one was touching the bed as she pressed the buttons and watched David’s body convulse as the electrical shock tore through his body.

"Still fibrillating," shouted Steve. "Go ahead and defibrillate."

The resuscitation team was working overtime. They continued compressing David's chest and ventilating his lungs. David's skin color remained pink and his pupils remained constricted, both good signs that the CPR effort was delivering adequate supplies of blood to the brain. Another shock of electricity rocked David. It worked. David's heart was back in a normal sinus rhythm. Steve took a deep breath and backed away from the bed.

"The heart rate is not very fast," observed the nurse.

"I know," said Steve as he watched the EKG monitor, "but 50 beats per minute ain't bad."

David was beginning to respond once again. He was trying to pull out the endotrachael tube and he was opening his eyes.

Steve shook his head as he watched the EKG monitor. "Down to 40 beats per minute." Steve reached for the Rhythodyne.

"You are not going to give him more of that," said Dr. Welsh.

"Would you like to stand here for the rest of the day and give him CPR, Winston?" Steve drew up 4 cc's of Rhythodyne and walked over to the bed where David lay near death.

"I can't let you do that," said Dr. Welsch.

Jacque came to the bedside and grabbed Dr. Welsch's arm. "Come on, Winston. Let's go get some coffee. There are too many people in here." Before Dr. Welsch knew what was happening, Dr. Marten was shoving him out the door.

Steve slammed the 4 cc's of Rhythodyne into David's vein. Barely a minute went by when David's pulse rate was counted at 80 beats per minute. David was moving his arms and legs and he was breathing spontaneously. In another five minutes he signaled that he wanted the endotrachael tube removed.

"I hope that you don't have to give him any more of that stuff,' said the nurse. "It scares me."

"Keep your fingers crossed and the defibrillator handy," said Steve.

Steve and his crew of nurses and respiratory therapists kept the vigil. Steve kept his eyes glued to the EKG monitor, and the nurse kept her fingers glued to David's pulse. The heart rate crept up to 140 beats per minute and ventricular extra beats were beginning to leave their ugly tracings on the oscilloscope. Everyone held their breath, waiting and hoping. 150 beats per minute... 155 beats per minute... 160 beats per minute. Then, the heart began to settle down. In fifteen minutes the heart rate was regular at 100 beats per minute. Steve removed the plastic tube from David's windpipe. Everyone began to relax.

Lisa came back into the room. David immediately recognized her and talked to her. The heart rate was 80 and regular. No extra heartbeats were contaminating the oscilloscope EKG pattern. After another hour, Steve, fatigued and completely drained both physically and emotionally, left the room and headed for Dr. Marten's office.

"I would have stayed, Steve, but I was not serving any useful purpose in that room. And anyway, you looked like you had things well under control." Then Jacque looked at Steve and he felt sorry for him. "If you want me to do anything for you do not hesitate to ask. I will do whatever I can to help you."

"Thanks for taking care of Winston," said Steve.

"I took him outside and kicked the shit out of him," said Jacque.

"You're kidding?" said a smiling Dr. McKay.

"Just kidding," said Jacque with a laugh, "but I felt like doing it."

Steve dropped into his favorite chair. "But we have another problem, Jacque."

"One more problem?" Jacque counted the fingers on both hands. "You will have to quit finding any more new problems, Steve. I am running out of fingers."

Steve pulled out the Rhythodyne vial and held it on his open hand in front of him so Jacque could see it.

"So?" asked Jacque. "The Rhythodyne vial. What is the problem?"

"The problem is, Jacque, this is it. No more Rhythodyne after this. I have been giving three, four, even five cc's at a time."

"Maybe David will not need any more," said Jacque with words moistened with hope.

"Maybe he won't," said Steve, "but more than likely he will. If we can pull David through the next few days we may save him. But we will need more Rhythodyne."

"But are you sure that you want to continue to use Rhythodyne?" asked Jacque.

"Strange that you should ask that," countered Steve. "You saw what happened in there, Jacque. David's heart would have stopped beating if it were not for the Rhythodyne."

"And the Rhythodyne almost killed David's heart," added Jacque.

Steve ignored what Jacque was saying. "Where can I get more Rhythodyne?" he asked.

Jacque spoke softly. "Do you still insist on using Rhythodyne in spite of what happened to David these past two days when you did use it on him?"

Steve dove into the depths of his mind and swam in the thoughts that had flooded his brain ever since he began using Rhythodyne on David. "I will continue to use the drug on David." Then he paused and rearranged his thoughts once more. "But it appears that Rhythodyne is not the answer to CM Disease. It is much too difficult a drug to use. It takes constant adjustment of dosage to tread a narrow line between adequate treatment for bradycardia and still not precipitate ventricular fibrillation. It is a dangerous drug."

Steve got out of his chair and walked to the window and gazed out at the courtyard below. "No, Rhythodyne is not the answer to CM Disease." He turned around and looked at Jacque. "We must find something else."

"There is no more Rhythodyne anywhere in the country," said Jacque, breaking the news to Steve as easily as he could. "I tried everywhere, Steve. I even tried the FDA. They know of no supplies of the drug in the country. Even the manufacturer did not retain any of the drug. They have dismantled their manufacturing process. It would be too costly and time consuming to make it in their laboratory. They might consider compounding some for you, if you could give them some reasonable assurance that it is beneficial in the treatment of the arrythmia of CM Disease." Jacque drove in the final nail that would seal the lid on the Rhythodyne saga. "And you do not have that kind of evidence, Steve. To put it even more plainly, Rhythodyne may keep a person with CM Disease alive for awhile, but it does not cure, it merely prolongs the inevitable."

"That is going to be tough to tell Lisa," said Steve, almost in a whisper. "She has been counting on the stuff to save David's life."

Jacque drew in a deep breath. "It is not ordinarily my kind of thing, but if you want, Steve, I will tell her."

"That will not be necessary. I'll handle it."

Steve left Jacque's office wondering where, how, and when he would tell Lisa that there was no hope. David was going to die.

Chapter 18

It was five a.m. as Steve walked down the hospital corridor. The echo of his walking seemed extraordinarily loud in the silence of early morning hospital inactivity. Steve stopped at Dr. Marten's Pathology office. The light was still burning inside.

"Good morning, Steve, and pour yourself a cup. The coffee is hot and fresh. Pour one for me, too."

Steve went about the chore of finding two clean cups and pouring the freshly brewed coffee. "Cream and sugar?"

"Black, no sugar," replied Jacque.

"And why are we meeting so early?" asked Steve as he handed a cup to Jacque.

"Late, not early," answered Jacque as he sipped coffee. "I have not been home since yesterday. I worked all night."

"She must have been good," quipped Steve.

"I have been working on some interesting leads," replied Jacque. "But how is David doing?"

"He is still hanging on, for how long I can't say. At least he went through the night without his heart going into fibrillation or asystole. After yesterday that is a major accomplishment."

"Have you talked to Lisa this morning?"

"No." Steve did not elucidate but drank coffee instead.

"I've received some new information from CDC in Atlanta," said Jacque. "They report that they have not yet been able to identify a virus with any degree of scientific exactness from any of the specimens that they have so far studied," said Jacque. "But they have detected and have grown virus-like particles, but apparently not viruses."

"A new organism, a new virus, or something else?" asked Steve as he groped for a simple answer to a complex problem.

"All of the above, or none of the possibilities that you have just mentioned. No one knows for sure." Jacque drank coffee again. "But, that is not the main reason why I asked for you to come here this morning, Steve.

If you remember, after Jim Street gave us the research money I began to put together an epidemiological map of the patients who have had CM Disease. I was especially interested in some of the first patients who came down with the disease. And I believe that I have come up with at least a feeble relationship."

"That sounds interesting," said Steve. "Finding the etiology would be helpful in tracking down whatever it is that is causing CM Disease."

"The relationship revolves around Bio-Medical Industries."

"That means that we have to involve Winston Welsch," exclaimed Steve.

"Yes it does," said Jacque dryly. "And I had to ask Winston since he is involved with BMI and should know something about the plant and its workings. I hated to ask him because it gives him the chance to be important again. But I had no choice."

Steve looked at his watch. "But why five in the morning? Do you suspect something clandestine about the relationship between BMI and CM Disease?"

Jacque rose from his chair. "No. Winston is leaving town on the company jet on business this morning and he invited us to come over for breakfast in the Executive Suite at the plant."

"Gee, I'm not exactly dressed to be meeting with company executives," said Steve.

"I can see that," replied Jacque. "But you can drive and your Jag will feel at home in their parking lot."

As they drove to BMI Jacque related his findings to Steve. "This is what I have found so far, and I'm not sure what it all means, if anything. It could all be coincidence. The first case of CM Disease at Good Samaritan Hospital was a former BMI employee, but he had not worked at BMI for about two months. Another of the first few cases was the son of a BMI employee. Another was a painter who worked at BMI during a remodeling project at the plant. Still another victim of CM Disease was a refuse collector who collected regularly at BMI. And finally, an air conditioning specialist who worked on the remodeling project at BMI died of CM Disease. Now how is that for a relationship?"

"What relationship?" asked Steve cynically.

"I know," continued Jacque. "It isn't much, but what else do we have to go on. I don't know why, but somehow I have a gut feeling that we may have something here. What it is I don't know, and maybe we will end up having the same information that I have just read to you and nothing more."

Steve could read the frustration in Jacque's voice that was mixed with a hope built on sand.

*

Dr. Winston Welsch played the part of the gracious host and had a beautiful breakfast prepared. After the three had finished eating and were on their after breakfast coffee, Jacque presented his findings to Winston, then he asked, "Can you add any further information concerning these people?"

Winston was enjoying every minute of his status as an expert. "Let me begin with the construction work that we did at the plant since a number of individuals on your list were involved in that. We closed down my research area and remodeled it so that it could be used for badly needed storage. The painter cleaned the old walls and repainted them together with the new partitions that were built. The refuse collector was one of many whom we engage, but this particular fellow was regularly assigned to collect from my laboratory area. When we remodeled we overhauled the ventilation and air conditioning system, so that is how the air conditioning man was involved. The son of the employee who died... .his father worked in the water filter assembly division."

Steve interrupted. "What do you mean, the water filter division?"

"BMI manufactures water filters for municipal water preparation plants. We send them all over the country, and in fact, all over the world."

"I did not know that," said Steve. "I thought that you were involved with the manufacture of laboratory equipment."

"That is our main line," replied Winston. "But we are also involved in the manufacture of water filtration and sewage treatment equipment; sort of a bread and butter operation. It pays for the telephone and electricity, if you know what I mean."

Jacque shook his head in an understanding way, although he was not sure that he did. He had other things on his mind. "And that leaves your former employee. What about him?" inquired Jacque.

"He had not worked for BMI for a month or more prior to the time that he came down with CM Disease."

"Where did he work in the plant?" asked Steve.

"Actually," began Winston, "He worked for me. I had to let him go because of his inefficiency. The final incident leading to his dismissal occurred when he knocked over the large cloud chamber...Winston stopped dead in the middle of his sentence, his face ashen, perspiration appearing on his forehead.

"Go on, Winston," urged Jacque.

"He dropped the cloud chamber."

And what was in the Cloud Chamber?"

Winston mopped his forehead. "I think that we should have some more coffee." Winston poured coffee for himself and for the other doctors. Jacque and Steve waited, speculating as to what Winston would tell them next.

"I am not sure of the significance of this, but the cloud chamber was used for the irradiation of organisms," said Winston.

"Winston," Jacque flew out of his chair. "You were warned and told to discontinue using irradiation on organisms because of the danger involved and because you did not have the proper credentials or facilities."

Steve interjected. "Let that be, for now, Jacque. Let's wait and hear what else Winston has to say about this."

Winston took a big gulp of coffee, swallowed hard, then cleared his throat in nervousness. "I realize that I had been directed to discontinue experiments involving the irradiation of organism, and you must believe me, I fully intended to do so." Winston looked beggingly at the two doctors. "But I had only one more or two more experiments and my data would have been complete. And I hated to see all of my prior work go to waste. After we had the accident with the gas chamber, I did stop."

Neither Steve nor Jacque said anything. They were afraid to speculate at to what might have happened.

"I swear I stopped experimenting right after the accident," said Winston in a tone of voice that was asking for understanding and forgiveness.

Steve broke the silence. "This gas chamber, I think that I know what it is, but will one of you please clue me in on the details?" he asked.

Jacque explained. "The gas chamber is used in the irradiation of organisms. Bacteria or viruses are placed in the chamber in a fog-like atmosphere made up of substances compatible for the particular organism that is being studied. Then the chamber with the organisms inside is irradiated with X-rays. It is a potentially dangerous process because no one is ever sure that a mutant organism generated by the irradiation process will appear."

Steve scratched his head and looked at Winston. "What kind of organisms did you have in that fog chamber, Winston? Viruses?"

Winston emptied his cup with a single gulp, then refilled it from the pot on the table. "No, not viruses. I did not have sophisticated enough apparatus for that. I was studying Chlamydial organisms. It seemed harmless enough. Chlamydia are known to cause eye infections, some venereal infections, and mild pneumonias in infants, but there have not been any reports of Chlamydia causing any fatal disease as far as I know."

"Up until now anyway," said Steve dryly.

Dr. Welsch rose from his chair and waved his arms to emphasize what he was about to say. "I do not think that you gentlemen understand. I had no intention whatsoever of experimenting with mutations of Chlamydia. I had to irradiate the Chlamydia in order to use the cell culture technique to propagate the Chlamydial organisms with McCloy cells."

Both Steve and Jacque thought that Winston was sincere in what he said. Chlamydia organisms are different than other bacteria. Originally they were thought to be large viruses because they appear as large particles in tissues. They are classified as modified bacteria because they have many of the characteristics of bacteria, but are much smaller. They cannot be grown on ordinary cultures like bacteria, but they must be grown either on the yolk sac of embryonated chick eggs or more recently, by tissue culture much like viruses. In order to use the cell culture technique to propagate the Chlamydial organism, the cell division is temporarily arrested by irradiation.

Jacque looked at Winston. "But you have to know what you are doing when you use irradiation."

"Chlamydia…that may answer some questions for us," said Steve. "The strange, unidentified particles that the Communicable Disease Center in Atlanta have been finding could be Chlamydia, not viruses." Steve turned toward Winston. "I'm still not sure what happened in your laboratory to spread this around."

Everyone remained quiet, Steve and Jacque looking toward Winston for an answer. "Go on, tell us what happened, Winston," said Jacque.

"My lab assistant knocked over the large fog chamber that was filled with Chlamydial material that I had recently irradiated. I fired him for that, of course."

"Of course," replied Jacque. "But it appears that he apparently was inoculated with mutated material from the fog chamber and came down with CM Disease. It is too obvious to discuss how the others might have contracted the infection."

"But how about the son of the employee. How was he exposed?"

Winston was asked to answer. "I really can't say, but his father was involved in the water filter assembly area."

"And where is that?" asked Steve.

"It was located on the other side of the wall separating the laboratory from the assembly area. The air from the laboratory was vented through the assembly area, but we had taken precautions by adding filters to the system."

Jacque tutored the two doctors. "The filters would be effective against bacteria, but not viruses, or other organisms as small as viruses like Chlamydia. Where do you send the water filters?"

"He told us once, Jacque. They send them all over the world."

Jacque shook his head in disbelief. "God, what a mess."

"But you surely don't think that I mutated the Chlamydia and that it is that mutation that is the cause of CM Disease?" asked Winston with fear in his voice.

"Yes, I do think that that is exactly what happened," said Jacque.

"So the organism causing CM Disease is probably a mutant Chlamydial organism," began Steve, "And that means…"

Jacque quickly continued, "It means that if we can stop it there is a ninety-nine percent chance that it will revert to its former non-virulent status."

"And if we don't stop it?" asked Winston with fear punctuating his sentence.

"Then the mutation may become fixed," replied Jacque. "And that means that the world is going to have to live, or die, with CM Disease."

"But, Jacque," said Steve, "Most Chlamidial organisms are susceptible to antibiotics, and we have been treating the hell out of our patients with CM Disease with antibiotics. I don't understand why they don't get well."

Dr. Marten was quick to answer. "Winston, by irradiating the Chlamydia, probably caused a mutant strain to develop which is not sensitive to antibiotics."

Steve looked at Dr. Welsch disgustingly. "Is there anything else that you screwed up, Winston?"

Dr. Winston Welsch was quiet. His hand shook visibly as he tried to drink his coffee.

"We have to report this information to the NIH and CDC soon," said Jacque.

"No!" shouted Dr. Welsch. "I will be ruined, BMI will be ruined. And there is no positive proof that my accident is the cause of this epidemic."

"Maybe not, Winston," said Jacque, "But it sure looks suspicious."

Steve got up and stretched. "I'm tired already and I can see that this is going to be a long day. Look, gentlemen, I see no real reason to announce to the NIH, CDC, or anyone else that all of this occurred. It is an after the fact information and will serve no useful purpose. What is done is done. They will have to be notified that they should look for Chlamydial organisms and that is the important factor, right now anyway."

"You are probably right, Steve," said Jacque. "I don't think that we should stonewall this, but on the other hand I think the emphasis now should be placed on doing something to find a treatment for CM Disease. The way it all started is not of prime importance. I suspect that there is a good chance that CDC may trace it down to you anyway, Winston."

"Oh God! No!" was all that Winston could mutter.

Jacque took control. "Now, for the present time, forget about this meeting. With this new information, my present experiments begin to make some sense. Steve, I want to meet you at my laboratory late this afternoon. And Winston," Jacque pointed his finger right in Winston's face, "Get your people busy and recall all of your water filters."

"But I have to fly to New York on business this morning," replied Winston.

"Winston," shouted Steve. "Today, this is your business. Can't you understand the trouble that you have caused already? You stay in this building until you get those filters recalled."

"But this is an important investors meeting..." began Winston.

"Do you want me to call the NIH and CDC and maybe the Justice Department?" asked Steve.

"I'll stay and get all of the filters recalled," replied Winston.

Dr. Welsch stayed at BMI to make arrangements to have the contaminated water filters recalled. Dr. Marten headed for the sub-basement and his makeshift laboratory to work on his experiment, and Steve went back to the hospital.

Dr. McKay gave David his dose of Rhythodyne, then insisted on taking Lisa home so that he could talk to her.

Steve and Lisa made themselves comfortable in the family room of Lisa's rambling ranch house. "Lisa, I realize that you are very tired, fatigued, and just plain exhausted. But there is something that we must talk about. We must reach an understanding about David."

Lisa was uncertain as to what Steve wanted to discuss, and her mind was clouded with tiredness. She could not give it a good think. "I will discuss anything that you want," she said, "About David or anything else."

"Lisa," said Steve clumsily, "David is going to die."

"But you are using the Rhythodyne and it is keeping him alive," said Lisa.

"I know," continued Steve, "But we are running out of Rhythodyne."

"Then we will have to get more," replied Lisa in a matter-of-fact manner.

"There is no more Rhythodyne," said Steve. "We have been in contact with the FDA and the NIH and anybody else who might have access to any Rhythodyne. They have all assured us that there is none available, anywhere. Jacque has even gone so far as to contact the developer and manufacturer of the drug, and again without success. When the Rhythodyne that we now have on hand runs out, that is it."

Neither Steve nor Lisa could find proper words to break the icy silence that overshadowed the room. Then Lisa said hopefully, "Maybe David will not require much more Rhythodyne."

"I would hope that that would be the case, but it does not appear that David can survive very long without the Rhythodyne."

Steve reached out for Lisa's hand, but she pulled it away and took a seat by the window. Her face was turned away from Steve as she peered out into the distance. After a time, Lisa turned toward Steve. "I guess that is the way it will have to be, but I am not giving up, not yet."

"Don't let your optimism get too high, Lisa. The higher it gets, the harder will be the fall when it comes."

"But Rhythodyne works so well," said Lisa. "So many lives could be saved."

"It is not the answer, Lisa. We have been keeping David's heart beating, but then it runs wild and we have been literally tearing it up with electrical shocks. The heart can take only so much of that, Lisa, and then something has to give way. He is going to die."

Lisa rose from her chair and the two embraced. There were tears in Lisa's eyes. Frustration and defeat were scribbled all over Steve's face. They held each other tightly, afraid to let go and face the world that was collapsing all around them.

Lisa clung closely to Steve, her head pressing hard on his chest. She spoke softly, quietly, and with deliberation. "Steve, if David lives, our relationship, yours and mine, can never be the same. But I want you to know that I love you dearly. I always will. That will never change. I don't know how I will live without you, but I will have to try."

The two stood still and unmoving, locked in an ever tightening embrace. Steve's voice was barely audible. He spoke as he embraced Lisa even more closely. "And if David dies?"

"I must be honest with you, Steve. If David dies, I will want you for my own, more than ever before, and I will not settle for less than having all of you."

That afternoon they almost lost David. His heart rate dropped precipitously to 30 beats a minute and Steve rushed to the hospital from his office and gave David one cc of Rhythodyne, but it did not reverse the severe bradycardia. Steve had hoped to be able to conserve the drug as much as possible, but he had to relent and gave David another large dose. David responded, then developed a ventricular tachycardia of over two hundred, and went into ventricular fibrillation that required two shocks before converting to a normal rhythm. He was stable when Steve left the hospital, but his heart rate was slowly dropping, and the Rhythodyne was running low.

After a quick supper, Steve returned to the hospital to meet with Dr. Marten as he had promised he would. Jacque was more excited than Steve had ever seen him before. "Boy, am I glad to see you, Steve. Have I got something to show you."

Steve whispered, but in mock anticipation. "How in the hell did you sneak her down here?"

Jacque took Steve over to the mice cages. "What do you see in the cages, Steve?"

"Mice, little white mice all running around like they are in heat," said Steve.

"Precisely," said Jacque "But not in heat, but all running around." Then Jacque pointed to another set of cages. "And what do you see there?"

"Lazy mice, dead mice, and a whole box of dead mice...that stinkith," said Steve.

"Now sit down, Steve, so I can explain." Jacque was still excited. "I knew that I might be onto something when I began this experimental series, but then this morning when we met with Winston I knew that we had something going."

Steve was becoming impatient. "Come on, Jacque, you are acting like a high school boy who just got his first piece. Just tell me about your experiment."

"Those dead and sick mice were injected with the same amount of homogenized heart muscle extraction as the live ones in the other cages, and at the same time."

Steve's heart began to pound as he sensed an exciting scenario developing. He got out of his chair. "Jacque, what is different about them?"

Jacque's sentences came out with a staccato rapidity. "The live mice have received serum from Charlie Teringo. Whatever Charlie has in his blood after surviving an episode of CM Disease is keeping these mice from developing cardiac arrhythmia and is preventing them from dying."

Steve was now as excited as Jacque. "It all adds up, Jacque. It is starting to make sense. CM Disease is killing people with toxins that are poisoning the electrical conduction system of the heart."

"Precisely," said the still excited Dr. Marten. "Obviously Charlie's blood and serum is loaded with antitoxin and prevents the arrhythmia's from developing."

"But, hold it, Doc," said Steve. "How come Charlie didn't die like the others?"

"I can't be sure, but I have a good theory," continued Jacque. "I have reviewed the slides of Charlie's heart biopsy that Winston did and Charlie had a myopathy alright, but I don't think that it is the Cardiomyopathy of CM Disease."

Steve exclaimed, "Charlie was an alcoholic and he developed alcoholic Cardiomyopathy, not a Cardiomyopathy like that of people who died from CM Disease."

"That's right," continued Jacque. "Now listen closely. For one thing, Charlie probably would have died if Winston would have given him Rhythodyne. If Charlie had died, then we would not be where we are today."

Steve began to speak, but Jacque interrupted and continued.

"This is the rest of my theory. I believe that there are a lot of people who develop an infection with Chlamydia that causes CM Disease, but all do not necessarily develop a serious enough infection to produce enough of the toxin to poison the heart. It appears that Charlie was one of these people."

Steve interrupted. "That makes a lot of sense. Chlamydia infections are known to lie dormant for long periods of time without being active; then all of a sudden -boom! They start multiplying and cause active disease." Steve let out a long whistle. "I can envision thousands of people who are infected but who have not yet come down with active CM Disease."

"That very well could be the case. But with this information CDC should be able to come up with a testing program to find those individuals who have high antitoxin titers, and from them, develop enough antitoxin from their serum to treat patients with active CM Disease. They can then develop some synthetic method to produce the antitoxin." Jacque was still prancing about the room like a show pony. "There are all kinds of possibilities. It will take some time to sort it all out, but it looks like we have at least found the hole in the wall that we needed."

"How much of Charlie's serum do you have left?" asked Steve eagerly.

"Not very much," replied Jacque. "Maybe a tube or so, not enough to do any good." Jacque noticed that Steve had all of a sudden become very sullen and quiet. "What is the matter, Steve?"

"The serum, Charlie's serum. I need it to give to David. It will save David's life. I have only enough Rhythodyne for about another dose or two." Steve spoke with grim determination. "We have to find Charlie."

Jacque's jubilation shifted to Steve's determination. "We have to find him soon. Antitoxin is passive, and does not remain in the blood forever."

It was after ten that night when Steve and Jacque found themselves standing on the steps of the ram-shackle boarding house where Charlie "The Trumpet" stayed while he was playing at Tilfer's Disco. Steve knocked on the door. "The police sure have not been much help," he said as the two of them waited.

"I thought that the FBI would have been more active than they have been. It did not appear that they have done a thing in the past two weeks," said Jacque.

Steve knocked again. "I would have thought that the NIH or CDC would have pushed them a little. Right now we have no good leads."

The door opened and the gruff looking German lady spoke through the screened door that was latched and locked shut. "You remember us I'm sure, Mrs. Schwartz. I am Dr. McKay and this is Dr. Marten. We were here a few weeks ago talking to you about Charlie Teringo."

"He has not come back and he still owes me rent, and I don't want to talk about it anymore," said the landlady.

"Don't be in too big of a hurry to send us away, Mrs. Schwartz." Steve pulled out his money clip. I have Charlie's rent and I'll pay you."

The landlady hesitated. She took another look at the money and then she unlatched the door. "Sixty dollars, he owes me," she said as she opened the door.

Steve closed his hand over the money as he and Jacque were in the house before the landlady realized what was happening. "But first, Mrs. Schwartz, we need a little information."

"Get out of here!" she shouted. "I knew there was some trick to it." She started shoving the two toward the door.

"Sixty dollars, Mrs. Schwartz, and another twenty, for interest," said Steve.

The landlady quit shoving. "Tell you all that I know."

Steve peeled off two twenties and handed them to the landlady. "You get the rest after you talk to us."

"I may just call the police," said the landlady.

"Wait, just one minute, Mrs. Schwartz." Steve looked carefully at her eyes, then he said, "Open your mouth, so I can check." Steve had put on his best bedside manner and Mrs. Schwartz complied. "I was afraid of that, the very earliest signs. I have seen so many of them that I don't make any mistakes any more."

"What do you mean?" asked the landlady with some degree of apprehension.

Steve ignored Mrs. Schwartz and spoke to Jacque. "Charlie had CM Disease, didn't he? Now if we find him we will be able to cure anybody with CM Disease."

"That is, if we find him," said Jacque picking up the cue. "That CM

Disease is so catchy, practically everyone who lives in the same house gets it."

"You don't think that I got it?" exclaimed a frightened Mrs. Schwartz.

"With a deadly disease like that we don't like to say until we are positive about the diagnosis. It does look suspicious," said Steve. "But, if we could find Charlie a lot of people would be saved."

"What do you want to know?" asked the landlady.

"We know that Charlie left town leaving a lot of his things behind. You must have them here. We would like to go through them and see if we can find a clue as to where Charlie might be."

Mrs. Schwartz remained silent, then she led them to a storage room and pointed to an old dilapidated suitcase and a few sets of coats and trousers hanging nearby. "Those are his."

Steve and Jacque went through Charlie's things but found very little that would give them definite information as to Charlie's whereabouts. They did find a bill that had been sent to Charlie at a St. Louis address and two paycheck stubs from an amusement park where Charlie had apparently worked. They also found a fairly recent photo of Charlie that he used when he applied for jobs. Steve stuffed the address and the picture into his pocket.

"The best thing for us to do now," said Steve," is for me to go to this address and the amusement park in St. Louis and see if I can find Charlie."

On his way out, Steve handed the rest of the money to the landlady. "And thank you, Mrs. Schwartz. I am sure that you will not regret what you have done for mankind," said a stone-faced Dr. McKay as Dr. Marten refrained, only with difficulty, from laughing.

"But what about me?" asked Mrs. Schwartz.

Steve took another quick look at her eyes and throat. Then he looked at Jacque. "I think that she looks a lot better."

"I think so, too," said Jacque.

Steve was half way out the door when he turned and said, "Take two aspirin and get a good night's sleep. You will feel a lot better in the morning."

Chapter 19

Early the next morning the BMI jet stood poised for takeoff. Steve would fly to St. Louis to try to track down the elusive Charlie "The Trumpet" Teringo. It had not been hard to convince Winston Welsch that it would be a good idea for him to offer the use of the plane for Steve's transportation. Jacque and Lisa had driven Steve to the airport and were waiting at the visitors' gate watching Steve mount the stairs of the jet. The engines were already whining with impatient anticipation of the upcoming flight.

Suddenly Steve stopped dead in his tracks, retreated down the stairway, and ran to where Jacque and Lisa were standing. "Now listen carefully, Jacque," began Steve. "We don't have too much Rhythodyne left so I would suggest that you ration it. One or two cc's will usually suffice. But, if the heart rate drops down to around thirty, then you have no choice. You will have to pull all the plugs and give more. Then you take the risk of David developing ventricular fibrillation. Lisa can help you if you run into any real tough problems."

Jacque rudely interrupted Steve and literally turned him around and shoved him toward the jet. "We have gone over that sixteen times, Steve. Now get on that plane and find Charlie."

The jet landed at Lambert Field and was berthed in the private aircraft section. It would wait for Steve so that they could whisk them back to Good Samaritan, hopefully with Charlie aboard.

Summers are hot in St. Louis and Steve was sorry that he did not leave his coat with the plane. He loosened his tie and waited for his taxi to arrive. Steve was carrying a bottle of Chivas Regal, a special gift from Dr. Welsch to Charlie. Steve was hoping that it would serve as a calling card that would help him gain Charlie's attention. Steve had a large number of twenty-dollar bills in his pocket that he thought might be used as further inducement for Charlie to come back to Good Samaritan if Charlie should waver in his decision to return with Steve.

The black driver pulled his cab up to the curb next to Steve. "You call for a cab, mister?"

Steve nodded his head and stepped into the cab. The driver had the radio of the cab tuned to a hep station and hummed along with the near-wild music. "Where's ya goin?" asked the driver in a melodious sentence in tune with the radio's music.

Steve dug into his coat pocket and retrieved the address he and Jacque had found in Charlie's bag back at Mrs. Schwartz's rooming house. He read off the address for the driver.

The cab slowed as the mustached driver nudged the breaks. "Oh, oh," he said, "I don't think I can takes you there, man."

Steve looked at the cab driver's license that was in a visible frame up front. Steve repeated the address to Simon. The cab was moving at a snail's pace and irate drivers were beginning to toot their horns with impatience. "That is not the place that nicely dressed men like you would go," said Simon.

"Just take me there," said Steve. "I will make it worth your time."

"Money ain't no object here, man. My object is to protect unsuspecting people like you from gettin hurt. Now why don't you pick another place to go."

"Look, Simon, the address that I gave you is where I want to go. Now if you don't want to take me there, I will get out and find a cab that will."

"Why don't you ask me why I won't takes ya there, man."

Steve wiped at his sweating forehead. "Okay, Simon, why don't you want to take me there?"

"Because if you live in that area and they knows ya, ya're safe, maybe. But if you don't live there, you ain't safe, period."

"I'll have to chance it," mumbled Steve with a bit of apprehension.

"There ain't no chance about it, man. You ain't got no chance of commin' out of there without a bump on your head, unless…"

Steve parlayed with Simon. "Unless what?"

"Unless you is a drug dealer and they knows ya. Are ya a drug dealer?"

"No, I am not a drug dealer. I am a physician, a doctor."

"Somebody sick there?"

"You ask a lot of questions," said Steve.

"Doctors ain't got no safety ticket any mores, man. They'll roll ya just as easy as anyone else."

"Look Simon," began Steve, "I am looking for a trumpet player named Charlie. It is very important that I find him."

"You got him," said Simon as he turned around with a great big smile on his face.

"Just watch the road," cautioned Steve as the cab barely missed hitting a parked car.

"What ya need Charlie for? You need him to play for ya?"

"No, I need his blood," said Steve.

"This gets weirder all the time," said Simon.

"Simon, just cut the crap and take me to the address that I gave you so I can see if Charlie is still there. And believe me, it is of utmost importance that I find Charlie."

"Okay, boss," said Simon as the cab skipped forward. "But if you is goin' in there, let me give you some advice. First of all, muss yourself up some. You looks too neat and you looks too much like a cream puff. Even the village wino would be tempted to try you." Simon checked the mirror to see whether Steve was complying. Steve was not, so Simon urged him on. Steve did not know whether to take Simon seriously or not, but as the cab made a right turn and Steve saw that they were in what could at best be called an undesirable part of town. He ruffled his hair, wrinkled his collar, loosened his tie and opened his shirt three buttons.

"That's better," said Simon.

As they drove through a wicked part of town, Simon continued to instruct Steve on how to survive in the city jungle. "Nobody gives you information," said Simon, "You have to buy it."

"But don't flash no big bucks around." Simon told Steve how much money to crumple and place in various pockets and he told him to hide the rest of his money in his shoe. His billfold; best to put all of his credit cards and whatnot in his stocking and leave only a few bucks in the billfold.

"You're not putting me on with all of this?" asked a skeptical Steve as he stuffed a handful of cards and papers in his stocking.

"Hell no, man. Take a look out the window and ya can see for yerself that there's lots of bad people out there and we is gettin close to wheres ya want to go."

Steve glanced out the window and he had to agree with Simon. A bit of fear began to creep into Steve's veins. He was not made for this sort of thing.

"Now remember, most of these guys is winos and is half crocked most of the time. They ain't nuthin in a rumble, but they do carry knives and they don't care if they use 'em. Hear now," said Simon in a voice trimmed with a definite warning. "They don't mind doubling or tripling up on ya if they have to. They probably will fight among themselves later fer what they gets from ya."

The cab slowed. "That's it right up ahead," said Simon. "Still want ta go?"

Charlie's address was a four story rooming house-hotel on the corner.

Small groups of derelicts of all ages, all races, and probably all religions and no religions, stood around and walked slowly down the sidewalk, stumbling over the winos who had already hit the pavement. It was a dismal place to be on a dismal, hot morning in St. Louis. Steve pulled out a twentydollar bill and flashed it up front. "Can you wait for me?" he asked.

Simon stopped the cab in front of Charlie's hotel. He turned around and said to Steve, "You don't stay parked here too long, man. It ain't safe, but I'll tell ya what. If ya gets out of there okay, start walkin south, and don't stop, just keep walkin, fast. I'll make another run past here in a short while and I'll have a couple of other cabbies do the same."

Steve handed Simon three twenties.

"Too much," said Simon. "One twenty does it easily tip and all."

Steve shoved Simon's hand away with the three twenties. "Keep it. That is my insurance that you will be here when I am ready to leave."

"No guarantee, man, but I'll try," said Simon as he put the crushed the bills in his pocket.

Steve stepped out of the cab thinking that his life was worth more than sixty dollars. He turned to go back to the cab, but Simon had already driven halfway down the street.

Steve looked around. Teetering drunks, seedy looking people, and mean looking guys stared at him. "What in the hell am I doing here?" Steve asked himself. Then he thought about David who was dying back at Good Samaritan Hospital and he thought about Jacque and Lisa struggling to save David's life. Steve turned and went into "The Royale."

There was only one person in the lobby, an old guy. He was dressed in baggy, brown checked pants, a shabby stripped shirt, and a poorly matching tie heavily spotted with remnant droppings from onetime meals. A crooked cigarette hung from the corner of his mouth. His face was wrinkled with the residuals of the long and ragged life that haunted him. The old man carefully watched Steve walk up to the desk.

"I need some information," began Steve. "I am looking for a trumpet player by the name of Teringo, Charlie Teringo. I was told he stays here."

The desk clerk studied Steve for a time. Then he said, "Why do you want him?"

Steve was not sure what to say, so he picked what he thought would be a safe answer. "I'm a relative."

The desk clerk snuffed out his cigarette in a big ashtray. "People who live here ain't got no relatives."

Steve tried again. "I have to see him. It is very important that I talk to him."

The desk clerk leaned with one elbow on the desk and spoke as he peered out the window. "Are you a drug detective?... a cop?"

Steve answered, "No."

"Who in the hell are you then?" asked the desk clerk as he shooed away the old man in the lobby who was creeping closer to the desk in order to get a better listen to the conversation.

Steve thought he might just as well lay it all out for what it might be worth. "I'm a physician, a doctor. It is highly important that I find Charlie Teringo. It has to do with the epidemic that is killing people. I am sure that you have heard about it."

"Doc, that epidemic is the last thing that is on the minds of the people in this part of town. Where they are going to get their next fix or their next bottle of booze is more important to them."

"Here is his picture. Do you recognize him?" asked Steve in desperation.

"I don't remember any Charlie Teringo and I don't remember seeing a guy who looks like the guy in that picture," said the desk keeper.

Steve was not only frightened by his surroundings, but he now felt the pangs of failure and the thoughts on his raid now centered on getting back to the airport safely. He started walking toward the door.

The desk keeper called out to Steve. "Hey, doc! I said that I don't remember seeing that guy you're talking about. But that don't mean that I have never seen him or that he doesn't live here."

Steve stopped dead in his walk and Simon's words, "Nobody tells you nuthin for nuthin," flashed on his mind like a neon sign.

Steve ambled back to the desk. The desk clerk had lit up anther cigarette and was looking into the distance. Steve held a wrinkled twenty in his fist on the counter in front of him.

"I might remember," said the clerk as smoke rolled from his mouth.

Steve shoved the twenty close to the desk keeper's hand. As swift as a striking rattlesnake, the desk keeper's hand retrieved the wrinkled bill. "I am beginning to see that guy in the picture in my head. I can also see another twenty." The desk keeper was still looking out the window and not once did he look at Steve.

"I have only a ten," said Steve.

"That will get you half way there," said the desk keeper as he took a long drag on his cigarette.

"What in the hell am I doing here?" thought Steve as he grabbed another twenty from his pocket and threw it on the desk. Again it was gone in a flash.

"You win the whole pot, Doc. Room 312, up the stairway and to the right. He may be in, maybe not. Works at the YESTERDAY'S TOMORROW

PARK, the Theme Park on the edge of town. It is one of the biggest in the country," said the desk clerk still not looking at Steve.

"Could you ring his room for me?"

The desk clerk turned and gave him a flabbergasted look. "This ain't the Waldorf, this is the Royale. We don't have phones in the rooms. If you want to talk to him you go up there and see him."

Steve took one look at the dimly lit staircase and was not sure that he wanted to go up to the third floor. The desk clerk sensed Steve's apprehension. He said, "Most of the guys livin' here are old drunks and some new ones. They ain't much, except that lots of them carries knives and they don't have no sense of conscience, if you know what I mean. If anybody shoves you, just shove back and hope for the best."

"Thanks," said Steve as he drew a deep breath and headed for the stairs.

The old man in the lobby got up and started following Steve but the desk clerk ordered him to sit down and wait until Steve was back. Then the desk clerk called out to Steve. "Wait, Doc." He pointed to the derelect. "This guy is sort of poor; maybe you got a little somethin that will make him stay in his chair better."

Steve looked at the package in his hand, the Chevas Regal, and said, "I've got something for him." He walked over and threw the package in the lobby man's lap, then headed for the stairs.

Room 312 was in front of him. Steve was glad that there was no one else in the hall, but it was daytime and these people are night people. Daytime was their time for sleep. Steve knocked gently on the door. He knocked again, then he tried the door. It was locked. He knocked again, this time a little louder. He knocked again; still no response. "Now what?" he mumbled audibly. Finally he banged on the door, real hard and real loud. No response from 312 but the door down the hall opened and a wobbling, unshaven, derelict stepped into the hall. The man looked at Steve with a grin then started walking toward him. Steve backed away three steps, then he realized that he was moving farther from the stairs that led back to the lobby so he held his ground. The man moved slowly toward Steve and stopped in front of him. "Charlie ain't here, pal. He is at work."

Steve said, "Thanks," and started to move down the hall, but the man stepped in front of him and blocked his way.

"A guy dressed like you should have a couple of bucks for a guy like me," said the derelict.

Steve reached into his pocket, his hand shaking badly. He pulled out a bill and in the process spilled three others on the floor. He reached down to pick them up and when he rose the man was edging him toward the wall. "I'll just take them all, pal," he said as he grabbed Steve's arm.

Steve heard another door or two open and knew that he was in trouble. He shoved the man in front of him, but the man bounced off the wall and came after Steve with his fist flying. "Fuck you," shouted Steve as he shoved the man again and ploughed into him with a flurry of hard punches that landed with a fury that surprised even him. The man hit the floor, his nose bleeding, his eye and cheek badly bruised, his brain that was swimming in the aftermath of last night's wine was drowning in the concussion from Steve's blows. The other men rushed at Steve. Steve went flying down the stairs two and three steps at a time, the derelicts running and stumbling after him. Steve hit the lobby with a loud thump as he jumped down the last four steps. He ran through the lobby but was confronted by the old man who was still holding the Chevas Regal. Steve came to a halt, took a quick look around and saw the others coming after him. He shoved the lobby man and sent him flying backward over a big chair into a glass door that shattered and sprayed broken glass all over. Steve rushed out into the street, the Royale people and now the desk clerk close behind. He ran for half a block, then was caught by two big, black guys who had no trouble subduing his frantic efforts to get away. One of the men waved his arms. In an instant a car screeched to a stop. One of the guys opened the back door and the other shoved Steve in and slammed the door. The car sped away.

"God, this can't be happening to me," mumbled Steve. Then he heard a familiar voice. He looked up and saw the driver of the car. It was Simon.

"I told you I'd be there when ya needed me." Steve did not know what to say, but he let out a feeble, "Thank you." Then Steve sat up in the seat, threw his head back and tried to piece things together. He began to feel the pain in his hand. He slowly brought his hand to eyesight level and took a good look at it. It was badly swollen. "I think that I broke it," he said.

"How is his jaw?" asked Simon with a laugh. I told ya it might be rough. But I'm proud of ya, man."

"Proud, shit," said Steve. "Stupid is a better word." Then he looked at his swollen hand again. "God, this hurts."

"We'll stop and git some ice," said Simon.

Steve suddenly became aware of his situation. "Those two guys, what about those guys?" Steve turned around and looked out the window expecting to see a car following them.

"They is on our side, man. I called them and told 'em to take good care of ya and they did," said Simon.

Steve shook his head in disbelief. "Thanks again," he said.

They stopped for some ice and so Steve could get cleaned up a little. Then they headed for YESTERDAY'S TOMORROW to see if Steve could trace down Charlie. Steve had tried to pay Simon for all that he had done to help him, but Simon settled for his fare plus a generous tip.

Steve draped his coat over his arm and walked through the gate of the theme park. It was hot, even by St. Louis standards. Perspiration poured from Steve as he walked down the road, the scorching sun streaming down and overheating everything in sight. Steve looked up into the western sky and noticed the makings of a summer storm rapidly coming up on them. He could welcome the break in the weather that the rain would bring, but he also knew that a heavy rain would close the park and that would make it more difficult for him to find Charlie. Steve had no overwhelming desire to have to return to The Royale.

Steve began looking for the bandstand where Charlie would be playing. There were three bandstands in the park and Steve was not sure at which one Charlie would be playing. He looked over the program and he decided that the best place to begin would be the Dixieland Bandstand at the far end of the park. He headed in that direction. But first he stopped for a lemonade and ended up drinking two. The heat of the day was taking its toll. Between the humidity, the heat, and his confrontation at the Royale, Steve was tired, fatigued, and wished that he were twenty again instead of forty-five.

Steve took his time as he meandered toward the Dixieland Bandstand. He could hear the rising crescendo of "High Society" in the distance as he moved closer to the Dixieland. He stopped when he heard the trumpet blare out and rock the air with a tempo that could come only from the horn of the best trumpet player in the country, Charlie Teringo. Then the music stopped. Steve wavered for a second, and then he hurried his pace to the Dixieland Bandstand.

It was break time when Steve arrived at the Dixieland. Steve looked around and finally saw someone who looked as if he might be in charge. Steve introduced himself and told the man that he was looking for Charlie Teringo. The man looked Steve over very skeptically. He was not very friendly and offered no assistance whatsoever. Steve offered to show the man his identification, but as Steve was reaching for his billfold, he suddenly remembered that all of his identification was stashed away in his stocking as Simon had told him to do. Steve was debating in his mind if he should reach down into his stocking to retrieve his identification, a rather unorthodox maneuver. As the debate went on in his brain, the man casually walked away leaving Steve standing alone, and discouraged.

A band member dressed in white trousers, red and white striped blazer, and straw hat that was the trademark of the Dixieland Band, had overheard the conversation. "I understand that you are looking for Charlie Teringo," said the band man as he walked up to Steve.

"Yes, I am. And it is very important that I find him," said Steve.

The band member gazed upon Steve for a short time, then he said, "Is he in trouble with the law?"

"If he is, I know nothing about it," said Steve. "I am a physician and I would like to talk to him about something very important."

"The FBI has been here looking for Charlie after he came back from wherever he was," said the band man.

"The FBI and myself are looking for him for the same reason. We literally need his blood." Steve reached into his pocket and rescued a loose twenty-dollar bill. He held the bill in his hand in front of him.

The band man pushed Steve's hand away. "No need for that. I do not expect, or want, any reimbursement for any information that I give to you. It is just that Charlie has been in trouble with the police so often that we have a hard time keeping him in the band. Never real bad things you understand, but things like writing bad checks, not paying his bills, and stuff like that." The band man looked Steve over very carefully once again. "And then there is the big stuff."

Steve looked at the band man with a quizzical look on his face "Big Stuff," he repeated. "Are you referring to drugs?"

The band man remained non-committal. "Charlie has used a little pot and a little coke, but then, who doesn't?"

"I don't," tersely replied Steve.

"But the loan sharks are the worst. That is where Charlie could really get into trouble."

"I am in none of the above categories," said Steve impatiently. "Now, can you tell me where I can find Charlie?"

"Sure," said the band man.

Steve dipped into his pocket again, and this time pulled out two bills that he held tightly in his fist. "How much?" he asked.

"For nothing," replied the band man. "I think that you are clean."

"Where's Charlie?" demanded Steve.

The band man pointed in the direction of a food stand. "Charlie is eating a bite of lunch."

Steve looked at Charlie who was dressed in the white trousers, red and white striped coat and holding his flat topped straw hat. The man who Steve had talked to and who was so unco-operative was now talking to Charlie. They were both looking in the direction of Steve and the band man.

Steve started walking slowly in the direction of the food stand. Charlie and the manager watched for a moment, and then took off in different directions. The manager had told Charlie that someone was looking for him and that it might be better if he took a few days off to let things cool down.

Steve hurried his pace, but so did Charlie. Steve began to jog lightly, but when Charlie saw that Steve was getting close to him, he broke into a run. Steve had no choice, he had to start running himself or he would certainly lose Charlie. Charlie took a couple of quick turns, but Steve managed to stick with him

Steve figured that he was in better physical condition than Charlie was and that he could wait him out without doing anything drastic. But Charlie also figured that Steve could outlast him. Charlie looked up at the sky and saw the storm clouds rolling in. The wind was starting to blow and it would not be long until the rain would be coming down. The crowd was already starting to disperse and that was bad, for Charlie. Charlie knew that he could get lost a lot easier in a crowd. He was beginning to tire. He knew that he would have to take more aggressive action if he were to lose whoever was chasing him.

Charlie went over the fence and into the area of the Frontier Railroad. Steve went over the fence after him. Charlie, with Steve in close pursuit, ran toward the tracks. Charlie saw the train coming down the tracks. He ran along side the train and waited for the last minute, then he crossed the tracks just in front of the train, hoping that the train would block Steve long enough so that he could get some distance between him and Steve and possibly lose him altogether. The whistle of the train blew long and hard and the hiss of steam escaping from the valves filled the air as the engineer hit the brakes. Steve had just made it. He was still in close pursuit. Charlie ran through the tall grass and down into the muddy stream, white pants, white shoes and all. Charlie climbed the muddy bank on the other side of the stream. He slipped and almost fell back into the stream, but he regained his balance and scurried up to the top of the embankment. Charlie looked back. Steve was closing in on him. As Steve splashed into the stream, the first drops of rain splattered his face and a flash of lightening crossed the sky closely followed by a distant crash of thunder. Charlie ran through a group of "cowboys" on horses, their faces covered by bandannas as they waited to "rob" the Frontier Train. Charlie yelled out something as he ran past them and one of the men rode up to Steve and reached out for him, but the whistle of the train and a shout, "Come on, here it comes," put an end to that.

Charlie was tiring and both he and Steve knew it. Charlie climbed the hill with difficulty and stood briefly on the blacktop road. He was panting and the pain in the center of his chest was getting worse. He remembered that Dr.

Welsch had told him before he left the hospital that the chest pain came from his heart, so Charlie ran the short distance to the HOUSE OF FRIGHT, one of the park's major attractions. Charlie, sweating, wet with rain and with pain in his chest, pushed his way past the line of people waiting to get into the HOUSE OF FRIGHT.

Steve managed to close the gap between them. The rain was coming down harder now and the crowd was dispersing. The attendants at the gate were surprised, first by Charlie rushing past them and then by Steve. They made a feeble attempt to stop Steve but by the time they realized what was happening, Steve was well inside the HOUSE OF FRIGHT.

It was very dark inside and Steve had to grope his way past the people in front of him. There was some yelling and screaming as Steve moved through the crowd, bumping into some of them and almost knocking down a few of the kids. Some of the people thought that this was part of the plot. Steve inched his way forward and found himself in a room splattered with flashing lights of weird colors and with coffins scattered about, the lids slowly opening to reveal gruesome sights of bodies that lay still, eyes half opened, some slowly rising and sitting up to look about the crowd and coming alive with ghastly noises, screams and laughs. The people were delightfully startled. Steve stopped to look about trying to get his bearings and hoping to find Charlie. Steve looked back and saw one of the attendants moving toward him so he moved onward, carefully checking to see if Charlie was hidden somewhere in the crowd or among the ghouls. It was pitch dark again as Steve moved through a dark tunnel-like passage. Steve, in his rush to find Charlie, found himself again bumping into people and knocking over little kids, causing a minor disruption.

Outside the thunder was crashing louder and the reverberations could be heard inside the HOUSE, adding to the already eerie atmosphere that was there. Another room and this time Steve found the famous monsters reaching out for the crowd, almost catching some and scaring everybody, but retreating to their haunts to await another group of people entering their lair. Steve continued to shove and push his way forward, noticing that the attendants were still stalking him. He moved forward a little faster. He entered still another of the fright rooms, this time a room with lights dinned just enough to allow a good look at what was there, but not bright enough to allow a detailed look. The walls were covered with heads hanging as if they were trophies collected by some ghoulish monster. The heads were well decorated to bring out the most spellbinding qualities of bewitchery that could be imagined. There were heads covered with blood, heads with eyes popping out of their sockets, heads with features horrendously disfigured in diabolical contrivances. It was really a scary room. The figures moved, watched the crowd, their eyes blinking with life. Smiles, grins, and grimaces alternated on the same faces. Steve slowly moved forward examining each head. Some let out groans or growls as he stopped to take a closer look. He was about to leave the room when something bothered him enough to make him turn back. He moved up to one of the heads. A hand grabbed him by the shoulder and Steve turned around to see that it was one of the attendants. Steve shoved the arm off of his shoulder and looked at the face again. "Charlie?" he said to the face.

In a flash the head was off the wall leaving an empty hole where the head had been. Quickly Steve moved to an Exit door. He felt a strong hand grip his shoulder and again he roughly shoved it away, saying, "Lay off, damnit!"

Steve went through the Exit door into a back room where the bodies of the heads stood on platforms, doing their thing. Steve rushed through a door leading to the outside. He ran out into the rain. Lightening and thunder were waning into the east. The wind had melted to a breeze that blew easily across his face. He ran down the road looking carefully in all directions with an attendant stalking close behind. Steve looked up the road and saw him, Charlie with his white trousers, red and white striped coat, walking along the deserted road. When Charlie saw Steve he started to run. Steve ran after him at full speed. Charlie was wet, tired and the chest pain was coming back. His run slowed to a walk and then Charlie suddenly stopped and dropped onto a bench by the road.

Steve saw Charlie hit the bench. He automatically slowed the pace as he saw that the end was near. The run slowed to a jog, then a fast walk, and finally a slow walk. Steve stumbled up to where Charlie was sitting. Charlie was panting, his hair was matted down with the rain, his white trousers were splattered with mud and grime, the red and white jacket was wet and dirty.

Steve fell onto the bench next to Charlie, soaking wet and near exhaustion himself. He was puffing hard and his heartbeat was beginning to slow down from the epinephrine fueled rapid rate of a few minutes before.

Charlie was still panting. He did not even look at Steve, but he said, "You win, whoever you are."

Chapter 20

Steve injected the Rhythodyne into David's intravenous tubing, and then he withdrew the needle and walked over to where Lisa was quietly standing in one corner of the room. Steve clumsily held the empty syringe in his hand with the cast. "That was the last dose of Rhythodyne. There is no more."

"The heart rate is picking up," said a nurse as she monitored David's EKG.

"But what about the antitoxin. That should be working soon," said Lisa, hoping for a positive answer.

"Lisa, we are not exactly sure how high a titer of antitoxin Charlie's blood has in it anymore. We have sent samples off to Atlanta to CDC, but it will be a few days before they can give us any results that we can count on. By that time we will already have the answer ourselves."

"The heart rate is up to 70 beats per minute now," interrupted the nurse. "I just hope that he does not fibrillate again," she added as an afterthought.

"I don't think that he will," said Steve. "He only received one cc. of Rhythodyne and we have not had any difficulty with a dose that small in the past."

Steve grabbed Lisa's hand and led her out the door. "Come on, we'll go down to see Jacque and see how things are going with him."

Lisa spoke as they walked toward Dr. Marten's office. "How much more of Charlie's serum are you going to give to David?"

"So far we have taken five hundred cc's of blood from Charlie. We centrifuged the blood and gave the red cells back to Charlie. We injected the plasma to David. Hopefully there will be enough anti-toxin in the plasma to begin to neutralize the myocardial toxin produced by the Chlamydia of CM Disease. Later today we will draw off another five hundred cc's of blood from Charlie, spin it down, give the red cells back to Charlie and give the plasma to David once again. We will repeat the process four times. At the end of that time Charlie probably won't have enough of the anti-toxin left in his serum to do any good."

Steve and Lisa walked into the Pathology office. "You may go right in," said the secretary. "Dr. Marten is expecting you."

Jacque was on the phone when Steve and Lisa entered his office. Dr. Marten motioned for them to take a seat. In another minute Jim Street walked into the office just as Jacque was putting down the receiver.

"That was Atlanta," said Jacque. "They are quite excited about the work that we are doing. They are going at full speed in an attempt to find a method for the detection of anti-toxin titers so that they can screen the general population and find those people who have high titers of anti-toxin in their blood. They also think that they can develop a concentrated antitoxin so that we won't have to mess around with plasma all of the time."

Jim Street spoke. "Have they said anything about us not having a license to do what we are doing?"

"That does not bother them since we have been transfusing plasma, which is a natural product, and not actually a drug," said Jacque. "It's a technicality that they and we can live with."

"But what about the Rhythodyne?" asked Jim Street.

"They do not know about that," said Jacque, "and I think that we can bury that in the avalanche of information that we have given them concerning anti-toxin for CM Disease. They will not find it difficult to overlook us using the Rhythodyne."

Steve's hospital pager went off. "Dr. McKay, call third floor right away. Dr. Mckay, call third floor right away."

Steve hurriedly dialed third floor. He listened carefully, then slammed the phone back down. "David is in trouble," he shouted as he ran out of the room. Jacque, Lisa and Jim Street followed close behind.

"The heart rate is up to 190 beats per minute," said the nurse, crying as she talked to Steve.

"Stop that crying," shouted Steve as he watched the heart rate on the monitor creep even higher.

"I can't help it, Doctor. He can't take much more of this," said the nurse. "We are going to lose him."

Steve grabbed the nurse by the shoulders and spoke directly at her. "We are not going to lose him. Now get those defibrillator paddles ready just in case we need them."

Jacque, Lisa and Jim Street watched the scene from a distance, wanting to do something, or to say something, but not knowing what to do or what to say. Finally Jacque motioned for the three of them to leave and allow Steve to do what had to be done.

"Jacque," Steve cried out before Dr. Marten had left the room. "Let them go and come here, please."

Dr. Marten came back into the room and took a place next to Steve. They both stood, anxiously watching the monitor, not saying anything and sure that the deteriorating electrical pattern would soon degenerate into ventricular fibrillation.

"Jacque, I want you to bleed Charlie, right now. I want that second specimen of plasma as soon as you can get it."

Jacque spoke softly. "But it has been less than two hours since we last bled him."

"He'll make it," said Steve. "Give him plenty of intravenous fluids and get me that plasma." Steve watched the EKG carefully. "There he goes. Get ready to defibrillate and be prepared to perform CPR."

Jacque did not wait to see the outcome of the resuscitation that was in process. He left the room and headed for the laboratory so that he could bleed Charlie once again.

It took three shocks to get the fibrillating heart to hold in a normal sinus pattern. And when the normal rhythm returned, the heart was beating at only 55 beats a minute and this bothered Steve. Slow heart rates were anathema for patients with CM Disease.

"He did not fibrillate after such a low dose of Rhythodyne before," commented the nurse.

"I know," smiled Steve. "I think that the anti-toxin is working."

David's heart rate continued to drop very slowly...50 beats per minute...40 beats per minute...35 beats per minute, and then it held. Steve anxiously checked his watch and was tempted to call Jacque and ask him to hurry, but he knew Jacque was doing his best to get the blood from Charlie so that they could infuse the plasma into David as soon as possible.

"What if the heart stops?" inquired the nurse. "You do not have any more Rhythodyne."

Steve looked up at the young, good looking, blonde nurse. "How long can you do CPR?"

She got the message and nervously waited, like everyone else.

"30 beats per minute," someone said quietly.

"An emergency pacemaker?" asked another nurse.

"No good," answered Steve. "We can deliver all of the pacemaker shocks that we want, but it won't do any good. The electrical conduction system of the myocardium is poisoned so that pacemaker shocks cannot stimulate the heart muscle to contract. That is why we get cardiac standstill with CM Disease. We will just have to wait it out."

Jacque brought the plasma to David's room. Steve hung the plastic flask on the I-V stand and connected a special pump in order to quicken the flow of plasma into David's vein. The heart rate was holding at thirty, barely fast enough to sustain adequate circulation. Any lower than that and David could end up a vegetable with viable vital organs but with a severely damaged brain.

Steve looked up at Jacque. "Now force intravenous fluids on Charlie, and get me another unit of plasma as soon as Charlie's red cells have been pumped back into him."

"This is your ball game, Steve. I just hope that Charlie will agree to this. This is not the protocol that we told him we would follow. And I also hope that his heart can take it." Jacque left the room to go downstairs to talk to Charlie.

"The heart rate is up to 50 beats per minute now," said the nurse with a big smile on her face. "That stuff really works."

Steve said nothing but he kept the vigil at David's bedside. David was not responding very well, but he would answer to his name and to simple questions that required a simple yes or no answer. Steve hoped that he had not sustained any significant brain damage from all that he had been through.

"Heart rate up to 60 beats per minute," said the nurse, with an even bigger smile.

Steve began to relax as the last of Charlie's plasma rolled into David's vein. David was beginning to answer questions and was more alert. As he left for Jacque's office, Steve told the nurse to send for Lisa to stay with David.

Jim Street and Jacque were quietly sitting in Jacque's office. "How is he?" asked Jim Street.

"Alright, for now," answered Steve.

"You look more dead than David," commented Jim Street. "How about lying down for awhile. We can get you a bed somewhere."

"Not right now," answered Steve.

"I will get the third unit of plasma for you as soon as we are able," said Jacque. "We are re-hydrating Charlie and we are pumping in his red cells as quickly as we feel it safe to do. We have to watch his fluids though. Welsch tells us that Charlie has a friable heart that could go into failure very easily."

Steve closed his eyes for a moment. "Winston is right. Go ahead and let him manage the fluid balance and withdrawal of blood from Charlie," said Steve. "He can handle it."

"Coffee, tea?" asked Jim Street.

"Fresh and black," replied Steve.

The atmosphere in Jacque's office was that of quiet optimism. No one dared say anything positive, or negative, concerning the unpredictable and precarious situation in which they were enveloped.

After awhile Steve meandered back up to David's room. David was awake and talking, although he was extremely fatigued. Lisa was at his side, holding his hand. Steve rapidly assessed David's condition, then walked over to the monitor. The heart rate had dropped to 50 beats per minute, but the decrease in rate was much slower now than it had been in the recent past. Steve decreased the rate of flow of the intravenous fluids that David was getting. He did not want to overload David's circulatory system with fluid and plasma. Steve then left the room to await the administration of another unit of Charlie's plasma to David.

David's heart rate had dropped to 40 beats per minute before Charlie's plasma was ready for administration. Steve gave the plasma as rapidly as he thought safe. David's heart rate rose to 70 beats per minute, and held. Steve waited for another hour, then he said goodbye to Lisa, thanked the nursing staff, and headed for Jacque's office.

"I think that the worst is over," said Steve. "We will not give the last unit of plasma until later tomorrow, unless something really bad happens. And if it does, I think that the whole damn business has been a sham. If the three units that we have given to David do not reverse his poisoned cardiac conduction system, then he is dead."

Jim Street got out of his chair and walked over to the window. "Steve," he began, "You have done all that could be expected of you. Why don't you go home and get some rest. We will handle things here, and we will call you immediately if anything goes haywire."

Steve was in a near stupor and his mind was so clouded with the veil of the past week's activities that he could not think straight enough to give Jim Street a coherent answer. He sat, eyes closed, saying nothing.

Jacque got out of his chair. "You are not going home. We are getting you a bed here at the hospital." Jacque looked at Jim Street. "Can you get Steve a room?"

"Consider it done," said Jim Street as he reached for the phone.

Steve dropped into the bed in room 655, a private room reserved for VIP's. Overwhelming fatigue put him to sleep in a matter of seconds and for the first time in months he dreamed of life, not death.

Both Steve and David had spent a restful six hours. David's heart rate had remained stable at 60 to 70 beats per minute, and Steve had gotten some long overdue sleep. Nature itself seemed to be speaking to both of them with optimism. The sky was cloudless and bright, the sun was shining, and there was a cool breeze rushing through the air that made the whole world seem alive again.

Steve examined David very carefully. David was very much awake, alert, wanting something to eat, and even talking about getting up in a chair for a while. Steve could find nothing from a clinical standpoint that would contradict that request, and he wrote a note in David's chart that he could get up after he had received the last administration of Charlie's plasma containing the anti-toxin.

Steve met Jim Street in the hall and they both went down to the cafeteria. After a brief bite to eat they headed for Pathology and Dr. Marten's office. Jacque was busy reading communications that were coming in fast and furious, not only from the NIH and the CDC, but from laboratories from all over the world. "Sit down, Steve, and you, too, Jim," said Jacque without even looking up. "By rights, you should be answering these requests for information, Steve you have done all of the important clinical work on CM Disease."

"You do the research, Jacque, and I will practice medicine," said Steve. "I like it that way."

Jacque watched Steve as Steve watched the pretty blonde secretary bring in fresh coffee. Jacque followed Steve's eyes that followed the secretary as she left the room. Jacque looked up. "Did you see that, Jim?" He asked the administrator.

"I don't chase any more," said Jim Street casually.

"No, I mean did you notice Steve?" asked Jacque.

"Committing adultery in his heart, again," replied Jim Street "So what else is new?"

"Just that he has not been doing that for awhile," said Jacque.

"I take that as a sign that things are getting back to normal."

"How normal?" asked Steve. "What about the anti-toxin and the Communicable Disease Center in Atlanta? Are they working on it?"

"Beautiful, simply beautiful," replied Jacque. "They are not only enthusiastic about it, but they think that it is the biggest thing that has come along since Salk and the polio vaccine. They already are developing a program to prepare the anti-toxin by using cultured Chlamydia stimulation and they have high hopes of developing a synthetic anti-toxin. It is so much easier now that they know what they are looking for. BMI has offered their facilities to develop and manufacture, at no cost, any of the apparatus that may be needed for the process."

"How come Winston Welsch and BMI are so generous lately?" quizzed Jim Street.

"Scientific interest, I guess," answered Steve.

"Maybe so," replied Jim Street, "but I think that there must be more to it than that. They have never had a demonstrable social conscience before."

Jacque continued to bring Steve and Jim Street up-to-date as to the progress that was being made in controlling CM Disease. "The people at CDC are very hopeful about being able to detect anti-toxin titers in the general population by a screening process that will be rapid and practical. Treatment will begin with the administration of plasma from well people who have high anti-toxin titers to patients who are dying from CM Disease. Then in the not so distant future they hope to be able to develop methods to concentrate the anti-toxin so that it can be given in smaller injections rather than having to give plasma. Then, finally, as I have already told you, they are very hopeful about developing a method of producing the anti-toxin in some synthetic manner. It may take a little time to sort all of this out and to get it into high gear, but at last there is hope for the future. The question no longer is 'Can we prevent CM Disease from being always fatal?' to simply, 'When'."

Jim Street, Jacque, and Steve remained silent, quietly sipping coffee. Jim Street broke the silence. "Is David still making satisfactory progress, Steve?"

"David is doing very well," replied Steve very softly. He put his cup on the table. "I have a few things to do this morning, and I want to check on David once more." Steve left to make is rounds.

Jim Street and Jacque again sat in silence. Finally Jim Street said, "Steve looked as if he had lost his best friend instead of having saved a life."

"He is just tired, that's all," said Jacque. "There is always a letdown after the sweet taste of victory."

Lisa watched Steve as he removed the empty flask that had just given up the last cc of Charlie's plasma. "That should do it," said Steve. "Tomorrow we can discontinue the I-V."

After a banter of words between the three of them, Steve offered to take Lisa home so that she could get some sleep and then come back to the hospital.

Steve parked the Jag in the driveway. "Come in for a moment?" asked Lisa.

"Sure," answered Steve with a smile. "But not for long."

They entered the foyer and closed the door behind them. They stood in complete silence, the tic-toc of the swinging pendulum of the grandfather's clock and the hum of the air conditioner creating a subdued, relaxing milieu.

"He is going to live, isn't he?" said Lisa.

Steve nodded his head in the affirmative. "David is going to live."

Lisa flung herself into Steve's arms as tears filled her eyes. The two clung to each other as tightly as they could. It seemed like an eternity for both of them and neither wanted to let go. Finally, Lisa looked up, and with tears streaming down her face, she looked directly into Steve's eyes as she said, "Thanks, and I am sorry, and I love you." Then she ran out of the room.

Steve stood in the quiet as he suddenly realized that so often the vintage wine and vinegar are drawn from the same cask.

Then he left for the hospital.

THE END

Printed in the United States
5942

9 781588 510174